In the Waters of Time

Bette Lischke

In the Waters of Time, Published January, 2015

Editorial and Proofreading Services: Shannon Miller, Kellyann Zuzulo
Interior Layout: Howard Johnson, Howard Communigrafix, Inc.
Cover Design: Alan Pearsall Art & Design, alanpearsall.com
Photo Credits: Author photo by Kirsten Lischke Norton

 **SDP Publishing**

Published by SDP Publishing, an imprint of SDP Publishing Solutions, LLC.

SDP Publishing
Permissions Department
PO Box 26, East Bridgewater, MA 02333
or email your request to info@SDPPublishing.com.

ISBN-13 (print): 978-0-9911597-8-9
ISBN-13 (ebook): 978-0-9905596-0-3

Library of Congress Control Number: 2013957055

Dedication

This book is dedicated to my mother and mentor,
Margaret Edith Wurster Hanlon—
writer, artist, musician, storyteller, and poet.

My mother was as gentle and graceful as a moonbeam. When she walked, it seemed that she stepped from star to star and when she spoke, her hands bracketed the air like birds stopped in movement. She had an expansiveness about her, a quietness, as if she were listening inwardly. Her hair was black and straight, her skin creamy and smooth, and although her heritage was German, Dutch and Irish, strangers thought she was Asian. She sang all the time, every song she knew. At dusk, she sang for us . . . songs like "Stars Are the Windows of Heaven" *where angels peek through.* She made singing carols next to the lighted tree the best part of Christmas.

My mother, a groundswell of water on fertile ground, nourished and enriched the best in each of her seven children. Her spirit feeds me still in these waters of time.

Acknowledgments

Thank you to my husband, Jerry Lischke, for his constant support, encouragement, and patience. It would not have been possible to hold this book together without the continued support of my son-in-law, Mark Wright, who monitored my play in the field of computer technology. Mark graciously deflected and bypassed technical meltdowns and computer crashes through multiple revisions and computers. Thank you to my most loyal and capable editor, Kirsten Norton, who also saved me in times of tech emergency. Thank you to Maggie Brewer and Nancy Rubinstein for editorial advice, to Patricia Hanlon Clark for reading, and to Janice Tangney for helpful prodding. Eternal thanks to both Larry Lewis and Stephen Roxburgh for pronouncing this book a viable novel, and special thanks to a young intuitive named Garrett Lischke, who said, "Go back to the beginning. See what it is you've got there." Thank you to all of my family for believing in me, to Alan Pearsall for his artwork, to Kirsten and Stan Norton for their generosity, and to all of my team at SDP Publishing Solutions, especially Lisa Akoury-Ross, founder, personal project manager, and agent.

Prologue

London, 1848

Missus Elizabeth Brewer closed the schoolroom door. Lately, while doing this, she wondered how many more times she would close that door, and now as she crossed the gloomy hall and opened the one to the teacher's room, she knew. It would stop now—she would not be here another day.

She took her bonnet from its hook, placed it forward of her chignon, and tied its blue silk ribbons to the left of her chin. She pulled on her gloves, collected her parasol, and left without looking back, her heels thudding against the sodden wood floor as she headed for the main entrance of the St. Luke's Parish Workhouse. She pushed through heavy doors, stopping on the high step as she always did—to breathe fresh air, to throw off the dankness of the place—and raised her shade.

Weariness splintered through her, ending all thought of teaching the poor. She hated the stink of the place and knew in her heart that she would never have agreed to the post of schoolmistress if not for the commanding new master of the workhouse, Jordan Locke.

Elizabeth and Jordan shared a kinship, a connection that livened each strand of her being. In Jordan's proximity, she was well tuned; strong, clear, in perfect pitch and resonance. When first they met, she sought out the harpsichord, playing more than she had since she was a girl, since before any of her five children were born.

The granite steps were as unforgiving as ever, and she held her skirt to the side and stepped carefully. At the street, she walked toward the avenue that would lead to the open market, her shadow short as she passed St. Luke's Church.

It was as if she and Jordan were made from the same thread in a tapestry of infinite fibers; each stood amazed in the other's presence. But it was her husband, Palmer, who instigated her teaching at the

5

workhouse. Her working pleased him, especially if she were tired. "Now you see how it is," he might say, as he rocked on the balls of his feet, his hands snug behind his back. He reminded her that she had wanted to teach before they married and insisted she use her meager earnings as she wished.

Elizabeth intended to keep Jordan in her life. She was giving up the workhouse, not him, and planned to act, from her home, as teaching adviser and go-between for charitable events. She would be spending her days with her *own* children, completely free of that jaundiced building. She longed to paint with Meridith and Emma; she would collect watercolors from the playroom and they would paint in the garden. And the boys, if they wanted. At the workhouse, boys and girls alike used the chalk colors, and whether or not they liked drawing had nothing to do with their sex.

Elizabeth craved vivid, bold color, and would try her hand with oil paint. She would need a lesson, but other people used oil and turpentine and so could she. They would need a cupboard with lock and key, perhaps in the garden room.

She was to meet him at the open market, which, pleasant as it might seem, felt ominous, for they half-expected the intrusive housekeeping matron of the workhouse to undo their dalliance. But it no longer mattered what the fool woman thought since Elizabeth was leaving the teaching post.

"Cabbage, missus, n' beans just picked!"

She waved away flies as well as the vendor, pulled a mint-scented hankie from her pocket, and scanned wagons for the flower cart. Jordan stood tall in his dark suit with ruddy face raised to the sun. She moved close, her wide skirt brushing his knee, and watched him brighten at the sight of her. Only his eyes were sad; dark, almost fearful.

They linked elbows and walked on. Elizabeth pressed her hankie to her nose against the reek of butchered cattle. Jordan had been talking about America. Once, when he was a constable, he had chased a thief across the ocean to a new brick city where young women lived in boarding houses and worked in clean textile mills. "*Wholesome* young women!"

Ducking through a doorway in the face of a narrow building took them into the walled yard of an old church. Steps led up to a burying ground where headstones pressed into surrounding buildings, marble cemented into brick.

"Saint Bart's." Jordan removed his hat and looked up to the top of the edifice.

Elizabeth closed her parasol. Standing next to him, she placed her arm across his lower back. He lifted his arm, and, as if dancing, she moved within its circle, into the harbor of his arms, and rested her head against his chest. They stood, each nourished by the other, energized, soothed and strengthened, in a gentle rocking. Sounds of carts and calls like bird song dropped on them from beyond the wall.

Pulling back, their gazes locked, she said, "When can you come to tea, my dearest? We must choose a time. Every day!"

Jordan stepped aside and, holding her hand and gesturing, invited her to sit on the large granite stone beneath arched oak doors. They sat with elbows linked, their sides touching, leaning into each other. The bright outer street was framed like a gigantic keyhole.

"I will be going, Liza."

Porous gray blocks of paving wept in dark blotches. She shivered and blinked the courtyard into clarity.

"I have *prospects* in America." He took her hands and played his long thumbs against her palms. "I've tried to tell you. You can't just keep brushing it aside. It's a whole new world! With my experience and ability to lead, I could be captain of police! I could as well direct a team of navvies. They're laying rail across the entire continent."

Darkness covered the sun, dimming even the world beyond the doorway. She couldn't speak. Her jaws were locked.

Jordan knelt before her. "My dearest. You must come with me." He closed his hands over hers. "We can be together there, Liza. As man and wife."

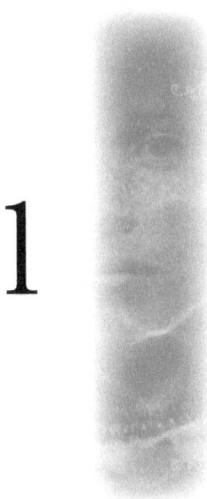

1

She looked at me! The thought reached in and pulled Jane out of sleep and bolt upright in bed. *This was different!*

The old dream of waiting to board a steamer had haunted her for as long as she could remember. Too anxious to breathe, legs trembling, she gripped a child's hand, prepared, waiting to step forward. Her shoulders leaned into movement, her foot lifted, and she was stopped when a man said something. But this time, the child—a little girl in a straw bonnet—turned her head back and up, squinted in the sun, and looked into her face! Sunlight. The dream had always been murky.

Her husband slept on in the dark. Very dark. Yes. They were at an island cottage. Jane threw her legs over the side of the bed and stood at the open door of the small, unfamiliar room, found the threshold, and crossed floorboards onto a braided rug. The chair with the floor lamp was diagonally across the room, and that was where she'd put her sketchbook and a new charcoal pencil. She cried out in pain when her shin caught the edge of a low table. Bending and groping, she found the overstuffed chair and the lamp beside it. She pulled the chain, closing her eyes to the bulb's glare, and tried to hold on to the child's image: cheeks baby-full, lips pursed in confusion.

She picked up the pencil and sat in the chair within the pool of lamplight. With the sketchpad on her knees, she rounded the cheeks and little chin, the brim of the hat. While blackening the curve of bonnet ribbon, she could see its French blue color. Nausea swept through her and she pushed the drawing away. Morning sickness? No, and anyway, the nausea was gone. Jane would have had a child that age if she hadn't miscarried. Twice miscarried. She pulled back from the pool of angst that she could so easily slip into and, repositioning the tablet, arched in the eyes, knowing that they were blue. And worried. She smudged in shadows with her thumb then tried again to see with her mind's eye. Her hand started moving on its own, and she placed it, splayed, on the arm of the chair. Jane spent a lot of energy trying to outsmart her spastic right hand. It did its wagging whenever she wasn't purposely using it.

She removed the stiff paper from the drawing pad and placed it against the back of a chair.

It felt so good to draw! Her right hand bobbed now, but it had behaved for her drawing. She turned the tablet from portrait to landscape and gave in to the urge to sketch. Her hand strummed with the charcoal pencil. As she thought of a bowl of fruit and put the pencil to paper, her hand stilled and then moved by her own design: the curve of a wooden bowl, the dimpled sphere of an orange, circles of grapes. Pausing, she gazed at the sketch of the child. Her right hand immediately moved to its own rhythm, marking circles above Jane's lines. With a gasp of annoyance, she threw down the pencil.

———•◦•———

Later that morning, David was cooking bacon for their first vacation breakfast. "As soon as it rains, I'm going home and getting my own frying pan. This thing's useless."

"No, David. Just because we live nearby doesn't mean you can go home when we're on vacation. We can buy a frying pan, today, because I need to get something."

"You just want to go for a ferry ride."

"Not just for the ferry ride. Guess what woke me up? I was having my creepy old dream and this little girl turns and looks up at me! She has to tip her head way back to see past her bonnet—in the sun—"

"Damn!" Grease spit had singed his arm.

"Just turn off the burner." She found a large dinner plate, placed it over the skillet, and said, "Here, I'll show you." She pulled him into the living room.

The sketch was propped against the back of the chair. A rush of love warmed her as she looked at the image.

David said, "It's not like the face you draw in your sleep."

"No. Of course it isn't! I drew this. But can you believe this child emerging from that nightmare?"

"I didn't know you could draw like that. My God, Jane, you're an artist!" The statement hung in the air. "Hiding your light under a bushel?" he asked, arms wide.

"My hand . . . wags."

"Yeah, I know. Did you used to draw?"

She nodded. "Uh-huh. I guess I'll try doing it again. Look." She picked up the second sketch. "But if I'm not careful, the wagging starts."

"I'm very impressed. Odd, how different it is from . . . the sleep drawing seems filled with rage."

She leaned into him, resting her hands on his forearms as he wrapped them around her.

"Now that you're finally talking about the wagging, maybe you can tell me when it started?"

"I don't know. It didn't happen all at once." She paused. "Maybe when I was around twelve?" Never comfortable thinking about her spastic hand, let alone talking about it, she moved out of his arms and went to the portrait. "But look what came out of my awful dream. Kind of like a lotus flower—grows out of muck, then blooms and floats on the surface."

"Well, *that's* prosaic."

"I've been *thinking* about it." She felt such promise. Something of worth had to come from this.

"She looks worried."

So worried that Jane was unnerved and turned back to the kitchen. "I need to go to an art store. We can take our bikes. Later in the day."

"I hate to leave the island when we just got here. Can't we wait till it rains? We'll buy a new pan, a really good one."

"I'll buy you a pan but I'm going today."

After breakfast, they took their coffee out to the porch and sat in old wide-armed rocking chairs, cane-seated and painted green. Scorched August grass gave off the sweet smell of hay. A tree line of oaks dropped down with the land, and beyond, Casco Bay sparkled white between them and Portland's sunny shoreline. One day, they would buy a place on Peaks Island. They loved its backshore road, where waves exploded in white shocks of spray and sent drafts of cool air and a misting so delicate it might have been imagined. But for now, Jane relished the surprise of a rental. Only by staying in a cluster of unknown houses could you find a sandy cove, approachable from yards, not roads, like nooks on the perimeter of a mountain. This cottage was on a clear high spot of the island, at least three tiers above the water, and faced west toward the mainland. David propped his heels on the porch rail.

"I don't think I'm ready for watercolor." She couldn't imagine sitting still that long. "Maybe some oil pastels. They're like oily chalks. I used them in school—grammar school."

"Maybe we better get to the library. If you're actually going to be sitting down for a change, I can do some reading."

"I don't know how much I'll be drawing. I'm just trying it, you know." She breathed in calmness and squeezed his hand. "Let's go out to dinner every night."

"Unless we have lobster—"

"Or we run into a fisherman with a fresh catch."

"I'm doing my own fishing, Jane."

"Okay." She'd buy some thick-skinned oranges. She imagined rounding them out and filling in their color and wondered how to make the skin look dimpled. With light, she supposed. She would just copy what she saw.

"I've reserved a day-sailer, but I'll fish from the pier."

"I'll get dressed," she said as she stood. "I'll ride my bike to the ferry. Do you want to come? To the art store?"

David dropped his feet to the floor. "Sure."

——•◦•——

They careened down hills and biked between shoulders of wild grass and outcroppings of granite that, like miles of giant hands, dangled fingertips into the sea. David raced down steep inclines, while Jane squeezed her hand brakes. She thought her husband was pretty competitive for an only child, but she was the youngest of three, so maybe she was used to coming in last. Her friend Louise said that Jane wasn't a typical youngest sibling, being more intense than playful. David, a CPA, strove for a conservative tone and, because his natural speaking voice was loud, made a constant effort to speak softly. He liked cars and racing, and followed autocrosses instead of the Red Sox.

On the evening of day two of vacation time, while the light was still good on the porch, Jane sat drawing a still life of strawberries.

David said, "You'll just have to put the crayon down, Jane."

"As long as I'm thinking about the drawing, I'm okay." But as she considered what was there, her hand started bobbing. She set the crayon back in its slot.

"What's with the black paper, Janikins?"

"Pastels look good against black, but the light is getting so bad I can't tell one color from another."

"Most artists work in daylight. Who's your favorite artist these days?"

"Van Gogh. I like how he manages to paint energy. Who is yours?"

"I like El Greco."

"Why?"

"I don't know. I remember him. And Sargent did great portraits."

She thought of the woman with the white neck and shoulders. Sargent had dropped one strap. "Yeah. He was fantastic."

"Artists look for north light."

"Well, this artist will be looking for shade."

——•◦•——

On a misty morning, they rounded into a cove where pink beach roses floated in rolling white fog, the clouds pillowing a mortared stone wall. Breathtakingly beautiful even on a clear day, Jane always stopped here to either lie on the wall or sit and dangle her feet. Today she gloried in the mist, closing her eyes to the soft crashing of surf, tasting salty air and welcoming its wetness on her skin. She broke off a pink blossom, five petals with a tuft of yellow at its center, and a white one, the same in all but color, and carried them across mist-shrouded rock. The blossoms were like the little girl—delicate white skin, flushed with pink. Perched on a stretch of rock with the ocean shushing around her, she compared the blooms' scents, finding the white spicier and lighter. She conjured the mysterious child as she sniffed the blossoms, seeing round blue eyes, golden curls, and a smile with lots of little white teeth. *Promise.*

———•◦•———

Jane chalked blue and white checks on a yellow paper and said to David, "Don't eat all the strawberries. Please." She sprayed the paper with fixative and started a line of glass plate in silver. "Where should we eat tonight?"

"Jane, look out!"

She quickly dropped the gray pastel and put away the crayons and paper.

On the following day, while coloring in the strawberries, she said, "I don't care if I really only need one strawberry, David. I want all five. Eat your cereal with blueberries." She had tried to turn the circular scribbles from the night before into a pitcher but, in the end, had to cut down the paper. "Don't distract me. The red smears easily."

Her best effort came on their second Thursday night. She picked up her charcoal pencil and sketched David reading his book. Much as she wanted to draw lush circles, the quick concentrated movements between her eyes and hand were the most successful.

As the second week ended, Jane focused on savoring all aspects of vacation. Now it was low tide, and she bypassed small boulders on the western shore and walked in wet sand, bending to something sparkly.

"Look!" She held a heavy, odd-shaped thing, flat on one side, round on the other, a little lopsided and curving into a kind of beak. "I think . . . is it silver?" She handed it to David. "Don't throw it in the water!"

"I won't!"

"Sorry. It's just that you're always skipping rocks."

"Something silver that melted in a fire." He tossed it in his palm and passed it back.

"It looks like a duck." The tip of her thumb fit in the curve of its beak. "I'm keeping it."

David pressed his hand to her back. "A lucky duck. C'mon. I'm hungry. Let's head up to town."

When they reached the concrete boat ramp at the bottom of City Point Landing, Jane said, "That's it? We can't go any farther?"

"Not unless you want to swim."

She remembered seeing this bluff before. It jutted far out in the water and interrupted the shoreline. They always studied its large house as they walked up the boat ramp to Island Avenue. "I thought it was a longer walk."

"I told you there wasn't any 'walk on the western shore.' If it were high tide, we couldn't even stand here."

West of them, Little Diamond Island lay solid black between the reddening sky and its watery reflection. The sun's yellow path rippled blindingly bright.

"If we hurry, we can watch the sunset from a table."

"I don't want to hurry on our last night!" Disappointed at the shortness of the walk, not wanting it to end, she sat on a thick board that edged the landing and wiped sand off her feet. Over her shoulder, a cottage on stilts crouched above incoming tide, a hammock glowing orange under its deck, suspended mere feet above surf.

"So how come only two weeks, Mrs. Eliot?" He lowered himself onto the board next to her and held out one of her sandals.

"I don't want the shine to wear off. If it were three weeks, I might get used to it." She wondered how he could possibly not already know that, given her obsessiveness. The little duck was warm in her hand, and she rubbed its back as she watched the sky and its watery reflection blush like the skin of a ripe peach. "Let's just sit here."

David thumbed the cleft in his chin. "Okay."

"We can time how long it takes the sun to set. From the time the ball touches the water to when it disappears," she said.

"No we can't." He gestured to his bare wrist. "No watch. No phone. Some people actually relax, Janey."

"I know." Her throat tightened with sadness. When it passed, she said, "I'm working on it. I'm relaxing right now." The prospect of going back to work was grim but she knew she could rely on its sustaining schedule.

That night, after hugging and extolling their days and nights on the island, just after David had dropped into sleep, Jane wondered at her reluctance to head back to the office. Maybe she was just tired of engineers. She decided she would ask to work the temporary placement desk for a change. *Forever finished with engineers*, she thought, and slept.

Pain.

Surged up from her foot, knife-sharp, along her spine, to her brain. Pain.

Her eyes flew open . . . and, now awake, the old familiar terror approached . . . goading her—again—to look, to look . . .

Moonlight flooded through the window, washed over the kitchen sink.

Her foot still hurt.

Forget that. There's something else, something worse . . .

Slowly, because she must, because she had done this strange ballet before, she forced herself to look, following a scent—sharp, invasive.

There! There!

In front of her, a woman's face had been drawn in black marker on a white window shade. Black eyes. Black hair. Black, black, black slammed Jane with mournful sadness that forced her to look away. She tried to forget the parted hair, soft cheeks, tiny neck and collar. Her fingers clenched and she realized the marker—reeking its chemical smell—was in her hand and beneath her foot, cutting into her sole, was its cover. Fully awake now, she put the pieces of the black pen together and dropped them into the open drawer. Shaking, she glanced at the untouched walls and breathed relief.

At least the shade could disappear. She pulled it all the way out and rolled the drawing away. *Gone. Like the nightmare it was.* She ripped the stapled fabric from its roller above the door's window. Removing the hem's wooden stick and setting it aside, she folded the vinyl into a plastic bag, opened the door and waited for the dark outdoors to separate into some degree of dimension.

There were no houses, only a bend in the road and trees. She could barely make out the name 'Porthole' spray-painted on the trash can. In absolute quiet, she stepped down the wooden planks, lifted the cover enough to slide in the bag and moved up the steps, closing the door behind her. It sounded different without the shade.

The marker's stink laced the dark. She took down the naked roller and—walking softly, quickly—carried it and the stick to the tiny bedroom where she kept her clothes. She tucked the parts in the bottom of her duffel bag, planning to replace the shade.

Passing their bedroom, she closed the door and remembered David's ranting. "Why didn't you just tell me, Jane? Why did you have to throw it out?" He had found his spreadsheet inked over with the same dark face, even more unreadable from having been crumpled. So she started leaving a sketchpad on the window seat in their bedroom. She'd brought it with her—but there it sat, blank, and the charcoal sketch was safe. She turned on the lamp to check and smiled at the child's face, at the warmth that flooded through her. She wished she could program her hand to draw *this* face.

In the kitchen, pressing her hand against the sink's white porcelain, she scrubbed her blackened fingers with cleanser, stinging the skin near her nails where her hand had held the marker. She squeezed a lemon wedge over her fingers to get rid of the Ajax smell and winced at the sharp pain. She had dreamed again of waiting to board the steamer but without the little girl, and now she felt as gloomy as she had after the dream. The stove clock read 4:44. Hoping chamomile tea would bring her sleep, she checked the kettle and turned on its burner. Fingering the cross at her neck, gazing toward the living room, she spotted the door's black window and a memory flashed before her . . . waking to her sister in red pajamas coming at her, yelling at Jane for drawing on her homework.

Her hand shook as she poured water into a cup. She wiped up the spill and carried the mug through the dark living room to the porch. Outside, across the bay, the city of Portland was strung with lights like a carelessly laid-out necklace. Her office building sat beyond in the blackness, three miles and three days away. Vacation was almost over.

Working at Port Placement as a headhunter had sustained her, filling the void made by loss, as well as the time to obsess about childbearing. Calling companies for openings and recruiting applicants used her days and nights. While other would-be recruiters grew shaky and left, she was competent—of a select group. Mornings, driving to work, she felt like she had a fat cigar clamped between her teeth. But lately, nothing seemed to fit. Clients and companies wouldn't gel, and an engineer she had recruited said he wished he'd never heard her voice.

Darkness pulled away, a silhouette of oaks distinct against the pearl gray sky. A single bird called. As she stood, the mug slipped from her hand, hit the decking and split in two. She squatted to pick up the two halves and went inside.

It was only a cup. But she trembled with a sinking feeling. *Losing my grip.* She turned on the oven and emptied the refrigerator, then beat eggs and poured them over leftovers in David's skillet. As she slid the pan into the oven with its ropey gasket burned black and brittle, she thought she smelled smoke.

David parked the Range Rover in line for the ferry, and they crossed the street for ice cream cones, hers vanilla and his chocolate. They sat on a low wall, and she held the cone with her left hand, clamping her right hand between her knees.

A young man with a bicep tattoo carried a toddler on his shoulders, his wan and slender wife wearing a happily bulging infant sling. They looked much younger than Jane's thirty-three.

David said, "Babies having babies. You, however, *are* a babe." His navy shirt had a collar, his straight hair was parted in a traditional boy's cut, and his long legs were tanned between khaki shorts and leather boat shoes. He used his free hand to needlessly smooth his short hair.

"Thank you." Still a size eight, and having kept her sensitive skin out of the sun, she'd held up pretty well. She licked her melting ice cream, noting how much her husband had to fold his legs in order to sit on the low wall. "I should think you'd move more at tennis with those long legs."

David would send her all over the court. Yet, when she delivered hard-to-hit balls, he discriminated in which to chase and never tired himself.

"I use discernment in all my expenditures." He let his sunglasses slide down his nose and fastened his eyes on her. "That skirt should be able to stand on its own by now. Haven't you worn it every day?"

"Only when we've gone biking." She held the dripping cone away from her.

"Or hiking," he added.

"That's because it's easier for a woman to pee in a skirt. How does it look?"

"It looks fine. How 'bout wearing it at home? In the bedroom."

Heat rushed to her face.

David wiped some ice cream from her chin with his knuckle. She handed him the rest of her cone and stood, sweeping grit from her backside.

"I'm not kidding, Jane."

She watched the ferry berth, felt her stomach knot. "Maybe I should add it to the list—things I need to talk about."

"You can talk to me. What's going on?"

His hand felt large on her shoulder. She moved her lips as if she had something to say.

He lowered his voice. "You were randy enough on the rocks. Why are you putting me off in bed?"

On the backshore, they'd walked away from sunbathers. Squeezing between hips of rock, dropping closer to crashing waves that smelled of kelp, they would lie flat on warm granite, and she would occupy her right hand by holding David's. While the ocean beat its rhythm into rock, then sucked back loose stones in a soft clacking, its watery sounds wakened her sexuality, until her groin grew heavy; and she arranged her skirt and pressed against her husband's hard thigh, her body so ready that she barely needed to move before waves released within her. The orgasm lasted until either the hard surface or his own frustration caused David to shift, and he wrapped his arms around her as if she were at risk of being washed out to sea. This was spontaneous and unpredictable, happening more than once but not at the same place. She meant to make it up to her husband, but the cottage was too sunny and hot in the afternoon.

Now she slid from under his hand and moved toward the waiting pedestrians, wanting the easy lift of stepping on the ferry.

"Don't block me out, Jane!"

She slowed, waiting for him and, side by side, they walked across the landing to the car. She climbed in and closed the door.

David threw his glasses on the dash, ran his fingers through his hair, then turned to her. "Look in the mirror, Jane. In the visor, dammit!"

She folded down the visor. Her green eyes, surrounded with straight black lashes, stared back.

"Look at your mouth."

Her wide mouth, closed in a straight line, pulled down on the right side. Strands of black hair criss-crossed her brow. She smoothed the hair from her forehead and folded the visor back. "So?"

"Your mouth used to do that when you were upset. It's like that all the time now." He started the car and continued in a low voice. "You have nightmares. You can't sleep and when you do, you sleepwalk—even *draw* in your sleep. You can't sit still. You barely eat. And now—" He hit the steering wheel with the heel of his hand. "What's wrong with you?"

Her back was sticking to the seat. "Can you turn on the A/C?" She lifted her hair off her neck. "I think—maybe you should wear a condom."

He stared at her, his dark eyes wide and still, the skin around them a pale mask.

She stopped drumming her fingers. "I'm sitting still now," she said, raising her chin and trying to lift the corners of her mouth.

"A condom." He looked straight ahead. "Why?"

She distracted herself by watching passengers debark, and tried to identify cottage landlords marching to chores.

"I thought you *wanted* to get pregnant." He edged the car forward.

"Maybe *you* should get pregnant!" From the corner of her eye, she saw David's face pivot toward her. She turned on the radio.

He shut it off and pulled the car forward, driving right up to the chain that kept vehicles from rolling into the ocean.

She reached for the door handle.

"Don't!"

She hated his saying that.

"Do not—open—the—door. Yet."

She stared at the churning water.

"What is that supposed to mean, Jane? Why the hell should I use a condom?"

Sadness rose to her throat. *I will not cry.* The ferry vibrated under them, jolted as one car bumped another. "I'm afraid."

David gazed through the windshield. "Afraid of what?"

She made herself flat. "Another miscarriage."

He opened his door, and she opened hers, and they got out and went up the stairs and up again to the top deck, crowded with people and carry-ons. She sat on a red slatted bench. He stood at the portside rail, facing away from her.

She got up and wrapped her arm across his back. "I'm sorry. It was a stupid thing to say."

He nodded, lips pressed tight.

The engines ground as the hull moved away from the landing. Skinny boys knelt at dock's edge, peering into the water. She was driving him away as surely as the boat's propellers cleared fish from the dock. Her head ached. Her breath grew rapid and shallow. She drummed her fingers.

David placed a hand over hers, stopped the movement. "It's all right. We're all right." He rubbed her back, idling among her vertebrae. "Bony beans." He squeezed the nape of her neck.

She leaned into his side, felt his arm go around her. *I'm sorry, David.* When she pulled back and looked up into his face, his normally curvy mouth was straight, the edges turning down. The green lenses of his sunglasses reflected sky. She stayed in his arm and gazed over the rail, lowering her hat against sun spiking off the water. Spray showed brown against white hulls. Feeling dizzy, she turned from the rail and sat on the bench. David watched her, and she reached out to him.

He pulled on a navy baseball cap and sat. The benches were back to back, and David spoke quietly, his lips close to her ear. "Are we giving up on having a family?"

"No."

A little girl with a mass of golden curls pushed a stroller past their feet. For a second the world turned sepia, and Jane opened her eyes wide. Suddenly thirsty, she reached for her water. She drank, choked a little, and passed the bottle to her husband. "What if I miscarry again? Strike three!" She began to shake and turned into David as his arm came around her. Unspoken words beat through her. *Barren. Not worthy.* She fought away sadness, sitting up straight, and reached into her bag for the aspirin bottle. "I have a headache."

She lulled herself with the ferry's vibration for a while, then looked around to see which lucky passengers would later ride back to the island. Thinking out loud, she said, "You know, if I were a teacher, I could have the whole summer off. We could buy a cottage." She warmed to the idea, began feeling excited about it. "I could fix it up and rent it out. It could be my job. I could ferry back and forth, bike from house to house."

"Do you want to buy a cottage or be a teacher?"

She saw her distorted image in David's lenses. "I don't have the patience to be a teacher. I'm just not ready to go back to work."

"Then don't."

"I'm an executive recruiter. A headhunter! I'm good at what I do. And I 'strut' when I walk!"

"Right." David placed his palms together under his chin in his thinking pose. "Long range, we want to have a family."

She made a brief nod. David Eliot prided himself on taking the long and short view simultaneously.

"In the meantime, if your work no longer challenges you, you need to look for something else. Right?"

There were times when she didn't trust her husband, and this was one of them. Numbers and figures were finite, clean and clear. She wasn't. She would rather rhyme. *Jane has pain. Jane wants gain.*

"Maybe you *should* be a teacher. But with a degree in marketing . . . ."

He lacks emotional depth. "I don't want to be a teacher." *Jane, pain, gain, grain, wane. Stain.*

David dropped his hands. "You can *have* a longer vacation. What do you want?"

Something bumped her foot and Jane looked up and into the face of the little girl with the stroller.

"Sorry!" Blue eyes peeked through wavy, blond tendrils.

Their eyes connected, held. Jane, unable to look away, said, "I used to wear dresses just like yours." Pink seersucker.

"My *baby* has a dress like this, too. See?" She pulled a large doll by its arm from the stroller. She smiled and returned it to the carriage, adjusting its legs around a strap. The doll had a cloth body and a smooth, painted head.

Jane moved to the edge of her seat and cupped the doll's head in her palm. "She's beautiful."

"I have hun'rets of babies, but I can only bring one to the hospital. We're going to see my grammy."

"Your grammy will feel better after seeing you." Pink and white like the girl in her dream . . . Jane sat on her hands to keep from reaching out and touching her.

The child's sandals flashed red as she pushed the stroller toward a man in a Red Sox cap, wearing jeans and work boots. He worked a pen over a folded newspaper and glanced up when the stroller hit his boot. The little girl used her round blue eyes to direct his gaze toward Jane, placing a hand over his ear and whispering. He listened and made an abrupt nod to Jane, his mouth unmoving under a rust-colored mustache, a hardness bordering on anger in his brown eyes.

She had expected blue.

For a rocking second, Jane felt a small hand in her own. An excited giggle pulled her attention to her side. Nothing. No one was there. But an image flashed before her—of eyes squinting up at her from under a straw bonnet.

"Mummy! Mummy!"

Again she looked, but no one was there.

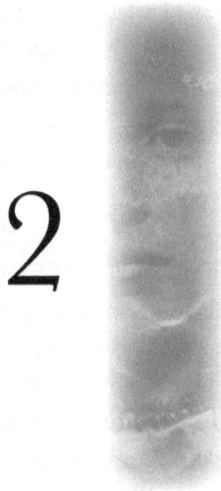

2

On Monday morning, Jane entered the green marble foyer of her office building and began to sneeze. She broke into a sweat as elevator doors closed her in, weight pressing into her lungs and blackness leaking into the edges of her vision before the doors slowly, slowly pulled apart. She slid sideways through the opening and ran to a window at the end of the hall. She imagined fresh air coming through, into her. Dry mouthed and headachy, she was breathing again. Sunlight reflected off her car, winking at her from the parking lot below.

As she started through her office door, an invisible wall left her hunched and gasping.

Louise walked her down the stairs and outside to a bench. "You're white as a ghost, Jane."

Pauline, the secretary, had followed them out and handed her a water bottle. "Is it claustrophobia again?"

Jane held the bottle with shaking hands and carefully swallowed. Her middle felt girdled, cinched tight. She was aware of Louise thanking Pauline for the water and sending her back upstairs.

Within five minutes of sitting, Jane was breathing normally. "I honestly thought I was past the claustrophobia, Lou." She pulled the little silver duck from her pocket, fingered it, moving her thumb against the beak.

"Jane, that was a full-blown panic attack." Louise studied her. "There's some part of you that does not want to be in this office!" She shook her head and looked at the duck. "What is that?"

Jane passed her the silver relic. "I found it in the surf."

Louise turned it this way and that, and passed it back. "What's the big deal? You can leave. We'll get you another job."

Humidity pressed Jane's temples. Sweat trickled down the center of her back. "It's just—" She stumbled over what she wanted to say. "I'm like a well-oiled clock. And this job is the oil!"

"Not anymore, it isn't!" Louise shook her head. "It's time to move on. It's time to face . . . I think you know what you've been hiding from."

Jane massaged the duck. "You know, I never even thought of having kids. But when a baby starts growing in you, everything shifts. Everything. I can't explain it, but it changes you."

"Yeah." Louise let out a deep sigh. "Probably by design. Hormones kicking in and all." She pressed a tissue to her neck. "That's why it's so hard, but you can't hide from your feelings, Jane. It doesn't work."

"Maybe my lucky duck isn't so lucky after all."

"A panic attack has nothing to do with luck. Your body's trying to tell you something. Did you *want* to come back to work?" Louise's tone was matter-of-fact, her lightly penciled brows still above round, red-framed glasses. "Trust yourself. You're stronger than you think you are."

Louise could deal with anything. She and Jack had long ago evicted their eldest son, telling him he could come home when he chose to be drug-free. He hadn't come home.

"You could choose to choke to death, I suppose."

"Very funny. Okay. I get it. I'll email my resignation from home."

"I guess you'll have to, since you can't so much as walk into the place!"

"Let's meet for lunch, Lou. Every week."

"How about Wednesdays? Starting the day after tomorrow."

"Thanks." The silver duck felt foreign and uncomfortable in her hand.

———•◦•———

Life without her job wasn't as intimidating as Jane had expected it to be. Some part of her had insisted she move on, and she needed to trust the good in that. Besides, keeping busy in the golden light of autumn was much more fun than rustling up jobs and employees, convincing and selling, and selling, and selling. Her marketing degree was built around creating visual lures, to sell concepts. She wanted to take an art course, but there was the hand thing. It was like hitting another wall whenever she considered it.

She cleared the patio and steps of green vines, cleaned gutters, and washed down windows and shutters with a garden hose. They'd lived in Portland for five years. Their house was built into a hill too steep for grass, so that it looked like a small cape from the street but was two-storied at the back. House and garage bordered a brick sidewalk, mimicking original carriage houses in their upscale neighborhood.

David gave her a carpenter's apron and hammer holster and taught her how to shingle. She poured nails that had been scooped like grain out of a wooden barrel at the hardware store into the apron pouch. When they stuck together, she laid them on the granite step and tapped them apart with her hammer. She covered the garage wall with sweet-smelling cedar, each wedge thinned to a delicate fringe, wide or narrow; pale, reddish or dark. She spaced the shingles one nail head apart and pounded two nails into each. Where there was a knot in the sheathing, the hammer bounced back and she nailed into a different spot, filling each row, alternating wide shingles with narrow. When necessary, she used a utility knife to cut a clean line and rapped a shingle into two pieces, until, like a life-sized puzzle, the wall was complete.

She seemed always to be counting things. While removing a pane from the garage door, she considered the current incidence of threes in her life—how three weeks had passed since quitting the job she had worked at for three years; from the age of thirty to thirty-three. Although she hadn't seen her a second time, the dream child was never far from Jane's mind. As she scraped out brittle putty, a monarch butterfly swooped up from the ground and flew so near that she felt the breath of its wing. *In spirit.*

Her friend Chester once told her about a man in hypnosis, who had, *in spirit*, before being born, hovered about a young girl at the beach who was slated to be his mother. Was little "Pink-and-white" hovering near her? If the soul of an unborn baby could have an agenda, maybe *her* baby, twice started, twice gone, was still waiting to be born. And maybe, just maybe, this had something to do with the dream child. An idea settled in her heart, like a promise, and secretly, without daring to put the thought into words, she expected to conceive a third time, in her thirty-third year, and this time she would carry full-term.

The fresh putty was a supple gray. A special tool made a clean line of its softness over the new pane of glass. With a happy heart, she would cover its delicate surface with white enamel, sealing and protecting it.

But soon every butterfly, every bird, and then any flying thing, suggested her secret prayer, nicking at its promise, until the sight of fluttery wings became an irritant. Afraid of obsessing and jinxing the whole thing, she put on her headset and listened to public radio.

When she wasn't working, the silver duck was in her hand. One day, she looked at the duck and wished it were clay, but she was running out of projects and getting panicky, and forgot about the clay. She tried drawing her dream child with colorful chalk and couldn't even blue the ribbon before severe nausea struck.

At lunch, Louise said, "I know you've been busy, but have any of the things you've done really pleased you?"

Jane fingered her cross. "I liked shingling the garage wall. I wanted to do more."

"Wow! Then you're in luck! Chester has a cottage at Peaks Island and spent his summer fixing it up. He came up short—on—guess what? Shingling!"

"I thought he moved away."

"He did. To New Jersey. I ran into him at the bank." Louise's straw pulled at the bottom of the glass and she signaled the waiter for more water. "Maybe you can help him," she said, pulling his card from her handbag.

Jane had hoped that Chester would easily land jobs for people at the placement agency because she so enjoyed his company. His straight eyebrows would shoot up and down when he talked, and after telling Jane about working nights as an exotic dancer and how he had lined his Dracula cape with red satin, she felt as if she had known him forever. They used to eat lunch together every day, but eventually Jane began to feel uncomfortable because she wouldn't have liked David always dining with a female co-worker. When, like a jerk, she declined Chester's next lunch invitation, she was filled with regret. He was visibly hurt and his confidence further shaken. Pay arrangements were drawn against commission, and, with no sales, Chester was gone before Jane even had a chance to talk with him.

Chester was happy to hear from her again. "I'm so glad you left that awful job, Jane. Tchtt. I wish I could go to Peaks with you! I have to confess I've never shingled. But I worked so hard getting everything *there!*" He gave a loud sigh. "It's only the front wall, and the place is so small, it's called Pigeonhole. It'll look like something from Nantucket when it's done, and that's saying something for Peaks!" His laughter was infectious and Jane was smiling when she hung up the phone and relayed the joke to her husband.

David said, "If we wanted pristine Nantucket, we'd go there. It's the difference between suburbia and country, and I prefer country." But he didn't like her plan. "There's no one out there, Jane. Summer's over."

"People *live* there, David. And didn't you tell me to do whatever makes me happy?"

He considered this, hands on hips, mouth clamped.

She noticed how good he looked in his dress pants as she tucked her trusty old headset into her pack. "I'm pretty much over the claustrophobia."

He leaned into the counter. "Shingling can be very 'zen'. What's with the headset?"

"In case I get bored. Or obsessive. I can listen to public radio."
It never hurts to add a little truth, and the statement brought him
over to her. She wrapped her arms around him and breathed his clean
smell. "You could come see me, and we could have f-u-n, fun!"

David stepped back. "We can have f-u-n right here, and you
better be commuting because I have no intention of going out there."

———————

Jane stood at the prow of the ferry with the engines humming like
a lullaby through the soles of her feet. She raised her collar, turning
her back to the damp breeze and considered her morning dream: *My
headset fell in the water. I dove down for it and came up choking.* She
had also dreamed of waiting to board the ship, once again without
seeing the little girl and, pushing away the glum tedium as she woke,
said, "I'd like us to get on the boat." *And see the child.* She picked
up a notebook and wrote in block letters: **GET ON THE BOAT. SEE
THE GIRL.**

Now feeling something cold touch her ankle, she looked down
into a dog's black eyes. She stooped to rub his shaggy white head,
standing when he waddled back to his owner.

"Max always gets nervous on zee ferry." The French woman's
wide smile creased into suntanned laugh lines.

The dog's serious gaze fixed on Jane, who chuckled and said,
"What breed is he?"

"He's a Tibetan Terrier, big brother to the Lhasa Apso."

I know this woman. "I'm Jane Eliot," she said, extending her
hand. "You came into Port Placement. Renee, isn't it?"

"Oh, yes. Of course! What a good memory you have!"

"That's because I was hoping you'd work at placement *with* me."

Renee's laugh was gravelly and husky. "Thank you. But I owe
you so much, Jene. You told me to think about what truly interests
me. I went back to school and I am doing my dissertation on hypnosis
and healing."

"Hypnosis?" Jane pushed her right hand into her jacket pocket,
hoping to keep her hand still and at least out of sight. "Good for
you!"

"Do you live on Peaks Island, Jene?"

"No, I live in Portland. I'm only out here for a few days—to shingle a friend's cottage." In answer to Renee's lifted brows, Jane said, "I'm taking a break from placement." Her face warmed. "Do you live out here, Renee?"

"Oh, no. We live just south—in Saco."

The engines were loud, the air exhilarating, the ferry freeing. Jane felt her own smile widen like Renee's. "And your kids? How old are they now?"

"They are big! Seventeen and fifteen . . . and with their friends today. We just got back from visiting my mother in Paris, where my husband also had a reunion at the Sorbonne. It was a wonderful trip, but we are desperate for a head-clearing walk. That's why we are here."

"I can imagine," Jane said. Thinking of Chester, she continued. "I have a friend who talks a lot about hypnosis." *And the spirits of unborn babies.*

"Hypnosis and healing is fascinating to me. I love doing my homework," Renee laughed.

Jane considered her right hand and plunged. "Well, maybe you can help me, Renee. I've been having a hard time drawing and painting. My right hand . . . wags."

"*Ooh la la!* I would love to work with you, Jene. And I need to practice with lots of people for my paper." Renee rolled her eyes.

"Renee." A man in a canvas hat held out a brochure to her.

"Jene, this is my husband, Bill." Renee pronounced it *Beel.* "This is Jene."

"How do." He nodded, blue eyes magnified by glasses, and looked at the pamphlet. Then, appearing distracted and perplexed, he raised his head and let it pivot from Jane to Renee and back again. "Odd. You two look kind of alike, with different coloring of course. Different coloring, but you both have green eyes."

The women laughed, assaying each other, and Renee objected, saying, "No, Bill! Jane is much younger with skin untouched by sun!"

Jane was flattered but perplexed. "I don't have such wide cheekbones—"

"You do. You look alike," said Bill, returning his attention to the pamphlet as the women looked shyly at each other. "The name 'Casco' is derived from the word Aucocisco, meaning 'Resting Place.' Fort Gorges was built on a rocky reef in 1858 with short range guns . . . obsolete by completion. That's it."

The building squatted low in the water, ominous and angry-looking. Grass grew on its roof, hanging over granite walls and black slits of windows. Water lapped at stones creeping up from the ocean's floor. The fort, flat and dome-less, grew out of the stones.

"Fort Gorges was never garrisoned."

Renee said, "I wonder if pirates used it. Can we go there?"

Shivering, Jane pictured a handful of men huddled in wet gloom, cut off from the world by cold, choppy water. A guard would stand watch. Other men steamed by the fire, and she sensed their shaking in terrible wetness, choking on thick curls of smoke. She coughed. Hot smoke tore at her throat, stung her eyes, burned in her chest. She covered her nose and mouth, afraid that when she stopped coughing, she would be dead. The world darkened around her.

———•◦•———

"Jene? Jene?"

Her head banged against something hard. She was being tugged at the shoulders.

"Can you hear me?"

She opened her eyes. Woozy. Sitting on the deck. *Why?* Her back was against the wall of the engine room. Renee's green eyes stared at her. *Oh, my God. What happened?* A jacket was draped over her. She managed to speak. "What is going on?"

"I heard you coughing, and then you dropped. No, no. Stay down."

She sat forward, testing. She remembered her throat feeling like it had been scraped raw. "Oh, how embarrassing . . . . " But she was surprised that her voice was not a croak. Her throat no longer hurt. "I thought there was smoke." There was none.

"Have you ever fainted before?"

"No. I almost fainted, but that was related to . . . claustrophobia."

Her head ached, pulsed with confusion. Two sets of eyes studied her mental disarray. Her face warmed. "I'm so embarrassed. But I can get up." She took Bill's hand and stood.

"Did you say something about smoke, Jene?"

A chill snaked up her spine, raised hairs on the back of her neck.

"Jene? You must tell me, Jene. I am your friend, and I can help you."

"You'll think I'm crazy, but . . . I was thinking of pirates around a fire." She paused to shake her head. "And then I was choking on smoke."

"You would be an excellent subject for my paper. May I call you?"

"Yes. Of course."

"How will I reach you, Jene?" They made their way down the stairs, and Renee turned to Bill for the brochure. "You may write on this."

Jane wrote down her numbers. "Thanks for your help, Renee."

"It was nothing."

"It was to me!" Jane listened to the whining of huge gears. The ferry bumped its ramp. Boat tenders lassoed tarred pilings, halting movement, metal to metal, pier to decking. They unhooked the heavy chains that fenced in the cars.

"Goodbye, Jene. I will call you!"

Jane waved and went back to the van, feeling mildly irritated about fainting but grateful to Renee. Hypnosis offered a glimmer of hope for her crazy hand that she had tried so hard to hide and would never take to a doctor.

Fort Gorges sat like the dull hull of a ship without upper works, its blunt bow toward Portland. *What happened to me? This must be how people with dementia feel.* She didn't dare think about smoke. *Now. I must focus on now.* She aimed the car up the steep landing and right on Island Avenue, following the bend that dropped down to glistening water. At sight of the museum's wide porches, she turned left up a short hill and onto grass.

A black lettered sign with the word *Pigeonhole* hung above the steps. Four narrow posts, located where a front wall might have been, supported the second floor, creating a deep porch. A freestanding roof on the left of the tiny house added a shallow porch. She drank from her water bottle. And sat. She didn't know what the smoke thing was about, but the thought of tidy shingles calmed her. She was to nail the cedar right over asphalt siding, *after* scraping green trim boards around windows and door, and painting them white.

Feeling as brittle as a stick figure, she stepped down from the van. Closed-up houses sat on six-inch posts, porch decks a full story above the steep hill. Shriveled geraniums grew from the center of an old tire. Nothing moved on the empty road.

Do I really want to be here?

She crossed spongy decking to a bulging screen door.

Turning around and leaving would be worse.

She took the key from a nail under the porch rail. She worked the lock until it released then opened the door wide enough to enter. Going from window to window, she raised loose bottom sashes, pulled back a dead bolt on a second door, and escaped onto the side porch. Hands clutching her arms, she paced. *I can do this! I can do this! I can do this!*

Back inside, she crossed the kitchen to the rear door, lifting and dragging it over worn linoleum. Despising attached sheds, she plunged through, unhooked the door and broke into daylight and the sweet-sour smell of over-ripe apples. Gray clothespins waited on rope tied to a box elder tree.

A patch of ocean gleamed like a silver plate as she climbed the back steps. Keeping the image in mind, she approached the inside staircase, extending her breaths, ignoring the dark strips of wood closing in on her, the pulsing in her ears, the throbbing at her temples. She took courage from the light coming in from the window at the top. "I can do this. It's only a staircase." *And there's no one to hear me.*

Sand from the steps stuck to her hands as she crawled up, until, pushing up the wobbly bottom sash, she stuck her head through and sucked in air.

She wore a headache like a watch cap. At the opposite window, she raised the sash and the curtain billowed. White chenille, stark against a dark wood wall, covered the bed beneath a milk-glass wall lamp. A ceiling fixture's string brushed her face as she headed for the stairs.

Downstairs, sun beamed through two windows, curtains wafting in and out on all three walls. *Phew. Maybe I am over the claustrophobia.* She was still ragged, but now she could look at the house.

Tweed swivel chairs and an ottoman faced the inside wall and fireplace. In the right front corner, a kidney-shaped coffee table curved in front of studio couches covered in Indian bedspreads, sarongs and scarlet throw pillows. A table made of two planks hugged the opposite wall, a straight chair at each end, and one facing the window. The floor was painted in taupe enamel around a large braided rug, and the walls were studs on sheathing, painted white.

Three strides into the kitchen took her to the sink, set in red linoleum, flanked on the left by refrigerator, on the right by a stove. She found the bathroom to the right of the back door. A cylindrical water tank stood next to the shower. She washed her hands. Light from the window above the toilet cast her face in shadow so that her reflection in the mottled mirror was unrecognizable.

3

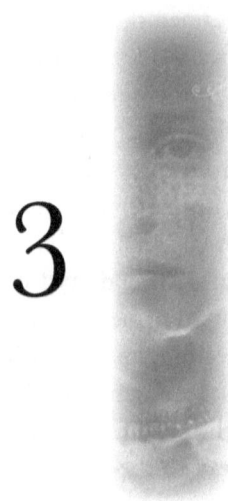

Jane ran water into an orange kettle, turned on the burner, and phoned David.

"This is David Eliot."

"Hey."

"Hey yourself. What's up?"

"Chester's cottage is pretty nice. Wanna come see it?"

"Tell you what. You come home tonight, and I'll see it tomorrow. Deal?"

"Take me out to dinner?"

"Twist my arm."

That's what David had said on the day they met in Boston, after a turning tide chased the college crowd into warm restaurants. Stirring hot rum and gazing through glass, she watched him hurry to the entrance. Nose and cheeks red from the cold, he stepped through the door and ran a hand through wind-blown hair that feathered against the gray wool of his upturned tweed collar. When he turned, their eyes locked. She felt her face color from her chin into her hairline as she looked into deep, dark eyes. She lowered her head, breaking the invisible link. He joined some friends at the bar, and when she glanced at him, he felt her gaze and faced her.

Her friends were laughing. "We're out of here!"

Jane shifted from him to them. "No!"

"You stay!" Her roommate had said, and then arched her neck to greet the tall man who had come up behind them and would someday be Jane's husband.

Jane looked into his face and the room disappeared around them.

"Hi. My name's David Eliot." His deep voice resonated through her.

She stood up and took his hand. "Would you like to sit down, David Eliot?"

"Twist my arm," he had said, and his lips pulled back in a wide, easy grin that hooked up on one side. They laughed as they sat, their hands still together.

Smiling at the memory, she carried her tea and peanut butter sandwich out to the sunny front steps and sat on the warm planking with a perfect view of Whitehead, the cliff at Cushing Island. When she had eaten enough to take away the edge of hunger, and when her mind was for a moment blank, her vision tilted and blurred, and though she was awake, her old dream came to the forefront of her mind . . .

———◆———

Standing rigid, she gripped a child's hand. A steamer waited, belched black smoke, its engines growling. She moved toward its deck. A man said something to stop her. With a jerk of alarm, she tried to pull back from the dream. Her brain seesawed, then her ears began to hum, and the world seemed to vibrate in muffled quiet. Queasiness roiled up from her stomach. The scene darkened and cleared to harsh brightness, and she was leaning into the ship's high rail, waiting for a water closet for five-year-old Sally to pee. Her mouth was sour, her throat raw from vomiting. Her head pounded to the creak and bang as passengers pushed out of privies and the doors slapped shut behind them. Water closets lined the bow below the foredeck. Her stomach lurched.

"It's nicer up front, Mummy. I'll show you after."

Woozy, she watched her child scratch her belly. "Mummy needs to watch for the captain." Sally's curls, frazzled at the crown, glowed like a wide golden halo in the sun. She wanted to redo the braids, finger-brush the thick curls—but her stomach recoiled at the thought.

"Feel the deck, Mummy. Smooth as kinder ash!"

"Kinder ash?"

Sally danced from foot to foot, digging at her head, then her leg. Their berth should have been washed with carbolic acid, corrosive enough to turn her hands into red-gloved retribution for bringing her child into such filth. They had slept in the six-foot crypt with an Irish couple buried under a quilt. Fevers and typhus oozed along with the ragged skeletons lying below-decks, but she herself was another form of scum, sliding away from her family like muck at the bottom of the sea. More vile than the worst of steerage until she could get them off this boat!

"Smile, Mama." Sally's eyes pooled with tears.

Passengers collided, shrieking, as the ship pitched, and she held Sally against her legs and clung to the rail. Her bonnet pulled low, she tried to scan for other vessels, but sunrays stabbed white from endless water. Saliva burst from the sides of her tongue and she stretched her head over the rail and heaved, her groans hidden from even her own ears by the sounds of the ship.

———•——•———

Jane opened her eyes to such a whirling that her hands flew out and grabbed on to the step. Her stomach lurched. Her ears thrummed. She fought nausea and spinning until she was again aware of sitting on the porch steps at the top of the empty road. A piece of sandwich lay on the plate next to her.

She sprang to her feet and wrapped an arm around the post. "Oh my God!" Her gut released short breaths, clenching and letting go. "Oh!" Her gaze took in the desolate short street. "Thank God, there's no one here to watch me."

With a moan, she sat back down on the step. She could almost forget that something had happened. Like a dream. *The little girl!* Jane felt such a squeeze of love that she could have wept. Sally. Then it *was* her dream, her old dream, coming to life. Coming to her when she was awake.

"Wait a minute!" She reeled. "We're *on* the boat. We were *always* on the boat. We need to *get off*!" She rose and strode to the car for her notebook. She didn't know how a dream could happen like that—while wide awake. *I'll make sense of this by writing it down.*

Dizzy, notebook and pen in hand, she returned to the porch steps. A space, an invisible, vertical space ran through her, made her wobbly; like a vacuous cylinder designed to keep her unsteady. *Focus.* She pictured a steel rod, straight and rigid. The spacey feeling disappeared, and she spotted her tea. She lifted the mug and recalled sickness. "The tea!" Was it drugged? But she hadn't sipped it, and the peanut butter and bread were her own.

Maybe she was possessed! "What in the name of God do you want?" she shouted. That was the way to address a ghost. *A ghost in my head?* She lifted out the tea bag, causing its dark stain to swirl, and put it to the side of the dish.

The tea was hot, not scalding, and it wasn't bitter for having sat too long. It had been more than a moment, more than a minute. She went over what she had seen and where she had been. All of it was beginning to fade, like waking from a dream, except for a headache at the front of her head. But it *wasn't* a dream. She was awake. She drank the tea. Gazing at faded leaves, she remembered her eyes blinded by sun glinting off water, and that the ship was noisy, but its sounds eluded her now. Jane heard nothing but leaves, occasional insects. Even the birds were still.

She opened the notebook and wrote:

> *Sally. Braids. Blue flowered dress. Blue sweater.*
> *Scratching!*

Why hadn't she held her, soothed her?

> *Sailing ship*
> *Water closets*
> *Captain*
> *Shame, remorse*

Carbolic acid
Steerage
Need to get off & back to other children

The woman's skirt had horizontal stripes in varying shades of blue that billowed and flattened against her legs. All those years she thought she was waiting to board a boat. *Not so reliable, those dreams.* "But this *is* my dream! Continued!"

Numb, she took her things inside, dropping her notebook on the long table. She rinsed her cup and plate and wiped the counter and replayed the scene as she climbed the step ladder, seeing barefoot women in ragged skirts and shawls, and men in hats crowding the deck, like New York's Lower East Side, thronged with immigrant workers. She saw Sally's shadowed eyes and flushed skin. *Thick hair for such a little girl.* Her neck prickled as she sensed other textures between her fingers, slippery thin, strong, and straight. *Other children, other braids.*

On the ladder, dead flies and spider webs stuck to her brush, forcing her down for a broom to clear the surface. She had the paint but forgot the brush. She shook her head and did some stretching exercises. She needed to focus, but she was intrigued and eager to know all there was *to* know.

She swept out cobwebs with a kitchen broom and climbed back on the ladder to cover the green trim board at the top of the wall with white paint. The brush left dark traces in its path. Reconciled to doing a second coat, she painted more quickly. Pathos deeper than sadness had filled the woman. Like muck at the bottom of the ocean being sucked away from her family. *I hope she gets off that boat. What if she didn't?*

Jane scraped at the board with a putty knife, put the tool in her pocket and wiped down the board with a rag that she tucked in her sleeve. It was as if she'd gotten hold of a strand of wool at the broad back of a knit sweater, and if she could just pull on that strand, she could reveal what's beneath. But an undercurrent of fear tugged at her. Her subconscious was revealing something in a dream—*it would have to be good for me. It's my subconscious.*

A gentle rapping is easily drowned out. Where had that come from?

Legs and back achy, she laid the brush on top of the paint can and stood tall, stretching her arms and back and then bent at the waist to dangle and stretch out her back. Her knuckles brushed the worn porch boards. *Those boards should be oiled the way Aunt Aleece's were each spring*, she thought, seeing again the dark oiled wood that swept so well. From a distance, the boards looked almost black against white risers. A wave of dizziness passed through her as she stood. *Aunt Aleece?* She didn't have an Aunt Aleece.

She decided to do it again, stretching high toward the unpainted underside of the porch roof, reaching with one arm and the other, and then bending at the waist and dangling. Old drips of green paint lay hardened near the railing and under the windows. Flooring near the steps had been walked down to unprotected wood that had gone punky. She lifted slightly as she inhaled, dropping down further, and pictured oiled wood as she had seen it, colorless, but appearing brown or black against white risers.

———— • • • ————

"A cottage in Dorset, porset, morset!" She can smell the grass, thick, almost as long as hay, as she tumbles. "Sit 'n watch the sunset, sunset, sunset!"

"Elizabet'! You moosn't toomble lak tha boys!"

She completes her somersault and pulls her dress over pantaloons. A black shoe bulges with ugly fat toes. She is yanked up, fingers squeezing into her arm. Her eyes burn with tears.

"Tha's noone way for tha' yoong lady 'a behave."

Elizabeth swipes the back of a hand across her cheek, wrenches her arm free and bolts. She won't even look at the old cow.

"Stop tha' roonnin!"

She watches the grass rush by her feet. She would tell Mummy, "It feels good to run, Mummy!"

———— • • • ————

Jane found herself still bent at the waist, dangling, and looking at her paint-smudged knees. Holding on to the porch rail, she straightened and waited for vertigo to pass. Green weeds and trees blurred as she waffled in her head, until she thought again of the steel rod. Steady, she stepped off the porch and walked through tough crabgrass to the back of Chester's cottage. The other grass had been fine wild strands, dense with summer growth. A bird skittered from the clothesline.

In the kitchen, she turned on the burner under the kettle and only then realized that she had walked through the shed room without even noticing.

She felt drained, as if a plug had been taken out of her head while she was hanging upside down and her energy had spilled into the floorboards. She got out a teabag, milk, and a cup. Her thumb stuck to the cup's handle. She washed her hands. Paper toweling caught at the web between thumb and palm.

The sun was at the back steps now, and she sat there, sipping her tea. The dangling trick felt perverse. Like tripping or something, although she had never done that. When the tea was gone, she went in to make more, recording the sight of Aunt Aleece's porch and the impressions of the little girl, Elizabeth. *I am seeing through this child's eyes.* Just as she had seen through the woman's eyes. Whose child was this? Were the two one and the same? Why would she see through *this* child's eyes and not Sally's? But the answer was obvious. *Plain as the nose on my face,* And unavoidable. She saw through the eyes of the child because they were *her* eyes.

Jane would call her mother. She could ask if there had been an Aleece in their family. She could tell her about hanging upside down to stretch out her back and thinking of the oil that had been used on Aunt Aleece's porch and ask about the product.

Her phone chimed. Water hissed on the burner. "Hello?"

"Hey. Which ferry are you taking?"

"David."

"Who else would it be?"

"I just . . . what time is it?"

"Time you were heading to Portland. I'll meet you."

"I'm a mess." Her hands were like sandpaper. She sat on the stool. "I forgot . . . to watch the time." She had lost track of their plan. Her mind raced.

"It's 5:15. You can be here in twenty minutes."

"David. I'm so tired I could cry."

"Why? What's wrong?"

"I fainted on the ferry this morning. And then I had that old dream while I was wide awake." She expected him to say something. "Remember that dream? Trying to get on a boat?" She waited, static in her mind.

"Jesus, Jane! Blackbirds?"

"Yes. That one."

"What do you mean you fainted? Are you sick?"

She sighed and it sounded like a moan.

"Just tell me how to get there. Can you hear me?"

"Yes. It's the last left before the Civil War Museum." She found her way to the couch and went to sleep, thinking that she needed to get the paint off her hands.

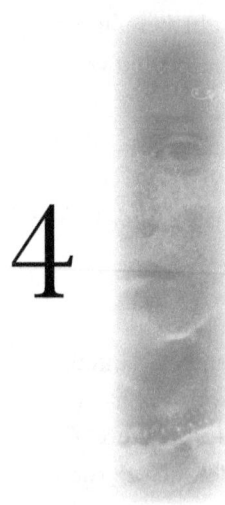

4

Waking to lamplight, Jane sensed something tall looming above her. David. When she felt her hand thick with paint, memory flooded in. He placed his suit coat like a heated blanket over her shoulders as she sat up. He sat beside her.

"I fell asleep."

"You're all right?"

She nodded.

"What happened on the ferry?"

"I fainted. It was so stupid." She wanted to use the bathroom and moved to get up.

David held her in place. "Tell me this first."

She let out a breath. "Renee's husband was reading from a brochure about Fort Gorges. She asked if pirates might have used it. I was thinking of being cold and wet and standing around a smoky fire. This doesn't make sense, but I choked on the smoke." She coughed. "It was like dying in a fire. And the next thing I knew, Renee was shaking me awake."

"Who's Renee?"

"She's someone I met at Port Placement—a really nice woman who just happened to be riding the ferry."

"And then?"

"And then I was fine." She stood and considered how to get to the bathroom, saying, "It's off the kitchen," and headed that way.

The room was bright when she returned. The painted studs on sheathing created shadowed alcoves in the glow of half a dozen small lamps. A ship's etching, schooner pitched against sky and water, smacked of the shipboard . . . visit? Experience? She adjusted a cockeyed shade, the movement careless and burning her fingers, as she focused on getting out the door to where David must be.

He stood on the front porch in a blaze of setting sun.

"Quick!" She pulled him by the hand down the steps and down the gravel road.

"I thought you were so tired you could cry." David's wingtips crunched in the grit.

"I'm not now." She hurried them across the street and up the steps of the Civil War Museum, the surf's *shoosh* and rattle growing louder as they walked to the back. Incoming tide crashed into the cove. The island yawned a cool breeze at their backs. She leaned into David's warm chest and he wrapped his arms around her.

"What about the dream, Jane?"

The flush of sunset picked up darkness like an impressionist painting, each dot blotting out light. She started to move away, to think.

"Uh-uh." He held her against his chest, his chin topping her head. "What did I tell you?"

"Something about your dream with the boat."

"Okay."

"When did this happen?"

"It was right after I called you. I made tea and a sandwich, and I was sitting on the front step in the sun." She told him as clearly as she could, saying finally, "I was *there*, living it! It wasn't like a dream at all."

He loosened his hold and they moved apart and walked back the way they had come.

"It's confusing—even to me." She told him about the dizziness and nausea, and as much as she could recall about coming out of the "dream."

It was dark when they got in the Porsche for the short drive to dinner. Both were quiet, each trying to make sense of the tale she had told. At the Landing Restaurant, they sat in a booth overlooking Casco Bay and a ragged line of lights on the mainland. Locals came in the front door and filed past, the door squeaking behind them. Camaraderie barked from the bar.

When the waitress had come and gone, David fingered the cleft in his chin. "I still haven't heard what made you so tired, Jane."

"I wrote down some things about that boat thing—I can show you when we get back, and then I started scraping and painting. But I was too distracted and kept messing up with cobwebs and stuff. I was stiff from being on the ladder and did some stretching to loosen my back." She told him about new knowledge of porch boards and an aunt with a name she had never heard in her life: Aleece.

"You're impressionable, Jane. You probably heard that name when you were two years old." He placed pats of butter on his potato and asked the waitress for more.

An image of the child tumbling in pantaloons crossed her mind. "What really made me tired—"

"Was scraping Chester's windows." He completed her sentence and squeezed lemon over his fish.

She could let him think that. She'd rather not put into words how she had purposely hung upside down, trolling for more of the strange scenes. That was what made her feel as if all her energy had spilled from the crown of her head into the old, punky porch boards. It had felt slightly wrong, unclean. She bit into her roll.

He raised his brows, waiting.

"I think forcing memories made me tired."

"Forcing memories? What are you talking about?"

"I purposely hung upside down again. A second time. To see if . . . it would happen again. I got a little dizzy and then . . . I'm little, playing in high grass. A cranky servant grabs me. I see her ugly shoe and pull away. I run away from her. The little girl, the one whose eyes I'm seeing through, grows up to be the woman on the boat. Her name is Elizabeth."

"I thought the woman and little girl were together at the boat."

"Sally is the child on the *boat*." She picked up her water glass. "But that's what made me tired. I think."

He stared at her. "How does anyone—?" He shook his head and returned to his food. He sipped his wine. "This can't be healthy, Jane. I don't want you out here."

"There are no distractions out here. Maybe that's why this stuff is coming through." She wanted to *keep* it coming.

David tossed down his napkin and went to the men's room.

Never before had the simple task of house painting felt enticing, like an opportunity for a story, a story from another time. *Enthralling.* She cut into her baked potato. She had always liked the earthy-tasting skin best. *Hunger makes a good sauce.* Was that her thought? It was a phrase her mother used.

"It's not *like* you to eat with such industry." David took up his napkin. "You haven't been hearing voices, have you?"

"No! David, you *know* about this dream! I've had it longer than I can remember. The dream is from *me* and this is just—more of it!"

He ordered coffee and asked for the check.

"I think it's pretty cool," she said.

They finished eating and rode in silence to the cottage, where she closed windows and wrapped herself in a blanket while David built a fire, laying down rolled newspapers, some twigs and sticks, and log wood on top. He struck an old fashioned match against the brick and held a flaming taper up the chimney to create a draft. After a "whoosh," he held the taper to the newspapers.

The fireplace was shallow and quick to throw heat. She sat in the swivel chair, stretching out her legs and feeling drowsy. Heat baked her face and she rotated the chair, her back to the fire. Parched and beginning to sweat, she went to the kitchen, turned on the tap and drank from her cupped hands, letting the water pool to her cheeks. She filled a glass and relished the coolness as she swallowed . . . and then she was choking.

David's jaw dropped.

She coughed. "I was concentrating on the wetness."

"Is this what it was like on the ferry?"

"No. That was smoke. And I fainted."

"You're not staying out here, Jane."

"I'll commute. I don't have to sleep out here."

"Good. We'll leave when the fire dies down."

"Let's just *enjoy* the fire. We can stay tonight. Okay?"

"Maybe. Where are the shingles? I'll move them for you."

"They're in the shed room." She sat on one of the colorful studio couches and watched small flames flicker, consuming with tiny blue licks. For a second, she felt herself pulling a needle up through a cloth taut within a loop of wood; sensed more than felt. It was just a shiver of time, like déjà vu. She had brought a tube of hand cream from the kitchen and rubbed the cream into her hands, so enjoying its fragrance that she read the label: *patchouli geranium cypress rose*. The smell was sensuous and she cupped her palms over her nose.

David said, "Never use shingles for kindling. They explode with sparks."

She made room for him and held his hand to her nose and inhaled the scent of cedar. Then she moved to his collar and inhaled his fragrance, running her nose up and down the side of his strong neck and into his shirt. His shoulder and chest were padded with muscle, his skin smooth and sweet. She unbuttoned his shirt and spread it wide, then pulled off her own, draping her breasts across his skin before raising them up to be caressed and sucked. Her tight jeans tingled against her crotch and she wished for a skirt, because now she had to disengage herself to take them down and peel them off. But it was easier for David, and before she had freed even one leg, he was touching her. Gasping, she struggled with the denim until it covered only one knee, and he was there, lapping her, and soon she was coming. David entered her while she was still in orgasm, and the strange howling she heard was coming from her.

———◆◆◆———

In the morning, as David rolled off the bed, she said to him, "I dreamed about you, but you looked different. You were tall. I was tall, too, but you were taller."

He stood up, crying out as he hit his head on the sloped ceiling. He held his head and crouched toward the center of the room. "Jesus, what a way to wake up!" He padded across the floor and thudded down the stairs.

The dream seemed so real, and Jordan so distinguished, tall and mustached. *Jordan?* But she knew it was David. She dressed from her backpack, revisiting the dream.

He was coming out of a large building, granite with yellow brick, hat in hand; his dark coat skirted. A "frock coat." Silver streaked his hair, mustache almost white against a florid face. Eyebrows alone were black above intense, dark eyes.

She walked toward him, heart-happy at the chance encounter. Their eyes held, and she dropped a polite nod as he tipped his hat. She kept her expression bland, grateful for the veil that covered her face, and continued past him.

Jane could feel the bonnet that sat forward on her head, designed to clear a chignon at the nape of her neck. Her wide skirt, purple, green, and black silk, belled out from her waist.

Electricity ran up her spine and prickled her neck. She was again the woman from the boat.

That's all there was. The man coming out, she seeing him, passing him. No. They looked at each other, cared for each other. And pretended otherwise.

"Maybe we can get coffee." David was bent over his shoes. "You have to come in case I can't get the car on." He stood up, revealing very wrinkled slacks, and headed for the front door.

She was smiling at the reminder of their lovemaking as she hurried down the porch steps after him, playfully pressing his broad shoulders from behind and wanting to kiss him. "We had such a good time."

Once they were both in the car, David cupped her face in his hands and kissed her on the mouth, before turning to the driving.

The ferry was already berthed. The Porsche went down the cobblestones, across the ramp, and on to the gray deck. The attendant pointed and David backed up and repositioned.

"I'll see you tonight at home." He gave her another solid kiss and looked at her, his mouth hooking up on one side.

She winked at him and skipped from deck to dock, wanting to hop on and off again just for the fun of it but, restraining herself, began plodding up the landing. She thought first of their robust coupling, and then of steaming hot coffee in the thick cups of the Cockeyed Gull. When her calves began to burn, she turned to wave.

A net of black dropped over her view. Her legs wobbled and she was light-headed. Diesel fumes pulled her stomach into nausea. Pier walls the color of gravel wore a brown stain at the water line. Jaundiced water churned around the ferry. The scene trembled under a muddy wash and black, heart-bruising remorse. Shivering in cold damp, she sensed thoroughly wet wood, a water-soaked hull.

She blinked to see better, and the picture brightened with the movement of a dog shaking off water. Dizziness layered through her. The ferry hadn't moved and David's arm was raised, wavering, waiting for a return salute. She waved back.

Screams of gulls jarred her. Marble specks on granite breakwater glimmered in the morning sun. The murky stillness was gone. She registered that it had been there, had left heaviness in her stomach. Remembering fumes, she breathed in clean air and walked fast to the café. She took her coffee and muffin to the deck, cupped the warm mug in her hands and drank, letting the caffeine and the ritualistic sipping lubricate her muscles and thoughts.

Sunlight burned away morning mist and covered the water with mirrored armor. She *knew* that David and Jordan were one. As she and the woman Elizabeth were. Her head began to ache. The muffin felt like it couldn't quite get past her esophagus. She went into the grocery store next door for aspirin and water, swallowed three tablets, and began her trek back to the cottage.

Raised Catholic and later harangued by Jehovah's Witnesses, she used the Lord's Prayer as a spiritual rudder, reciting it as she passed the skeletal pier with its patched-up path to lobster pots and seagulls still as woodcarvings. She longed for more of Elizabeth's story—this mystery/history—and vowed to be patient, to *wait* for the vibration and shuddering change. Underfoot, tough shoots of grass would probably survive winter's snow.

———•◦•———

David texted that he could meet her ferry as late as 5:45, but after that he'd be at a trustees' meeting. She repositioned newspapers and the ladder and climbed up with the bucket and paintbrush. New cobwebs caught in her cap's beak, tickled her face as she spread thick white paint. *Unlikely that Elizabeth would have painted like this.* Even before completing the thought, she saw shiny black paint over uneven bricks and bulbous mortar. A rancid smell engulfed her. A hornet flew close. She swallowed saliva and climbed off the ladder, set down the bucket and reeled into the porch rail. Holding on to the post, she sat on the step and dropped her head. Nausea passed. Her head stopped spinning. A soft rustling of leaves and insects was all she heard in this quiet place. She felt a pinch.

The hornet glided away.

Panic flashed through her. The sting throbbed at the back of her arm. Hair bristled away from her skin. She left the porch, mixed some dirt with spit into the size of a quarter and pressed it to the back of her arm. She drank some water and paced the gravel road.

When she had calmed, she took her FM headset from the car. While painting, she listened to accounts of an earthquake in Indonesia. She imagined women running with babies pressed to their chests, and recalled a tsunami photo of a placid young woman in a refugee line holding a toddler whose face betrayed an old person's terror. An interview followed, the novelist contending that time is an illusion.

Finished with the higher places, she folded the ladder and set aside the headset. She painted window frames, missing the excitement that had been pricked like a balloon. She wanted yesterday's wholesome lust, the confident attitude of patience and reward. Her feet safely on the porch decking, no longer at risk of falling off a ladder, she took her thoughts back to pre-sting, pre-hornet. She pictured shiny black paint over lumpy mortar. There had been a bad smell.

———•◆•———

Her hands ached with cold. Her dress was ruined with black paint at the hem and she wondered if she could give it to someone at the workhouse.

———•◆•———

Nausea swept through Jane as she dropped drunkenly to the spongy deck.

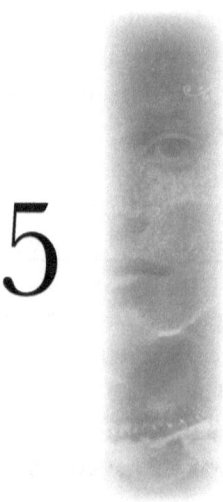

5

When the vertigo passed, she lay flat on the decking with her knees bent, studying the underside of porch roof. She sat up carefully, kneeling before standing. *Okay.* She drank some water and put on her headset.

Shingling soothed her. Every movement made perfect sense, each shingle a puzzle-piece that fit, a game you could always win; and she played until she reached the top two rows. Those shingles had to be cut down, but there wasn't enough daylight for that. She began collecting cedar scraps and tucking them in a cardboard box with her tools. "Bummer. Too late to finish and too late to meet David."

She left a message on their home phone because his cell was off. "Sorry. I worked too late and messed up our date. Call me? Please? Love you."

Showered and dressed in sweats, she built a fire and, deciding to sleep on one of the studio couches, pulled curtains across black windowpanes. She turned on the old radio to a male crooner: *Honey, I'm lonely. I'm so lonely for you, and I wonder if you're missing me, too.* Bulbs from a two-headed lamp glowed through pink translucent shades dribbled with lines of black paint. *Are you missing me, too?* She traced her finger along a raised squiggle of paint on one of the lamp shades and jumped when the phone rang.

"Hello?"

David growled, "What happened?"

"I was trying to finish shingling."

"I picked up *your* favorite pizza. Onions, garlic, and fresh tomatoes. I'm hanging up to eat it while it's hot."

She sat on the couch and decided to call her sister. When there was no answer on her cell phone, she dialed the house. Busy. After reading over her notes about dreams, scenes and strange happenings, she tried again. Still busy. On the staircase wall, a yellowed chart of Casco Bay showed Fort Gorges in the path between Peaks Island and Portland. She was reminded of her choking on the ferry. That was delusional, the worst of anything. As radio commercials shouted and rambled, the earlier song tugged at her, the words repeating in her mind. *Honey, I need you. I need only you, and I wonder, are you needing me, too?* She got up for a glass of water. *Oh baby forgive me, take me back in your arms . . .* She tried her sister again. This time Eileen picked up.

"Your phone has been busy for the longest time."

"I took it off the hook for dinner. Are you coming this weekend?"

"I have to visit Mom first."

"You can stay here Saturday night and drive down to Mom's on Sunday. You'll be that much closer."

"I'll talk to David."

"We can go to Tom Tam and you can tell him about your claustrophobia, and we can go out to dinner after."

"The man who hammers on the doll? Chinese voodoo. Okay, but that's not why I called." She told her sister about Pigeonhole.

"Nothing you do surprises me, Jane. Of course you'd leave home to shingle someone's house! Anything to keep busy, right? What's he paying you?"

"Listen, Eileen. Can you just listen?"

"I'm listening."

"Remember that dream I've always had?"

"Uh—no. I only pay attention to my own dreams."

"The recurring dream!"

"What recurring dream?"

"Waiting to get on a boat? A child?"

"Oh, right! I forgot about that. Blackbirds?"

"Yes."

"It never made sense that there could be birds on a boat."

"Eileen!" Irritation bolted through her.

"All right. I'm sorry. Go ahead."

"Yesterday when I was having lunch, I kind of went into a trance—or something. Really weird. It started with that dream, and then . . . " She told her all she could remember of the shipboard vision.

"Oh my God!"

"I see everything through the woman's eyes, just like the dream."

"You never said that before!"

"Well, how else do you dream?!"

"Holy cow, Jane! This is so cool!"

"Yeah, it is, but sometimes—I don't know. I fainted on the ferry, just thinking about smoke. Then there's this sense of gloom that literally clouds the day, and I almost fell off the ladder. I was so dizzy I slammed into the porch rail."

"Hold on a second."

Telling Eileen both livened and exhausted her. Maybe her mind was playing tricks on her.

"Jane, Harry has to use the phone. I'll call you right back."

"On your cell?"

"Your eldest niece has it. I'll call you back."

Now that Eileen was working full-time, her calls to Jane were less frequent. Three years her senior, Eileen had practically been a second mother, shadowing Jane as her self-proclaimed protector. Whenever they played house, Jane was the baby, dutifully calling her sister 'mummy,' which was strange because they used 'mommy' for their own mother. As a tiny child, Jane thought of them as little mummy and big mommy. She had been doglike in her devotion to Eileen, following her around and waiting on her. Her mother would say, "Jane, you tell Eileen to do that herself," and, "Eileen, Jane is not your slave. Get it yourself." After years of climbing into Eileen's bed, she was told, "You're a big girl now. Four-year-olds sleep in their own beds."

Pulling up her feet, she laid her head on a scarlet pillow. Her cheeks burned from the day's sun and wind. The words of the song played through her mind: *Oh, baby, forgive me. Take me back in your arms.* She was sleepy. But the phone would ring. It would wake her up and then she might not be able to get back to sleep. Still, she crossed her arms, put the phone on her chest, and snuggled down further. David. David and Jordan were the same. Her eyes popped open. The phone hit the floor as she stood up.

The radio was all static. She rotated its orange plastic dial, bypassing clear rock and fuzzy classical, and stopped at a soft ballad. *Said he'd love me forever. Now he's gone with another. And I am alone . . .*

She brought down bedding and was tucking in the top sheet when her phone made its chirping sound. She hoped it was David. "Hello?"

"Hi," Eileen said, "Your husband just called. Don't tell him I told you."

"Oh, for crying out loud!"

"He's a man of few words."

"That's because every word has to count!"

"Uh-uh! I didn't tell you."

"Okay."

"So. This really blows my mind, Janey. I'm jealous. It sounds like you're *remembering* something from the bigger you. The part of you that *makes* your dreams."

"You mean the 'superego'?"

"Well . . . let's just think of it as the soul. The point is it can only help you. My friend Ruth took a psychic awareness course." She said this as if it were a question. "The teacher, a psychic, told her that in another time Ruth didn't finish things, so now Ruth's purpose is to finish everything she starts."

"Hmph."

"It makes sense to Ruth. She waxes the kitchen floor before going on vacation. Drives her husband crazy. She said that with psychic awareness, 'You just know.'"

"Right. When you think about it, you know it's true? That doesn't make a lot of sense, Eileen."

"It might take a little time. Just let it sit. Remember when we first heard about intercourse? How you couldn't believe it? And then you started paying attention to what people said?"

Jane laughed. "Right."

"The important thing is to stay calm. Trust the good in you—the God in you."

Jane rolled her eyes. Eileen was always preaching at her.

"Remember I taught you the muscle testing? The yes and no—with your fingers, Jane. The yes is strong. The no is weak. Have you practiced it? And the next time you feel dizzy, try putting your hands in prayer position right at the breastbone. It centers you."

"You've done this, Ei?"

"Yes. When I do my Tibetan spinning. Remember the five rites I showed you?"

Her mind did backward somersaults. Her sister was forever telling her things and she couldn't find "spinning" in the pile of tidbits. "No. I can't quite place it."

"I showed you at Mom's last April. You do each exercise twenty-one times. The first one is spinning with your arms out, right thumb up, left thumb down. Like dervishing."

She remembered Eileen spinning in Mom's bedroom. "You almost hit your hand on the bureau, and you put your hands in prayer position. Where did you learn that?"

"I read about the hand position in a Christian Science magazine. I sent the article to Mom for her vertigo."

Jane turned off the radio, ending static. "I went upstairs for sheets and a quilt after we hung up. Zero claustrophobia. Can you believe it?"

"Yeah, well, I guess I can believe just about anything. "

"Why though? Why would this suddenly start happening?" Jane waited. "Hello? Are you there?"

"I'm here."

"What? What's wrong?"

"Nothing's wrong. You're asking what I think and I need to put it together—without offending you."

"Oh! It's about my being tense?"

"Don't get defensive! This is your higher self trying to get through to you. You weren't always like this you know."

"Like what?"

"Busy all the time. Brittle. You know how your hand spazzes whenever you relax?"

Jane had worked hard to hide that. "Yeah?"

"Ever since you started the violin. It was like an excuse to keep moving! Then it was knitting. And the house! Painting and painting, until you got a job that let you work night and day. We're mind, body, and spirit, Jane. I think your spirit is trying to find a chink in your armor. Are you there?"

"Yes."

"So what if your hand spazzes out. Let it. This is a good thing."

She wanted to cry. "I kept my hand busy so that it couldn't—*do its thing.*" She had always been afraid someone would notice and say that she had a brain tumor or something. "You knew?"

"Jane. Whenever you're not involved in something—it does it when you're in between—when you're deciding what to do with it. Remember when you used to draw in your sleep?"

"I remember you yelling at me." She quickly changed the subject. "How long can this go on?" She moved the phone to her left ear and let her right hand just sit there on the sheet, letting relief spread through her. *Nothing physical.* Eileen was slow to answer. *Out of character*, she thought, watching her hand twitch back and forth against her thigh.

"I don't know, but would you want it to stop? I wouldn't."

After hanging up, she stayed where she was, letting her hand skitter around on her thigh. Her hand moved with a purpose of its own, up and down, side to side; as if someone else were pulling the strings. It seemed familiar, but it had been doing this for a long time. Maybe if she just let it wag, it would get out of her system and leave her alone.

Her sister spoke with bravado whether she knew what she was talking about or not, but this relaxing about her hand ... *This*, Jane was happy to accept. The place Eileen was touting involved hammering surrogate acupuncture dolls to remove blockages from people.

Chinese voodoo. She was afraid to ask her sister why she thought the hand thing had something to do with spirit, afraid of disturbing the layers of tension lifting away. *It's okay.*

David. "He doesn't want to give me the positive reinforcement of a phone call!" *He's worried about me.* "Well, let him worry."

She went to the kitchen, spread peanut butter on two slices of bread and poured a glass of milk. While eating, she checked the brown paper bags on the dining table to see if they'd been drawn on. They lay as she had left them, held flat by a rock, the borrowed doorstop, with pen and pencil in a mug. She'd slept pretty well lately, had barely encountered that nighttime scrawl. *Nothing physical. How nice.*

David wasn't going to call and she wasn't about to call him. She massaged the arches of her feet that ached from standing on the ladder. Turning off the lamp with the pink shades threw the room into darkness, the fire a shallow glow of ashes. She placed her hand on the sheet and let it shift on its own. In spite of being annoyed with David, she felt more relaxed than she had in a long time and drifted into sleep to the rhythm of spacing shingles and pounding nails.

A baby suckled at her breast. The tugging created a painful pull deep beneath her stomach. She rocked away the pain and focused on the milk being drawn out and the kiss of baby's mouth, stroking the delicate brush of hair on a tiny pink head, cupping its roundness in her hand. The touch was enough to distract the infant, and the baby choked, losing her rhythm of suck and swallow. She sat the baby forward with easy competence and dabbed at the wet mouth with a nappy, as three skinny streams of milk shot out of her nipple, flooding the baby's cheek ....

She felt around in the bed, groping for the child. Gathered her up but couldn't lift her, tried dragging the small body. What was tying her down? She felt a neck, a shoulder. A head. Her husband's head. Not the baby.

She lay crying in quiet sobs and jagged breaths. He hugged her, but his arms were awkward and not comforting. "I love you. You are my life."

She blew her nose and sniffled. He was an orange tallow glow in a nightshirt with a candle in one hand and a cup in the other.

He sat on the bed, looking out in front of him. "I bring you down slowly."

Headachy, eyes swollen, she said, "How?"

"By pulling away from you. I have to stop."

———•◦•———

Jane woke with sadness on her like an invisible blanket. She went over the string of dreams. The baby. That tissue-fine skin—a newborn! She cupped her small breasts, remembering that deep pull—actual nursing—and laughed about the milk hitting the baby's face, so close to the tiny ear. Opening the curtain to let in some light and finding none, she turned on a lamp, its discolored shade evoking the man with the candlestick and thinning ginger-colored hair. *Sarah.* Baby Sarah. The name was in her head.

Baby Sarah became Sally on the ship. She didn't know how she knew that. "Maybe I made it up." The echo of her words pushed her to find her notebook and record the dreams. Feeling the promise of a baby, she went back to bed and lay in pitch dark, focusing on the fuzzy-headed infant. She felt again its delicate skin, counted fingers and toes on little pink feet, but finally reverted to counting seconds of her own breaths in order to sleep.

And when she dreamed, she passed through a hedgerow, white with tiny blossoms, brittle with winter's brown, and dripping with heavy rain. In and out, again and again, until heavy wet drops chilled her shoulders.

She woke to wet wind and rattling casements, a downpour drumming the roof and the acrid reek of sodden ashes. She heated the chimney and lit rolled newspapers under logs. Dampness rode drafts from windows and doors. Shivering, she turned the swivel chair to the fire. It hissed with spits of rain. When a downdraft billowed smoke, she placed a screen over the opening, wiped her stinging eyes, and wrapped herself Indian-style in a blanket. She was aware that fire, chair and blanket all belonged to Chester, and she wished he were there. Chester knew about past lives. Her gaze rested on the flickering flames. A howling started in her ears. Darkness fell over firelight.

———•◦•———

Blackbirds. Standing rigid, she gripped a child's hand. A steamer waited, belching black smoke, its engines growling. She moved toward its deck. A man said something that stopped her. With a dizzying twist, she is on a sunny street. She sees her friend Harriet and calls out to her, but Harriet doesn't respond. Surely that was she, in the new striped dress. Together, they had selected the silk—green with rose—and a thin black line in between. The skirt swung like a bell as Harriet's step quickened. She chased after her friend, waiting for a slow-moving gig to pass before crossing cobblestones.

"Harriet?"

Face smeared with hurt, nose red, brown eyes guarded, Harriet held her chin high.

Elizabeth said, "Roger?"

Harriet nodded. "She isn't new. But an open carriage?"

They hurried on, looking straight ahead in silence, and passed large houses before stepping through the Bryants' wrought-iron gate. She took Harriet's arm as they walked up marble steps. A brass kick plate reflected their approach, their skirt colors muted and dark. She lifted the knocker, letting it fall loudly, and prepared to ask the maid for tea in the morning room. The door opened, and as she peered in, the dimness of the interior swelled to darkness.

———•◦•———

Caught in a nauseating swirl, Jane pressed her palms together. The spinning stopped. She didn't fall out of the chair. Her stomach roiled, as one thought rounded through her mind. *Chester was Harriet.* She held on to the chair while picking up her journal and sat back down to write, leaving wide margins to record what she was doing when the scene occurred. She wrote: *Thinking about Chester.*

Trees had glimmered bright green against a blue sky. She held a turquoise and green twill skirt away from ankle boots with canvas-like cloth and black leather insteps. A rose-colored hat sat forward on

Harriet's head, a short cape ending just above her waist. "Pelisse" came to mind. She would look in a dictionary. She had seen a Webster's—there, on top of Scrabble in the bookcase. She looked up the word: "A long outer garment, originally of fur or fur lined." And what the heck was a "gig"? "A light, two-wheeled open carriage, drawn by one horse."

The horse's feet clip-clopped in the quiet morning. Metal wheels grated against cobblestones. *Chester was a woman in that life.* Now he was gay.

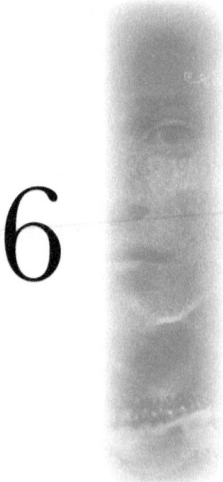

6

Jane heated a frying pan and broke an egg into it and watched the egg white solidify. When she added water, steam escaped, ineffective, because she hadn't thought to get a cover. Toast collapsed into crumbs under cold butter. In the living room, rain pelted on the roof as she cut egg on toast into pieces and ate it.

While she stared absently at the crumbly plate, her vision shrank to a cinched keyhole of gray light, dark all around.

———•◦•———

Blackbirds. Standing rigid, she gripped a child's hand. A steamer waited, belching black smoke, its engines growling. She moved toward its deck. A man said something that stopped her.

Candles shone on the altar and in sconces on the walls of the stone church. Stained-glass windows of deep-hued red and blue surrounded a cross, a bleeding heart, lily of the valley. Faces glowed in the dimness, reflecting candlelight. She smelled incense and burning wax and wet wool. When the choir director stood and turned to them, and lifted his palms, she sang.

"Glory be to the Father, and to the Son, and to the Holy Ghost.
As it was in the beginning, is now and ever shall be,
World without end … Amen, amen."

The choirmaster, with a pleased look, gave a slight nod and gestured for them to sit.

Sally was sick with fever and Elizabeth was anxious to be home with her. She watched the rest of her family, the girls disgruntled, each at the mercy of the other in getting there. Meridith, her first-born, filled blank books with numbered life lessons, and bossed her siblings. It was a relief to see Emma's emerging defiance of her overbearing sister. The boys conspired, heads bent. Lines etched her husband's mouth and the natural bow of his bottom lip had been drawn into a straight line. He framed a smile, delivered it to her, and allowed his mouth to resettle as he turned back to the minister.

Reverend Paul stood in the carved wooden pulpit and shouted. "The Union House of the Parish of Saint Luke's is proud to introduce Mister Jordan Locke as our new workhouse master. He brings a new approach to aiding the poor, and hopes to encourage the charitable services of the ladies and gentlemen of the parish to the mutual edification and benefit of the poor inmates and the benefactors. Give so that ye may receive."

Lurching, Jane grabbed on to the table and fought to get her palms together, working her hands together and apart, until she could get her notebook. She pushed aside her plate and wrote details in a center column.

Meridith and Emma were thirteen and eleven, freckled and tawny, one more orange like her father, reed thin with a small face. She longed to see the little boys.

And there was the ginger-haired man from the dream of Elizabeth crying. Elizabeth's husband. Heavier now. He wasn't Jordan. Jordan was being introduced.

Jordan, tall and dark, was the man she related to David.

The girls wore matching blue-gray cloaks with dark braiding. Their bonnets were dark felt with white ruffles inside the brim.

Quarreling had pinched their faces, and she had been cheated of their glances. She began to feel sad, missing them, and the love that had been so deep a part of the woman singing in the choir that it had gone beyond comment. More than that, she began to feel anxious.

Jordan Locke. The name rang like a bell through her.

She washed the dishes, the sound of the faucet drowned out by the rain hitting the shed roof. She could clean windows, but after that she might as well go home to a hot bath, and to "Jordan." Hairs rose on the back of her neck.

Chagrined, she found newspapers and vinegar and worked on the windows. While running the backs of her finger against a clean pane, a draft of cool air brushed her face. Her vision darkened to the sound of wet spatter.

----------•◦•----------

Rain streamed against the glass all around her, the world the tarnished white of dripping sky. From high up in the watchtower, she looked down at empty yards, mostly paved and surrounded by tall brick walls. It was shameful to hate the workhouse when she was free to come and go, dispensing knowledge like the holiday biscuits she delivered as a child.

Her shawl reeked of wet wool. Shivering, she rubbed her upper arms and did a kind of dance jiggle to stay warm in the small area, remembering to stand back from the glass. Her nose was cold. If Jordan were to come in now, his embrace would warm her. His lips would be hot on hers, his mustache familiar and comforting. She sat on the small bench that was bolted to the floor in the center of the room. Just thinking of him brought a flush through her, a kind of throb in her pubis, followed by a heaviness there. She felt her nipples erect in her chemise. No longer cold, she wanted to bare her breasts to him. His footsteps sounded on the stairs.

She saw only his face, his wavy, silvery hair, before they closed the door with their embrace. "My darling," she whispered. "I'm ready for you."

"You won't be cold, love?"

"No," she breathed, and she straddled him, and kissed his neck and his mouth, rubbing her breasts against him, warmth connecting through layers of linen and tweed. She melted around him, and she groaned until the waves subsided, leaving her barely able to breathe within the bones of her corset.

Jordan rocked her, tugged at her skirts to cover her thighs. "Shhh . . . rest a bit." He stroked her back. She kept her nose and mouth tight into his neck. She lit up with every movement like a harp string caught in deep reverberation, her moans changing to a birdlike mewing.

———•◦•———

Dizzy and breathless, Jane found herself rocking back and forth as she squatted on one knee and held on to the windowsill. She dropped onto both knees, pressed her palms together and waited for a semblance of stillness. Her hand went between her legs and she trembled and moaned as Elizabeth had. She climbed the stairs, her hand gliding along the smooth banister, and passed through warm air that lingered at the landing.

She took a pillow between her legs and lay face down across the bed. The pressure of the pillow meeting her own movements brought her gasping to orgasm, and her feet were quickly cold as she had never noticed when she was with David. She touched her own delivered wetness, opaque, silken, and sweet smelling.

Dismayed and humbled by her suggestibility and actions, she dressed and went downstairs. Grit scraped the stair treads under her sneakers. Her own chagrin blended with embarrassment for Elizabeth, as sordidness snaked its way in.

Not until she had washed two more windows did she think of Elizabeth's husband. As if by instinct, she collected her notebook. Turning to a clean page, she wrote *Husband theme*. "Am I supposed to be cleaning up after you, Elizabeth?" Her words echoed in the room, and she wondered if that were her karma.

With a sense of dread, she considered not looking at this thread of memory, as if it had all before been a cryptic entertainment, but now it was as serious as paying the bills. "Our Father, who art in heaven . . ." She recited the Lord's Prayer, having to start again and again. "Forgive us our trespasses as we forgive those who trespass against us, and lead us not into temptation but deliver us from evil, amen."

Her phone rang. She jumped and ran across the room to it, thinking it must be David and wondering how she was going to tell him about this. "Hello?"

"Hi, Elizabeth."

The misnaming boggled her.

"Jane, it's Eileen. Are you okay?"

"Yes." She sat down on the edge of the couch and pushed away her confusion.

"I wanted to see how you were doing."

She was quiet.

"Sorry about the joke. I won't do that again. I promise."

She dropped her pen on the coffee table. "I'm glad you called."

"What's going on?"

"I dreamed I had a baby, and I was nursing her. The milk started coming too fast, almost squirting in her little ear. Thank God you called. Some of it's weird." She sighed. "I dreamed I was sleeping and woke up worried that the baby might be smothered, thinking that I had fallen asleep while she was suckling. I was trying to pick her up, but I couldn't because what I was dragging around was a man's head—my husband's, I guess. I dreamed about him, too. I was in bed, crying and crying, and he brought me milk. He said, 'I bring you down slowly.'" She let out a breath and sat back on the couch.

"What was he talking about?"

"He was talking about making me feel bad. It was horrible. I almost forgot about it." Now she sat forward, on edge again. "This morning after lighting the fire, I was thinking of Chester, and suddenly I was in a park on a beautiful spring day. My friend Harriet was mortified. She had seen her husband and his mistress in an open carriage. I walked with her to her house. But here's the amazing part. Harriet and Chester are one and the same!"

"Soul," said Eileen. "Hmm"

"Oh. Right. But do you think that's why Chester's gay?"

"Is he?"

"Yes."

"Holy cow, Jane."

"I know. And then I was in a church, singing in the choir—with

Harriet. And I saw my children—two girls and two boys, and my husband sitting in a pew . . ."

"Who were they?"

"I didn't—I don't know. Don't distract me, Eileen. I have enough going on."

"Okay. Sorry."

"The minister was introducing the new workhouse master to the parish. It was Jordan."

"Jordan is David, right?"

"Yup."

"Wait a minute. He isn't her husband?"

"No." She got up and paced back and forth as she talked. "There was one more scene. Elizabeth meets Jordan in the tower of the workhouse. It's cold and rainy. There's nothing there but a small bench. She has sex with him. She straddles him."

"Oh!" Eileen laughed.

"Can you believe it? I'm blushing."

"They had an affair!"

They both said: "Some things never change!"

Jane crossed to the porch door and locked it.

"You shouldn't be alone, sis."

"Don't worry. I'm leaving now. It's raining and I can't do any shingling. I'll call you from home."

Thank God she called. She was beginning to wonder if some other consciousness was trying to crowd out her own.

She thought again of Renee, how she might help Jane, and knew she was depending on the *promise* of hypnosis. Mistaken or not, it at least gave her hope, just as seeing the little girl in the dream had. But it was all the same dream, the same story. Unchangeable history. Was there to be a child for Jane and David? Or was it the other: a demonstration of why there couldn't be?

She could handle that. It was the not knowing, the doubting and questioning that disturbed her. She could choose a worthy career, maybe with children. She wanted to paint and to squeeze clay into smooth shapes, but that led right to her spastic hand, a block to everything. This brought her full-circle back to Renee.

She got her backpack and poncho from the shed room. Her phone needed a charge but she dropped it in the pack with notebook, wallet and pen. She put on the backpack, then pulled the poncho over her head, and turned off the lights. She stepped out the door and felt freer. Wanting only space and movement to clear her mind, she locked the door and strode down the hill.

7

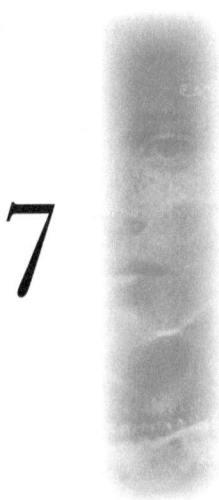

A foghorn's hushed bleat marked the rhythm of her feet and the swish of her poncho. At the bottom of the short road, before turning left and starting her walk to the ferry, she crossed the street. Through the steady rain came the sigh and rattle; the sigh of a wave pulled back, the rattle of stones dropped on shore. She detoured up the steps of the civil war museum and across the canted decking to the back rail with its overlook. White foam frothed the rocks, like lace disguising powerful haunches. Bay and sky blended beyond the dry-leafed branches of an ancient oak.

She closed her eyes, smelled the smoke of woodstoves. The crashing waves, the gusts of blustery wind, boxed and buffeted her ears into a strange, vacuum-like quiet.

Knitting needles clicked in her hands. She paused to recount the number of stitches she had cast on. Yes, eighty. She began the first row with a pearl stitch and started her pattern: knit two, pearl two. There was something refreshing about starting a new jumper. Gives a kind of lift. Knit, knit. Pearl, pearl. The wool was a soft tan. She had stopped making white sweaters. With the thought she saw blackened cuffs on those she had knitted before knowing better. Tan would look wonderful with Matthew's brown eyes and she would knit a soft gray for Owen. Owen and the girls had fair eyes; her own were changeable, sometimes green, sometimes gray. Of course, everything of Owen's found its way to Matthew in time. She started the second row with a knit stitch.

"What did you think of the new workhouse master?" Palmer lit his pipe, drawing in air until the bowl sparked and smoked. He dropped the match into the ash decanter. It snapped shut with a ping.

"I thought it was very accommodating of him to stand for the entire congregation at the church. It was a lengthy introduction," she answered. Pearl two, knit two.

"Why? We were the ones being imposed upon. He's getting paid, isn't he?"

She nodded and said, "Yes, of course." Pearl, pearl, knit, knit. "Did you speak with him?"

"Yes. I told him I was the man to come to for his medicines. Asked him to come round to the shop."

"Wonderful. I should think they would need a lot."

"Umm . . . Did you know they've had no doctor over there?" It was more a statement than a question.

"Really?" She looked up with surprise. "What of those carrying the pox and all? It's the poor that are most diseased."

Palmer took the pipe from his mouth and glared at her. "Don't you think I know that?"

She returned to her knitting. "Of course, you know." She finished the row, and started the next with a pearl stitch. Her husband's silence was eloquent. "How have they managed?"

"The Smythes didn't bother about the sick. Let the poor buggers suffer. Hoped they'd die, they did."

"Palmer, you can't be serious."

"Why not? The whole system stinks. Even Locke says it." He relit his pipe. "Smythe used to brag in his cups, 'Savin' money for the crown all round, we is!' Down at the Hog's Head. Was proud of himself for saving more quid by 'puttin' 'em outta their miseries.'"

Her hands collapsed in her lap. "Those people ran the workhouse for years!"

Palmer knocked the bowl of his pipe against the inside edge of the decanter. "I thought he favored another dispenser. Figured him to be in a kickback situation."

"What of the mistress?" She pitied his wife.

"No help there! Mistress Smythe was distrustful of her husband's leering ways. Kept the women filthy. Assigned nursing duties."

She watched her husband polish his spectacles with a hankie, clip them over his ears, and wipe his pocket watch, closing it with an impressive snap before opening the newspaper. "Locke says conditions in most workhouses run from bad to worse, but none comes near being as bad as our own St. Luke's."

———•—•———

Her head whirled, ears buzzing. Jane leaned into the railing of the museum porch and pressed her hands together. Surf crashed. The foghorn called. She opened her eyes to see surf still crashing into foam on boulders below. She steadied herself and closed her eyes again, remembering how she had watched the tan stitches grow. Her hands longed for the feel of her own needles that had clicked to life as soon as she learned to knit. This memory was simple, its ordinary aspect as comforting as the foghorn, but it hadn't stayed that way.

She retraced her steps on the wide perimeter of porch, past the museum's stained-glass windows, down the steps, across the front lawn of granite and grass, and out to the street, going over all that she had seen. A glimpse of sweet Matthew with fat cheeks was followed by the briefest glimmer of Owen and only a hint of the eyes of the girls. Palmer. The husband's name was Palmer. She had been sitting near a window. Palmer had knocked his pipe against a "silent butler" that sat on a large round table with photographs and stacks of books. His mustache clashed a little with his pink face. Light reflected off his glasses and he was wreathed in blue tobacco smoke. Sweet cherry pipe tobacco. She could almost smell it.

A truck ka-thunked and splashed in a pothole, its cargo of ropes and tools lifting and dropping in its bed as she approached the ferry landing. The bay lay gray and quiet with no ferry in sight, and the cement ways leading to the dock, even the pavilion with its dry benches, were empty of passengers. This pleased Jane because now she would have time for lunch. She crossed the landing's breadth and continued past the ice cream shop and the post office to the Cockeyed Gull.

Inside, she peeled off her wet poncho and hung it on a hook. The red-stenciled menu board boasted clam chowder. She ordered a bowl, removed her backpack and sat at a small table near the steamed-up window. A waitress placed a package of oysterettes before her. Jane fumbled with it, giving up when it didn't open, and pulled notebook and pen from her pack. Writing out the knitting scene, she grew annoyed with Palmer. *A peevish man.*

When she smelled the chowder, she traded the pen for a spoon and ate until, sustained, calmed, she set aside the spoon and rested her hands in her lap. She closed her eyes, felt a heaviness.

———•◦•———

She barely touched the handrail as she ran down the staircase. Exeter had been preparing for an outbreak of cholera since before Christmas, and Papa still ranted that they'd be "caught at sixes n' sevens and rightly deserving of it."

Mama turned from her writing table as she rushed in.

"Mum, I need an apron for the infirmary!"

"Darling, I know it's hot, but you must wear stockings if you plan to leave the house."

"No one at the infirmary will care."

"What is it you plan to do there?"

"Paperwork, Mama. To keep order when the sick start coming."

"Put on some stockings, Liza, and I'll meet you in the kitchen. Cook will put together a lunch for you."

She did as she was told and was soon breezing out the half-door, across the yard, and out onto High Street. She cut through a stand of fruit trees and into a courtyard, almost faster than squawking chickens could fly out of her way. Her feet sent up clouds of dust from the dry reddish earth, covering grass and shrubs in rouge-colored talc. Rounded paving stones formed a gutter in the center of the road to catch horse droppings.

Every parish was to set up its own Board of Health, but Exeter was a corporation of parishes. Tea times had hummed with harangues on "bloody politics" and "infernal peevishness" until St. Sidwell's set up its own board.

Starlings took flight as she burst into the barracks yard, and she slowed her pace and tried to look somber. "The bloody spot isn't even being used!" Papa yelled when the health board had been refused its use. The Poor Corporation later refused a site near the workhouse, and then disallowed the building of a hospital in the brickyard. Papa, pretending that the board had permission to use the barracks, took her with him to sweep and plan. When the bleaching factory was turned down, Lord Melbourne intervened. By then, the empty barracks were all set up to be the hospital.

Voices carried from the ward as she waited for her eyes to adjust in the cool, dark anteroom.

Papa and other men surrounded a tea service.

"Plymouth has put together a 'bed on wheels,'" Doctor Shapter, the leader of the medical team from London, said.

She tried to listen without staring.

"Although the parade ground would be perfect for a soup kitchen . . . ."

As she concentrated her gaze on the oak wainscot midway up the olive green wall, she could see through the corner of her eye a face turn toward her. A flush burned up her neck and chin. She felt childish and out of place. When it had turned away from her, she looked down from the wall and stole a glance at the group, being careful to move nothing but her eyes. The face instantly looked straight at her. A lanky young man with ginger-colored curls and big blue eyes stared at her, and she let her head rotate toward him. Their eyes locked in helpless embarrassment until the group at the table broke into movement. He stood, red-faced, and gazed back at her.

"Can I get you anything else, miss?"

Jane sat up, startled. "Oh! Coffee, please." Quivering inside and out, she placed her palms together. Hot. As if she were wearing the young blush. She cooled her hands on the water glass and pressed them to her cheeks.

She wrote it down: *Exeter*. The mother wore a light muslin dress gathered beneath the bust. Awareness that this woman was now Eileen washed through her. *No wonder she's always bossing me around.*

A plague of cholera in England . . . . She would look it up. The year was 1832, but she didn't know why she thought that. With second-floor overhangs and open-shuttered shops, it might have been the middle ages. Hovels crowded a bridge, and she had skirted pigsties and chicken runs and manure heaps. Actual walls of red stone surrounded the town—Rougemont.

The waitress set down a mug and filled it. How odd to know the peevish and resentful man before meeting the boy; to know how grim that fresh-faced, love-stricken youth would become. The thought reminded her of a song that had haunted her mother when she was newly widowed:

> *Would I make the same mistakes,*
> *If he walked into my life,*
> *today . . . ?*

Her hand shook, and the coffee spilled, burning. She wiped up the spill, balled the napkin and cleared a spot in the steamed-up window. Leaden Casco Bay swelled beneath the leafed boughs of an old tree. *Grey. Elizabeth and Palmer Grey.* House Island lay like a foothill to Portland half way across the bay. *Learn to trust.* The scene shivered.

———— • ————

They were climbing a high meadow with the sweet smell of freshly cut hay. Pausing to catch their breath, they turned to see if they were yet at the crest. The valley fell away to the river, buried from view by trees that grew near it, dark against the sunny hay, darker almost than hedgerows that sauntered up and down the meadows.

"There it is! There is the glint of the sea."

Palmer spread out his brown plaid cape. She turned her face to the sun, stretching her legs in front of her and leaning back on her hands. Far to the west, nestled on a thread of river, a cluster of reddish buildings gave off tiny squares of meadow.

He lay on his elbow facing her. "We can come back for holidays, to visit your lovely Devonshire."

His whole being seemed to fill his eyes. She kissed him then. Before they kissed again, for their lips were very good together and it lasted a long time, she said, "I would teach in London."

"What?"

"But you don't mind?"

"No! I don't mind. I'd be that proud of you."

"And when we have a baby, I'll stop."

His face pinked. "A baby? Oh, of course, then you would stop." He laughed and hugged her hard, then kissed her well. His lips felt wonderful against hers, and his nose, and face. She felt like she could do this forever, and they lay back against the tufts of hay and kissed until she got a kink in her neck. She rested her head against his upper arm. His eyes looked like the sky, pale blue with white speckles, like a forest of white leaves against a clear blue day.

———•◦•———

With barely a quiver, the moving planes of Casco Bay glinted back at Jane, cold and gray, through the glass window to the booth where she sat. Her stomach slanted. She rubbed the back of her neck where Elizabeth's had cramped. She felt no need to write anything down. She wouldn't forget it.

She focused on drinking the coffee, still hot enough to sip, but not scalding. The sky had lightened, and when she saw the ferry churning toward her across the bay, she checked the price of her lunch, pulled her wallet from the backpack and took out dollars for lunch and a tip. She returned wallet, notebook and pen to the backpack, stood to shrug into the pack, and pushed in her chair. She left the money with the check, took her wet poncho off its hook, opened the door and stepped onto the sidewalk. The rain had stopped.

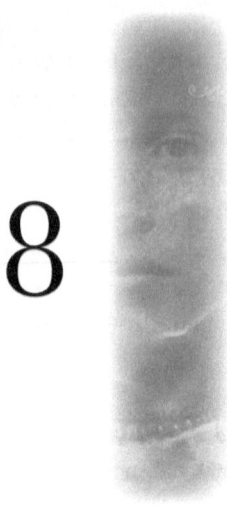

8

She passed the post office and gift shop and, at the top of the landing, heard the ferry's engine shift into neutral to coast into dock and then engage reverse to stop. A woman—unaware that the rain had stopped—opened her umbrella before stepping out from the pavilion. Jane hurried down the incline and joined the trickle of passengers waiting to board, the words of the song playing through her mind. *Did I ever really know . . . the boy . . . before I lost the man?*

Feeling that she'd been on the island longer than two days and nights, she reminded herself that just the day before yesterday, she had driven off the ferry. The car! Well, she didn't need it to go home. She had to cut a last row of shingles and nail them in place, and then she would need the car to bring home her stuff. She stepped from the dock to the deck and was immediately soothed by the engine's vibration moving through her feet and up into her body. All based on a dream that she had gotten wrong.

She climbed two flights to the top deck. Engines pulled the ferry around and when they throttled forward, she brought the poncho back over her head, and sat lee side of the engine house, facing aft. She wanted a hot soak in the tub. She'd walk straight up from the ferry terminal on Commercial Street and along the ridge, and when she ducked into the front door, she'd hear the ticking of her own clock.

Clumpy gray clouds separated, opening a patch of blue that brought back eyes "blue as the sky." Elizabeth and Palmer, in love and trust, had married and made babies. Yet she ended up with Jordan, loving him the way Jane loved David. No. There was nothing sordid in her love for her husband. But David was forever saying, "You never listen to me. Don't you trust me?" And sometimes she didn't trust him, but she didn't know why. He had never given her reason to doubt him.

Did it stem from that time? She shook away dizziness, but the world darkened.

———•••———

Standing at the door with her arms folded inside her cape, she noticed how little light came through the window. She could see her breath. A narrow bed with a stretch of rusted wire had a mattress rolled at the foot, a coal bucket opposite announcing a hearth of sorts. Hooks protruded from the wall.

She stepped to the window and used her hankie to clear a spot in the dirty pane, and, turning to a knocking at the opened door, jumped at Master Locke's booming voice.

"Missus Jaines has brought us some tea, schoolmistress."

The housekeeper marched through the door. "'Ere you are, Mum. Tha's nice on a cool day."

"Missus Jaines is in charge of housekeeping at Saint Luke's, Missus Grey."

A dirty-looking cloth covered the teapot. "Thank you, Missus Jaines. I'll just put it on the table."

Locke shouted, "Do you suppose you could send a pail of hot coals in for the grate, Missus Jaines? Right away?" And to Elizabeth, "You'll have to forgive my yelling. Our housekeeper is hard of hearing." His voice was still too loud. "Sorry it's so cold. It's disuse that does it. Here, now." He bent to remove a cord from the rolled mattress. It fell open, and he turned it over to help flatten it. "This will have to be your settee, Missus Grey. You may wish to bring in a coverlet of your own."

She found his manner as straightforward as his eyes. Almost liquid black, they were the largest, darkest eyes she had ever seen. She pulled a chair away from the table and sat to pour. "Sugar?"

Smiling, he said, "Will you take off your gloves to pour?"

"Oh, goodness!"

His eyes laughed back, which made her smile, and he let out a great big stomach kind of laugh, which sounded so funny that she chuckled. Grinning, Elizabeth poured the tea.

As the scene faded into sepia, Jane felt nauseated and as if her head were in the wrong place. She placed her hands in prayer position and imagined a rod running from beneath her feet and up through the crown of her head.

The brown wash continued, disclosing Missus Jaines, looking sideways at her, eyelids lowered over rheumy pale eyes. One corner of her down-turned mouth lifted, powerful with knowing. Elizabeth felt her stomach drop. She held her head higher to spite the flushing of her face and twitching of her lips.

Jordan's door opened almost instantly to her knock and closed behind her.

They stood apart, each looking at his own dumb shock in the other, as coal hissed in the grate and tin plates clanged from the dining hall. No more comfortable time to dine and laugh and forget about the sad, sorry workhouse. Jordan's irises had turned solid black.

Elizabeth whispered. "What did she say?"

"Nothing. She couldn't really know anything. I love you, schoolmistress."

"That's what she knows."

Lifting her chin, he kissed her lightly. "Right. Well, we'll get used to that, won't we?" But his eyes stayed melancholy and dark, velvety with sadness.

Elizabeth's shock left a bad taste in Jane's mouth—like old bananas. She had a clear, sickly picture of Missus Jaines in her widow's cap with its faded brown ribbons. To rid herself of the odious housekeeper, Jane closed her eyes and visualized Jordan's eyes, focusing on their blackness.

Her hands were on his back, smoothing his soft shirt. He rolled over on the cot so that she was on top and she kissed his neck, forcing herself off it and into his collar. She fell into deep, all consuming rhythm, until—sharp as an ice pick—a crash of splintering glass broke through. She clambered off Jordan, hands shaking as she buttoned. Seeing Jordan's mussed hair, she smoothed her own, opened the door and ran into the schoolroom and shrill, high-pitched hysteria.

Marlon's blood pumped bright red out of his forearm. His eyes glazed over, and she held him to her and sat them both down and removed a triangle of glass from his skin. She squeezed his arm above the gash and stared at the blood arcing out. He fainted against her, and she squeezed harder, as hard as she could, while Jordan and Nurse worked at tying a tourniquet.

"Missus! Missus! Can I take care of me boy?" A poke bonnet moved outside the window, the woman stretching, trying to see through the broken glass. A whole flock of bonnets bobbed in response to the screams. "Please, missus! Me boy!"

Elizabeth nodded dumbly, and the woman was at once frantic to climb in.

Jordan shouted, "He's going to the infirmary! Nurse, try just the tourniquet. Missus Grey, let go now."

"Don't take 'im to the 'firmary! There's the typhus!"

"'N the pox!"

"Yas' can throw the youngun' in wi' the dead as well!"

Nurse said, "Finger's turning blue."

"Missus Grey, send Missus Jaines for needle and thread!" Jordan scooped up the boy and called out the window, "Send a seamstress to the housekeeper's room!"

The children gaped.

She held on to the sill and pulled herself out of the mess of broken glass and, following their eyes, fixed on her bloody dress before giving the skirt a shake. Shards chimed delicately to the floor.

"Marcia, bring Missus Jaines from the dining hall! Quickly!" To the others, she said, "Marlon is going to be fine. The cut will heal. Can anyone tell me how this happened?"

They were all looking at her, yet as she looked at them, each turned his eyes away, even the small ones. She looked at the jagged hole in the whitewashed window, smelled and felt the draft of fresh air.

"It was stuck!"

The words were so quick that she had no idea who had spoken them. "It was stuck?" She looked back to the window.

"Aye, stuck!"

The windows were nailed shut. "Was Marlon trying to open the window?"

"Aye. Twas. Thas' it."

The housekeeper surged toward her.

"A boy has been cut, Missus Jaines. Fetch a needle and thread and take them to your rooms. A seamstress will be waiting. Go quickly."

Missus Jaines leered under half-closed lids.

The world dimmed around all but the sallow woman and then she too disappeared in a wave of brownness that left Jane stunned and glum, head hanging low. The blue skirt had soaked up blood like a blotter. She saw it brown, stiff and hard.

Her right hand wagged as if strumming a banjo. She crossed her arms and clamped her hands under them, noticing two women a few benches forward, one half turned to the other.

She groaned, feeling the Funhouse doors close behind her, as she edged, helpless, toward the House of Horrors.

Ask for fun—You'll be undone . . .

The cryptic message cinched her belly—an invisible girdle squeezing, squeezing; and while she suddenly dreaded what was to come, the air dimmed, murky as an old tintype.

"What is that smell?" She pulled out a hankie.

"The boys' dresses are being cut."

"What is it?"

"Flax. The odor washes out as it softens. Wears well and the cost is low." He scowled. "I thought that you might bring some students into the sewing room to learn how to cut."

Silhouetted against the whitewashed window, two women with shears stood cutting the rough fabric. Six inmates sat on a bench stitching. The one closest to her caught the thread between her teeth and bit it, looking sideways at her dress and up at her hair.

She hurried to keep up as Locke swept down the dark hall. They might have washed the cloth before sewing it! The poor boys, wearing such a dirty smell. In dresses, for God's sake! If they could get the whitewash off the windows, the place wouldn't be so gloomy. Their footfalls echoed as they passed the gray-striped bonnets of women humped on benches or leaning on walls. A moan tore into a scream. Locke put out his hand to steady her. "The Lying-in room," he said, as they pushed through dirty green doors.

———•◦•———

Jane uncrossed her arms and pressed her palms together, grateful for the clean air of Casco Bay. The cloying, oily smell of fabric was familiar to her. *Linseed oil.* The stink of the workhouse was as noxious as the reeking rafts of silvery fish that swam up river, only to die en masse in fresh water. Outhouses, lavatories, passageways, and inmates stank. The fabric's putrid odor irritated Elizabeth because it seemed so unnecessary.

She wondered how Elizabeth became schoolmistress to the poor in the first place, and clearly recalled Palmer saying, "You won't have to fill your time with silly teas and charity fairs. If we have to feed and house the poor, we might as well see that they learn something. Ignorant bullies are paid to keep order in schoolrooms. And you always said you wanted to teach!"

She remembered this as though it were her own conversation, as if her consciousness had merged with Elizabeth's. Heaviness as solid as wood had lodged in her heart, and Elizabeth had prayed. Dear *God, keep me from becoming a bitter woman.*

Palmer wanted his wife to teach at the workhouse. His apothecary work had grown dull, learning had stopped, and the customers seemed more callous. He was miserable when he was working and miserable when he wasn't. "All used up," he would say, with nothing left for men's clubs.

Elizabeth reminded him of the blessings they had: their children, their health, their comfortable station in life. Palmer's face flushed when she said that. Instead of being calmed, he became more irritated. But Jane suddenly understood that Palmer couldn't say what he felt because it would sound childish, even blasphemous. Palmer wanted to scream, "Don't thank God for our well-being! Thank me! I'm the one responsible! Me! Me! Me!" His wife's happiness told him that she didn't care about his suffering, and he ached inside whenever she was happy. Jane didn't know how she knew this, but she was just as certain that Elizabeth did not.

Suddenly off-kilter, Jane looked down at herself, tiny, on the deck of a ferryboat. And slap! She was back on the deck with her back pressed against her pack. The water, a trillion planes of light and movement, divulged nothing.

Anxious for more, she called in her mind, *Come back, Elizabeth. Come back!*

Elizabeth walked up the aisle on her father's arm. When she saw Palmer, tension melted away, and she glided gracefully on, as gentle and natural as petals on a breeze. Her gaze dropped on Aunt Pearl like a benediction.

Elizabeth battled to keep the love lines open between them. When something felt wrong, she wanted to know why and fix it, just like turning back the leaves of cabbage to find a worm. But Palmer liked to put his irritations behind him, and *not* talk about them. If Elizabeth sensed evasiveness in her husband, she would ask what happened, persisting until he finally told her something, forcing him to revisit some unpleasantness.

"I don't get mad. I get even," Palmer would say about a customer who let his account run up or a supplier who didn't deliver. *He gets even with me, too,* Elizabeth thought, every time she tried to find out what was wrong. When she felt that all was well and they could once again be loving and close, he would slowly get even. He would share table, parlor, and bed while withholding thoughts and feelings, keeping her at arm's length until she was crying with loneliness.

When Elizabeth felt their love renewed, Palmer felt abused. She sensed contempt in him, a hate for her that she couldn't comprehend. She learned that he was not like her and that it was not possible for her to understand him. Since she needed to understand him in order to feel close to him, the vibrancy and closeness went out of their marriage.

Jane's ears buffeted as if in a vacuum, the air stilled, and she steadied herself for whatever would come.

———•◦•———

Elizabeth watched Harriet pour from a luminous blue pot into a wide-lipped cup, its yellow background decorated with tiny pastel flowers. Distracted and nervous about the news she was about to drop on her friend, she focused on the tea, reddish amber against the cup's white interior. Harriet's husband imported teas and this one tasted of mango.

"This is very good, Harriet," she said.

"Yes. Roger does bring home the best, cad though he is." She offered small shortbreads that Elizabeth declined and said, "I can't wait to hear your news, Liza." She drank some tea and waited, dark eyebrows lifted high.

Elizabeth set down her cup. "Palmer wants me to teach at Saint Luke's."

"At the workhouse?" Harriet's dark eyes flashed. "You? A schoolmistress at the workhouse?" She put down her cup and stood. "Why in the world would he even think of such a thing?"

"I wanted to teach before we married, but the children came so quickly, it never happened."

"It's absurd, Liza! Pay no attention to him." She breathed a short laugh. "Here I've been thinking Palmer's such a good husband. Trustworthy." She stopped moving and faced Elizabeth. "I've been jealous of you, my dear." With that, she sat, somber and so saddened that her eyes teared up and her nose turned red. Sitting straighter, she refilled their cups and sipped some tea. "Surely, you are not considering this."

"I thought I'd try it—"

"Why? You don't believe that hogwash about a man being the head of a family? Do you?"

"Of course not." She reached for a biscuit.

"Then why?"

Elizabeth took a bite of shortbread, but it didn't hide her blush, and she choked a little on its crumbs.

"Oh, no! If it's the new master of the place, *you* are being the fool!"

"It can't hurt for me to try it, Harriet. It might teach Palmer a lesson or something!" She looked away from Harriet's stare. "I do like the man …'

"You can have him in your life, Liza. You don't have to work there. Think of your children. What will you bring home to *them* while you're acting out a stupid man's stupid idea!" Harriet crossed her arms over her small breasts in a graceless pose that was totally unlike her. "Men are worth no more than their seed, Liza, and Jordan Locke is just another man. Remember that."

———•◦•———

Jane pressed her palms together, breathed. Sadness washed through her, the sadness of a wife feeling uncherished, on the brink of going elsewhere for love. While Harriet's cheating husband kept her on the verge of tears.

Elizabeth ignored Harriet's counsel. She cancelled out Palmer's peevishness with dreams of Jordan, accepting the position of schoolmistress quite happily, wearing a separate wardrobe and bathing before greeting her children. She thought it was wonderful that thrilling Master Jordan would pay her. She expected Palmer's brow to clear, but when it didn't, she no longer cared.

Jane knew all of this as she sat with the ferry's vibrations running through her. And she knew that the boys' smocks were a poor quality of linen made from undressed flax that included stalks, leaves, and the seeds from which linseed oil is made. She didn't know how she knew that. The gray of Casco Bay shifted to brown. The air turned dank and still, and she was back there.

———•◦•———

Round, square, lumpy, smooth, or scarred, their shaved heads were visible like none she had ever seen. Shorn at different times, some had just a shadow, while a fortunate few had almost a full cap. Most were in between with scalps displaying fleabites and barren spots from pocks and blows. Except for scars, the hair grew with precise perfection, but their ears looked large, their heads odd.

Heavy, hobnailed shoes made their movements slow and clumsy, and whitewashed windows heightened their pallor. They waited with donated books at long narrow desks, a taller version of the benches on which they sat. If she happened to catch an eye, it was turned away.

"Children, I am here to help you learn. I want you to look at me. Good. Tell me your names." She beckoned to a girl and smiled. The girl's wide brown eyes stared—fearful, alarmed.

"Liza," came the scratchy whisper. She wrote down the names: Beatrice, Jeremy, Marlon, Malachi . . . Their eyes were skittish and they seemed to have a hard time holding their heads straight.

She had donned a red paisley shawl to brighten up the place and wanted to hang colorful things on the walls, but Master Locke said no. If she could get some paint and some brushes, each child could do a painting. Each would have a spot on the wall. They would draw them first. They could each use a piece of coal.

The cuffs of her wool sleeves turned black in the coal's wake. The walls had been painted to seal the brick, the lower portion in glossy black to resemble a wainscot. Mortar had been plugged into holes made by rodents and painted over like so many lumpy black protrusions near her feet. The coal broke down into black crumbs as it bumped over the painted bricks. Black dust settled onto the folds of her skirt. She stepped back from her drawing of a tree. "When we have colors, we can make the leaves green."

Heads cocked, they stared at the tree. As if weights had been removed from the bottoms of their faces, there were scowls of interest, the beginnings of smiles.

"A tree."

"I saw it at Cheapside." The voice seemed without timbre—rusty.

"Aye. Silhouette," scratched another.

She said, "What can we make that would have more color?"

"The sky."

"When it's blue."

She taught them writing and sums and dreamed night after night of dull, mind-snagging repetitions. The sounds of their voices were like chair legs scuffing against the floor. She recognized with new appreciation the untarnished luster of her own children, and stopped urging Emma to speak up or Meridith to be less bossy.

Her greatest gift to the pauper children was the colored chalks that livened the walls. She let them draw what they liked. Those who chose to draw loved it. Harriet held teas to raise money and donations of yarn, fabrics, and hand-me-downs for the inmate children. The money was used for chalks, pencils, and even drawing paper.

With deliberate eye contact, she learned who was timid, lewd, fearful, angry or sad. She could guess future choices by the degree of innocence or slyness and was stunned by their steely strength.

"Some will take the high road," she told Master Locke.

He raised a brow. "But in service to which others?"

"They require confidence, sir."

Locke fingered his mustache. "Confidence comes with competence. I'll bring in an abacus, schoolmistress."

"Elizabeth. Please call me Elizabeth." Shared tea breaks perked through their days, lifting their steps and their hearts.

Like a ship at sea, Elizabeth rode the waves. The early days rocked her with griminess, with fever sores and sleepless nights, as she struggled to figure out how best to teach the pauper children. Jordan's emotional approval anchored and encouraged her until, in time, her ineptness gave way to a sense of accomplishment and competence.

It was at the beginning of this stage of eager self-confidence in the schoolroom that Palmer and she dined with Harriet and Roger. After brandy and cigars, Roger brought out a tray of aperitif glasses and an elegant bottle of chartreuse, and Palmer, in black tie, stood and bowed to Elizabeth. "My dearest, I commend you for your goodwill and hard work, as does the entire parish of Saint Luke. You have made a great gift to the helpless children of the poor. I offer a toast to my beautiful and altruistic wife and say, well done, my dearest, well done!"

"Here, here," added Roger, as they lifted tiny glasses.

Elizabeth beamed in the compliment and said, "Thank you, Palmer," and to Roger, "This is the finest liqueur I have ever tasted!"

"Only the best for the best," he purred.

Harriet and Palmer exchanged a look, and Harriet said, "Liza, I would love it if you would teach me to draw and paint. It's wonderful that you've filled that post, and I'm sure the school will benefit from all that you have created and instilled. But isn't it time to offer the position to a teacher who needs the free room and board offered by the workhouse?" All three watched Elizabeth.

"Oh!" Stunned, she set down her glass. "But I've just now got the hang of it. I finally know what I'm doing!" A brief urge to cry stiffened her back and she sat up straighter. "Uh, no, I don't think so." Her eyes locked on Palmer, her smile gone. "I feel good about what I'm doing."

"Of course you do, dearest," said Harriet. "Just know that when it begins to pale, we'll do all that we can to find a worthy replacement."

Elizabeth didn't miss the look of scorn Harriet directed at Palmer. When his face pinked, it clashed with the color of his hair.

As this time of working buoyed with learning stretched on, the love she shared with Jordan blossomed into coupling. But in the backwater of grim poverty, the tide turned on their liaison, leaving a shoreline of scum. In less than a year, their lighthearted love grew sordid and demoralizing, the workhouse repelled, and the classroom lost its reward.

Harriet's words rang in her mind again and again: *You can have him in your life, Liza. You don't have to work there.*

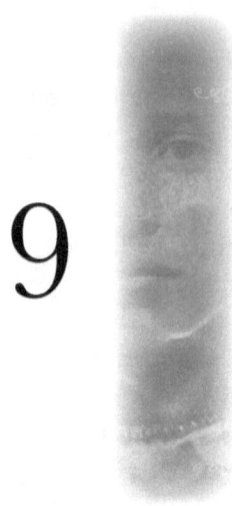

9

London, August, 1848

Elizabeth's longings converged into solid decision, and in the space of closing one door and opening another, she knew her time at the workhouse was over.

Harriet hadn't really expected art lessons, and it was just as well because Elizabeth wanted only to bask in good things that poor inmates would never have. Yes, some needy and capable person could sleep in her office and take her post, and the thirteen-year-old inmates, Cara Dempsey with letters and John Dodge with numbers, would help the new teacher.

Delighted with her decision, she was looking forward to meeting Jordan at the open market and delivering her news. A murkiness (of which she had not previously been aware) lifted away from her, and she relished what felt like escape as she moved down the granite steps. When she reached the tree-shaded avenue, she folded her parasol and ran its tip along wrought-iron fencing in chinging, ringing staccato. *Reminiscent of playing with my babies.* She could spend lots of time with Sally now. *Only the pull of Jordan has kept me there.* Almost a year, since Sally was four. They would visit parks mornings and afternoons, she thought, studying the depth of green leaves overhead. And Jordan could join them there, take tea with them. They would carry a hamper and have picnics. Their recent meetings inside had been full of constraint, adding angst that Jordan could do without.

Painting would be done in her own garden and at her own house. Using oil paints, she would do a backdrop of sky, and build the greens and colors on top of it. She considered painting her girls at watercolor easels in the garden with a backdrop of pink; green plants would vibrate. She smiled.

At the market, she saw the sadness in Jordan's eyes. Anticipating lightening his mood with the news of her resignation, she waited until they stepped into the walled yard of an old church and said, "When can you come for tea, my dearest? We must choose a time—every day!"

But Jordan was so full of his own plans that he didn't seem to hear her. He sat them both down and announced his decision to sail for America. Dumbfounded, she could barely hear his words and watched the day darken as clouds blotted out the sun.

He knelt before her and said, "We can be together there, Liza. As man and wife."

What? What did he say? Her head, her whole upper body, turned as she tried to see him, to place his face with the strange words. "What? No! No we can't!" She stood, reeled. Her stomach felt immense.

Still on one knee, he was below her and seemed small. His bottom lip dropped in surprise, his mouth open like an obscene cave, partially barred by the stiff white bristles of his mustache.

Standing tall, her gut leading, she turned and left him there, not feeling her steps and not opening the parasol until she was far down the street. She had never told him her news. He had denied her the chance to resign her post and ignored her attempt to speak.

Unbidden, Harriet's other words charged out at her: *Jordan Locke is just another man. Remember that!*

She felt the parasol in her hand and thought belatedly of whacking him with it. With one knee pressed to the bricks, he had been off balance, and she could have pushed him over with her foot. But her midsection, distended and long, taut as a board, kept her moving forward.

———•◦•———

She was a pigeon with no wings, a lump of gray, suspended. When the day was clear, the sun was no more than a harsh light through which to walk, and she craved something to shroud her. She took a cab to the workhouse as if to teach and went to Jordan's oak door. A brass plate read, *Master, Workhouse of the Parish of Saint Luke's*. She turned the knob and let herself in. His face lifted and froze, naked with hope.

She sat in a heavy armchair and folded back her veil, letting her sober demeanor speak for her and fingering the gold cross at her neck. "What of Mrs. Jaines?"

Jordan's hand swept through his hair. "I'm supposed to be away for two weeks. As soon as she knows I'm not coming back, she'll do whatever she wants."

"Why are you not giving proper notice? Why are you leaving all at once?"

Quick white pressure marks barred his face when he dropped his hands. "My father-in-law could make trouble for me. He could stop me." His shoulders were narrow beneath his large head, and he didn't look at her.

"You haven't lived with Dora for years."

"He likes to keep up appearances. I was planning to leave when he told me about this opening." His right hand again brushed his hair. "You were my reward for staying." His dark eyes found her gaze, the chair leather creaking as he shifted his weight onto his elbows and leaned toward her. "We can't go on like this, Liza. We must either change or part."

His shirt was too white, too bright, she thought, for this dingy place. She recalled his introduction to the parish as she watched from the choir. Faces glowed, reflecting candlelight in the dimness of a rainy Sunday service. He stood and bowed his head, tall and commanding, swarthy and intense. His hair and mustache were streaked with white, his black brows scowled, and his collar shimmered.

"The leaving is enough. If I gave proper notice—" He lowered his voice. "I should have no privacy at all." His eyes were heavy, the brown so dark no pupils showed. "Liza. You must . . . at least *think* about it." He rocked back in his chair. "Arrange a tour with the children."

And so she could dream. Perhaps when the children were grown, or maybe he would come back. "When do you leave?"

"My ship sails in three days."

Her stomach dropped.

Mrs. Jaines opened the door as she knocked. "Tea, suhhr." The housekeeper placed the tray on his desk. "Oh, suhhr! 'As Mrs. Grey 'ad a shock, suhhr?"

Jordan's face reddened as he pressed the woman out the door. "Yes! Mrs. Grey has had a shock," he shouted. "Mrs. Grey has only just learned of her mother's illness." He closed the door hard.

The sides of his mouth etched down. She poured the tea, gripping the blue-enameled pot with a tea cloth so smudged with stove black it dirtied her hands. "That woman is a disgrace." She set down the pot. "And, as my mother is . . . 'ill,' I resign my post. I had already decided to leave, but you never gave me a chance to say it!"

"I'm sorry. I was preoccupied."

"Well, I needn't concern myself with how or when I will see you. This will be our final tea, such as it is." She would like to see the slovenly housekeeper replaced.

"Then I must pay you for the rest of the term." He opened the cash box and dropped twenty-five pounds, one by one, into her purse. "You've been a fine schoolmistress, Missus Grey. The children have been blessed with your calling."

She had taught sums and letters, basic good manners, stitching and knitting. She brought in potatoes and carrots and nasty smelling turnips, which they took turns peeling. She read from Dickens and Punch, letting them draw on the walls with colored chalk as they listened. She collected pipe cleaners to make into people and turned kitchen crates into the Queen's castle with guards, doormen and coachmen, the smithy, laundry, gardeners, cooks, servers, and maids. She drew London Bridge on the whitewashed window, and they added shops and made-up stories. While she chipped away at all she knew to find the elements of decency and necessity, she was spent and useless to her own children by the time she bathed and re-dressed.

"Have you anything to collect?"

"No." He had scolded her for bringing in a red paisley shawl to brighten the place, saying she should have more sense then to flaunt her finery. Instead, she used it as a throw on her settee where the inmates never saw it. She swallowed the harsh, burned-tasting tea, letting its heat ease the weight in her chest. "Where are the children, Jordan? Are they in?"

"Well, yes, I suppose they are. What would you have me do?"

"Let them go out, for God's sake!" She saw again the jagged break in the white-painted glass where Marlon had tried to open the window; heard the delicate tinkling as shards of glass fell from her blood-soaked skirt.

Failure faced her on all fronts, and she cried because she didn't want to see them. She didn't want to even think of the poor lumpy-headed waifs, as if they were the cause of her own fallen state, her own shame-faced misbehavior.

She brought out her hankie and blotted her tears. "I don't want anything from my room, but promise me, Jordan, that you'll cut my red paisley shawl into seventeen pieces. Seventeen! One for each of them." She blew her nose. "Don't come near me!" Now her head ached.

She knew even as she said it that you couldn't cut something that way. "I'll cut the shawl myself, but I need some paper." She made a pattern with six folds and three lengthwise. "You can have the eighteenth piece if you help me do this. It's the last thing I'll ever ask of you."

He gave a wan smile and stood. Together, they walked down the grimy hall, through the paint-chipped doors. Jordan unlocked the door to her room and she took the shawl from the cot that served as her settee. They hadn't been together here since Marlon broke the window.

Her face warmed as her eyes met Jordan's and he started to close the door. "No!" She pushed past him and, for once keeping ahead of him, strode to the cutting room. The narrow room was lit by daylight from a tall window.

"We make a good team, Liza." He held the fold while she cut the fabric. "At least the shears work now. They didn't, you know."

"Do not distract me." She would have to hand out the cuttings to her pauper students.

Avoiding the coach with its quick delivery, grateful for the curtain of lace on her bonnet, she walked home, ignoring shoeless and ragged poor who wanted water and couldn't always get it. She once donated hours to church fairs, but she had grown callous at the workhouse. Unable to imagine Jordan forever gone from her life, she wouldn't have minded being crushed by a lorry or mowed down by horses. Yet she moved with habitual caution.

She would use Jordan's tale and send a message round to Palmer that she was going to her mother in Exeter. *I'll bring Sally with me.* Meridith and Emma, so close in age that no one considered taking one without the other, had gone to the shore with Palmer's parents since they were toddlers. The same was true of Owen and Matthew, but her youngest child, already five, was always left behind.

She'd wear the plaid silk and have her maid pack a skirt and some blouses for the country. She'd carry a shawl; Sally a sweater. She could be free of prying eyes for the long hours of the train ride.

At their final goodbye, she had studied him and thought, *This is how I shall picture you, my strong and handsome man, with black eyes that express pain and love simultaneously.* "I will love you forever," she said as she stood. "Please don't get up!" And they laughed because it had been one of their jokes. She went to his side of the desk. "I want you to stay seated while I let myself out."

Bending at the waist, she pressed a hand to either side of his big head and kissed him. Jordan took her hands and kissed each palm. She backed away, picked up her bag and parasol, and walked to the door. "Take good care of yourself for me. Forever." With her hand on the knob, she looked a final goodbye and let herself out. In the end, she behaved well.

She stopped on the shaded walk outside Harriet's house, its tall windows curtained, the drapes pulled fast. The Bryants were still at the shore, would probably stay at Blackpool through September. A breeze from Highbury Fields blew the veil into her face as she continued up the walk to her own house, the tip of collapsed parasol dragging. Harriet would know. *Harriet! I need you now!* She could tell her how to cope. How she longed to hear her words—in spite of the 'I told you so's. *I told you not to teach there, didn't I? I told Palmer it was a bad idea. I knew it was Jordan Locke! I knew it all along!* What would she say now? *What did you think was going to happen?*

She opened her own gate and stepped into the front garden, pausing in its quiet privacy, hushed from the street by the old hedge, high and thick. She sat on a Roman bench in the thicket of bushes that bloomed purple in spring and yellow and white throughout the summer. She had laid out the garden when Meridith was a baby, planning to have it paved for a quiet tea, out of the way of the back garden where the children played. How she had loved to sit there, and how the birds had trilled for her. Now they were still.

Reaching in her bag for a hankie, shifting among the coins, she found a stiff paper, folded and sealed. Her memory felt as fogged as her vision. She blinked and dabbed at her eye with the back of a finger, until she could read her name in the thick black sprawl that was Jordan's handwriting. *Oh, my heart. When did you put this in here?*

> *My dearest,*
> *This will be my first and last letter for, if we part now, we will part forever. My heart will break but once, and I will leave knowing that your own will soon begin to mend.*
> *I will ride the rails to Liverpool, where I will stay at Missus Farrady's guesthouse.*
> *My ship is the Ocean Monarch. She sails on Thursday, the 24th.*
> *   All my love is with you. J.*

A flush seared through her. Knowing she would keep it forever, she tucked the note into her bag and, standing tall, prepared to instruct her maid.

———•◦•———

Sally slept at the bottom of Elizabeth's and Palmer's bed, a spot of drool the size of a baby's fist darkening the pale green counterpane. Nuzzling her, she breathed in Lily of the Valley toilet water. "My Sally-O." She covered her with a crocheted throw and turned to her wardrobe.

The doorknocker rapped hard and she heard Addie's feet stepping down the stairs and across the tiled entrance hall.

"Where is Mistress?" Palmer. She heard her husband charging up the stairs.

She expected to see his shop attire, but he appeared, winded and pink-faced, in his frockcoat.

"I came straight away," he said as he put his arms around her. "Do you need me to come with you? How bad is she?"

She picked up the hairbrush and said, "Mother always feels blue at harvest. Father enjoyed it so . . ."

"Melancholia?" A scowl etched white in his forehead. His hands still comforted her shoulders. "Is that what's wrong?"

"No, well—I don't know, but that's probably at the base of it."

Palmer dropped his hands. "Where is the letter?"

"I'm sorry I frightened you. It was just a note, but she wrote it herself. I don't know where I put it," she said with genuine sadness as she gave a quick look around.

"What did it say?" Palmer's eyes had stepped back from her.

Her face heated with shame. "I'm sorry, darling. I didn't mean to alarm you." She sat on her vanity bench, and Palmer dropped into the slipper chair. "Mother wrote: 'I am feeling poorly and desire your presence for a tonic. Do you think you could come?' I don't think there's any cause for alarm. Do you?"

"No." He stood up quickly. "But the message you sent me was alarming. Is it necessary to leave straight away?"

She looked at the clothes spread around the room. Her flowered dressing gown hung from the inside of the open wardrobe door. "I was . . . anxious . . . to get clear of the Union House."

Palmer stood away. The color had left his face, leaving him sallow and sad.

"You don't mind my going, do you?"

"No. Of course not. I only wish I were going with you." He reached for his billfold. "You've told Jordan, have you?"

"Yes."

He stopped for a moment, his stare blank, then opened his wallet and emptied it. "You can't have too much money when you travel. Use your secret pocket." He handed her the cash and replaced the billfold before sitting again.

"Thank you."

"You seem so sad. Is the workhouse ... getting you down?"

"Yes. I'm not going back."

He removed his spectacles and rubbed his eyes. "Yes. Well I thought you'd done enough long ago. I'm glad it's finished." He took out his handkerchief and cleaned the lenses, suddenly terse. "I can see you to the station. I've left Rutgers in charge of the place."

"I'm not even close to being ready. You needn't wait." She stood to hug him.

"I'll send round a cab then, shall I? In an hour's time?" His pocket watch snapped shut.

"Yes." She kissed him lightly on the mouth. "I will be taking Sally. You'll want to tell her goodbye."

"Quite. Safe trip then." He bent to the sleeping child. At the door, he turned. "I'll catch up with you at Exeter, and we'll head for the shore. Our week's almost here."

She nodded. "Yes. Of course."

"Take care, then. Give my best to your mum." His footsteps were slow on the stairs.

In the mirror, she studied the somber droop of her eyes that seemed to have slid down her face. Lines pulled down the corners of her wide mouth. All her life she had been stared at. Her mother had said, "People look at you because you are beautiful. They are only admiring you." Now her nose was red and there were pouches around her eyes. Large eyes, large pouches.

———•◦•———

"Are we off to the shore, Mummy?"

"No, sweetie." Elizabeth pushed tickles of thick blond hair away from Sally's face and let her maid, Addie, struggle with tiny buttons and loops on Sally's dress and shoes. "We're going to Gramma's in the country. To Exeter, where Mummy was a little girl."

Sally trembled with excitement and wrapped her arms around her mother's neck. "Have I been there?"

"A long, long time ago. Let's hurry now. We're going to take a train."

"Will we go to the shore, Mummy?"

"Yes. But our holiday is two weeks off yet." They would join the family in Weymouth, south of Exeter.

"Would you like me to pack for the shore, Mistress?" Addie was brushing out Sally's thick hair.

"That would be lovely, Addie. And some things for Sally—to be ready with my husband's bags." She shut off the thought of it.

They sat for tea before leaving and for the long train ride, Cook packed a hamper, which was placed in the cab with their bags.

The cab jounced and lurched, metal wheels grating and squealing on paving stones. Sally swayed with the carriage. She reached up and touched her mother's face. "Don't be sad, Mama."

Taking the little girl onto her lap, she hugged her and felt sustained.

"We're goin' for a ride, Mama!" Excitement lit her eyes, her wide smile showing all of her tiny white teeth and deep dimples. Her happiness was contagious.

"Yes! And I'm happy as can be to have my weeniest girl with me!"

Sally chortled and slid down to the seat and the window, her back straight in the blue flowered dress, the brim of her straw bonnet curving across her cheek. Palmer had said that her teaching at the union house would prevent Sally's becoming a spoiled youngest child. Maybe he had been right, at least about that. Sally certainly hadn't been doted on in the past year.

Palmer. *I still have Palmer. Jordan has no one. No one even to see him off.* What an adventure they should have if they were to say "*bon voyage*" from the docks of Liverpool. She closed her eyes to imagine the surprise, picturing them walking toward Mrs. Farrady's boarding house. There, just before they reached the gate, Jordan would step out of the door, about to put on his hat. He would pause in mid-step, frozen at the sight of her. They would run to each other, and the whole world would be only the space that was shrinking between them. She saw him again and again, the light seeping into his face and eyes, his mouth stretching into a great smile.

"Look, Mama!" Sally shrieked, pointing at the horse guards.

"Shhh . . . Not so loud. You'll frighten the horses."

"Aren't they warm in all them clothes?"

"Those. Those clothes. Yes, they probably are."

"How come they walk like that, Mummy?"

They moved their arms and legs like wooden things. "Jordan said it was to keep their boots from creasing." They didn't look as if they *could* bend.

"Do they make their hats from cats, Mummy?"

She laughed. "No. I don't know what they use. Perhaps they come from bears." *Jordan would know.*

"Who is Jordan, Mama?" Sally asked as if reading her mind. All the laughter had left her face.

"Jordan is Mr. Locke, darling. He is master of the workhouse where Mummy taught school. You know Mr. Locke, love. He has come for tea."

But she didn't appear to remember and once again turned to the street. "Does he have a little girl?"

"No, but he has two big boys." She hadn't asked about them and she wondered how he would tell them goodbye. The strong reek of hot horses was overwhelming. *Horse guards! What were they doing up here?* "Good heavens! We're on Whitehall!" She rapped her parasol on the glass pane at the front of the cab. "Driver! Driver!" It was no use. He couldn't hear her above the traffic.

The face of Big Ben read three-twenty. They'd never make the four o'clock out of Paddington. The street teemed with hansom cabs trying to overtake coaches and lorries; horses, sheep, and pedestrians squeezing between and around them. The coach stopped opposite Westminster Abbey, and she held on and slipped her upper torso through the opening of the left-hand window.

"Driver. Oh, driver!"

"Some thick traffic, marm. We'll get t' movin' soon." He faced away from her, a silhouette in his high hat.

"Driver, this is not the way to Paddington Station!"

"No, marm, it ain't. This y'ere's the way to Waterloo Station, which is where marm directed me. We're ta' be movin', marm. Yer best ta' git back in."

She pulled herself in and fell into the seat.

"Did we go the wrong way, Mummy?"

She nodded.

The driver slid open the speaking door with a quick thunk and waited.

"Continue on to Waterloo, driver." The door closed with a snap of affirmation. At Waterloo Station, she handed the driver a crown and said, "I will find a railway guide before we proceed. You will wait right here, will you?"

"Aye, marm. Right 'ere. Thanks be to yer, marm." He helped them down and tipped his hat.

Their footsteps clacked and echoed in the vaulted marble interior. She hurried to a kiosk and studied a map of the country with railway lines shooting out like stars from London's stations. In the index of cities and towns by county, she looked up Exeter in Devonshire. The slow, many stopping south/southwest train from Waterloo ran twice daily, at ten and two. An express train from Paddington left at seven. They would have a long wait.

Sally studied a group of young Germans with carts of luggage, the girls colorful in round skirts and embroidered vests. They wore pinned-up braids and kerchiefs.

On the railway map she found Southport, just above Liverpool. Southport was Harriet's stop—a cab ride to Blackpool. Her breathing slowed while her heart beat faster. Lightheaded, she identified a first-class express train that left Euston Station for Liverpool at five o'clock, heading northwest in a diagonal line.

"Mummy, why do they talk like that?" Sally's eyes always appeared shadowed, like great-aunt Emma, her mother always said. *It doesn't mean a thing.*

She kissed her, letting her nose sink into sweet soft cheek, and whispered, "Where they come from, everyone speaks that way."

She longed to talk with Harriet. Since they were already heading that way, maybe she should try to see her. They could leave in an hour, spend Tuesday in Blackpool, and be in Exeter on Wednesday. She studied the railway lines. She could share her heartbreak with her friend, maybe attune herself to it. She couldn't breathe a word to Mummy, who would want to know what grieved her daughter. She trembled inside and decided to go to Harriet first. "Darling, we must run!" she said as she stood and took Sally's hand.

Looking back at the pretty strangers, Sally called, "Good-bye," and the men and women waved and laughed, saying all manner of things.

10

The train went faster and faster, pinning them against the seat, causing Sally to squeal with delight, and Elizabeth to imagine them thrown dead by the side of the tracks. The wrong tracks. "Don't stand against the door, Sally. Stay on the seat to look out the window." Suddenly warm, she removed her hat.

A shade tapped against the glass as they rocked and passed brick-walled gardens, until sheds, wagons, livestock, and long stretches of farmland replaced them. "Look, Mummy! Look!" Sally's short braids stuck out beneath a halo of golden tendrils as she pressed her nose to the glass.

"Yes, my sweet. I see."

There would be no locals to Southport at midnight. They would stay at a hotel in Liverpool and ride to Southport in the morning. Jordan couldn't be there yet, but she allowed herself to imagine an encounter, somewhere at the terminal, tomorrow—surprise twinkling to joy, his face opening in delight. Her imaginings were mere glimpses. She would close her eyes and think, *Now I am going to play the whole thing out.* But since there was no ending, it became a series of beginnings, fragmenting and starting over, again and again, and stopping with, *Oh, Jordan*, which had long ago become a kind of prayer.

They ate tea sandwiches from the hamper, cheese with cucumber or onion, and jam, and drank lemonade from a jar. The conductor held a taper in the flame of a special lantern and used it to light the wall sconce, blowing out the taper and leaving a tinge of black smoke in its wake. As Sally snuggled in her lap, Elizabeth—resolving to make consideration of her child the basis of every decision—pulled a carriage robe over them and began singing "Rockabye Baby," softly, quietly. Swaying with the car, they slept.

She woke dry-mouthed and disoriented in an unmoving train. Alarm coursed through her. *Alone in Liverpool in the middle of the night!*

"Train's stopped, Missus." White collar and cuffs glowed in the dimness.

"We'll just be a minute. Sally girl! Wake up!" She pulled back the blanket and prodded.

"No hurry, Missus. Not leavin' for seven hours."

"My little one doesn't want to wake up."

"Would some tea help?"

"Oh, yes. That would be wonderful." Shivering in a draft from the opened door, she closed it after him, locked it, and used the chamber pot. *Hotel. We need the hotel.*

"Sally. Darling, you must wake up now." Her cold hands cupped the small face. "Do wake up, darling. We're to have tea. That's a good girl. Sit up now. This is a good time to make water." She helped her with the porcelain pot, unlocked the door, and re-tucked the blanket around her.

"Mummy! Where's Gram?" Sally rubbed at her eyes and cried.

"We're not there yet, sweetie, but here's tea! Thanks awfully," she said, as the conductor bridged the seats with a tray. She gave him half a crown.

"Thank ye', missus. I see tha' young' one has joined us. Tha' tea'll perk ya up, Missy. My, this world was prettier the day this'un was borne. Will there be someone waitin' on tha' platform, missus?"

"No. We'll need a hotel."

The man reeled. "Liverpool's full up, mum! The Irish are leavin' bad potatoes, don't ya know?" He shook his head, quiet and somber. "Ye'll be needin' conveyance. Is there someplace you can go?"

She looked down from his gray eyes. "There's a guest house. Missus Farrady's."

"I will be happy to assist, Mum. Enjoy your tea." The door clanged shut.

"Mummy." Sally pushed a crumb into her mouth with the back of her hand. "Mummy, when will we get to Gram's?"

"Not for a while." The letter shook in her hands as she reread it and crushed it into her pocket. Her heart pounded. If there were no room, they'd have to come back to the train. Maybe they should stay right here for the next seven hours. She gulped her tea and waited for the conductor. When he returned, she asked if they could stay.

"No, mum. Train needs to be cleared out and locked until boarding time. I can see you to the platform and scare up a porter for you." He placed the tray under the seat and lifted her carpetbag.

She tied their bonnets with trembling fingers and put on her gloves. Collecting shawl, parasol and purse, she decided to leave the hamper under the seat and, taking Sally by the hand, stepped off the train in the dark, the city so damp that cobblestones stared wet under street lamps.

"Wait here, mum, while I find someone." Blackness throbbed around them. The lights in the train went out, and she jumped as a door banged shut. Doors shut and re-shut.

The porter emerged from the darkness without a sound. "'Elp ya, miss?"

She stepped back, keeping Sally at her side. "Yes. I should like passage to Missus Farrady's Boarding House."

He just looked at her.

"I require a cab."

"I can 'elp with that, then." He scooped up her bag, and she hurried Sally, pulling her by the hand and keeping her eyes on his back until they were on a curbing. He whistled and a horse clopped into the circle of street lamp, an open carriage trundling behind. "Missus needs to get to Mrs. Farrady's Guest House. What street was that, missus?"

"Near the sailing ships!"

"H'it's a big, dirty area down to the docks, missus," said the porter. "'Ow well do you know the docks, George?" he asked the driver.

The driver took a fat cigar out of his mouth. "I know the Farrady's on Fourth Street. It ain't far but it's rough by daylight." He paused and put the cigar back in his mouth, clamping down on it at the side of his mouth and talking around it. "I ain't never been fool 'nough to be there at night. Them Irishers fight when they drink and they're drinkin' all the time." He took the cigar out of his mouth again. "They're all of 'em just lookin' for passage money."

Sally twisted in her skirt, hanging from her hand.

"Would you be willin' if I rode guard for you, George?" shouted the porter.

The horse broke into a thunder of movement. The driver pulled and called "Whoa!"

"Papa! I want Papa! Papa!" Sally screamed.

"It'll cost a quid," the driver spoke when he could be heard and moved the cigar in his mouth.

"Mama! Where's Papa?"

She picked up Sally, placed her in the carriage, hoisted herself up and pulled the child onto her lap. The rig lurched to one side as the porter climbed in. Horseshoes shot like bullets against the cobblestones and metal wheels shrieked. Echoes bounced off hulking buildings. Panic seared her stomach. *Ladies don't travel without husbands.* She had never traveled alone. Foulness seeped from walls, river and paving, overlaid with smoke. She wrapped her shawl around Sally and kept her in a tight grip while reaching through her skirt to the pocket tied at her waist to remove equal coins for driver, porter, and Missus Farrady.

They tilted downward, past rickety buildings and blazing fire pits, and turned into a narrow road. "Nay, nay to worry, girl," the driver said softly to the horse. "You're wearin' yer' blinders." A clot of men passed a jar without banter, their quiet ominous, eyes wet in the firelight. A blazing torch was lifted toward the cab. Feeling its heat, she lowered her head and held her breath.

What if Mrs. Farrady's is full? Her face warmed and her underarms grew wet. *Staying at the guesthouse until his ship sailed.* Would they be holding a place for him?

The horse stopped. They rocked and creaked to a standstill. Discordant strains of music keened from the dark. "Would this be Missus Farrady's place?" called the porter. The horse blew and stomped. A shiver ran down its hide.

Dark forms clogged the entrance. No one spoke.

"Is this Missus Farrady's house?" yelled the driver.

"'Tis."

"Herself is to bed."

"Fer sarten she is."

"I have a guest. I'll thank ye to call her up." And to Elizabeth, "What's the name, mum?"

She called out, "The name is Locke!"

Sally woke with a high-pitched scream. "You skeered me, Mama! You skeered me!"

The porter told her she was expected and began helping them down. Carrying Sally with both arms, she climbed up the steps as bodies peeled back from the stoop. She tripped on her skirt and the porter kept her from falling into the vestibule.

"Sally. Stand! Let go, so I can pay the man." Trembling inside and out, she handed over the coins. "Thank you."

He gave a quick nod and said, "Thanks to ye, then. Safe passage, mum." He turned and was gone.

"What are ye doin' arrivin' in the middle of the night?" The woman blinked in a red sleeping cap. She held the guest book under the light. The sleeves of a gray plaid robe were rolled back on thick wrists. "Twenty-third, Tuesday. Sure and I'm not knowin' what day it is." She looked at the calendar and back to the booking. "It was Monday when I went to bed—Locke is booked for tomorrow night!" She turned as Elizabeth placed a pound on the table. "Well, I wasn't plannin' on shovin' yas out the door." Pale eyes staring, she picked up the coin and, looking from mother to child, said, "Now isn't she the spittin' image!" She led them across the hall to a room with a long table. "I'll start a kettle." She raised the lamp's flame and left them.

Elizabeth dropped onto a chair.

"Tea, Mummy." Eyes heavy and half-closed, Sally smiled. "Isn't that nice? Tea."

"Yes." She lifted her to her lap. A portrait of Jesus hung above the mantle.

"Where's Gram, Mummy?"

"We haven't gotten there yet." *Jesus, just get us to my mother and I promise I won't dream about that man again.*

Before long, they were trundled down a dim hall, vaguely wallpapered in some floral pattern. The straw mattress was still warm from some stranger, but there was clean water for mouths, faces, hands and feet. *Shame on me—bringing my baby here.* Sally was quick to sleep. She brushed her silky cheek. *My salvation. My redemption. I'll get us back to the station tomorrow morning. I'll keep us safe . . .*

She slept and, when she woke, was stunned to find Sally in her bed, until memory crashed in. She flung herself onto her back. *I'm in Liverpool! I'm in Liverpool! Oh my God! Palmer! This is your fault! Your fault! You sent me to teach at the workhouse!* She sat up and pounded the mattress. *You put me there!*

And now the man that gave more purpose to her days than her own children was leaving. *Leaving me grieving.* And her husband, the one who made the whole thing possible, would never even know the heartbreak he caused. Her love affair served him right. Putting his wife, the mother of his children, in that filthy place! Let him have his moods and insecurities. She no longer cared about him.

She turned on the coarse sheets. *Oh, Jordan . . .* gone to America. She would stay out of the vile workhouse forever. All those hours at home . . . . She could sit at the parlor desk and write letters. Letters written and posted in private. Filling a void, building normalcy around each session. *My dearest, what is it like where you are living?* She would post them to— She didn't have an address! Her eyes blinked open. It was good she was here, in spite of the stuffy room, so shabby in the gray light of false dawn. Water stains mapped a curtain tacked to the window frame. Wallpaper staggered unevenly under the ceiling.

All she had to do was wait. He would be here—right in this room. She would get an address, see him onto his ship, and then she and Sally could go on. A foghorn began a steady rhythm. The fog could detain a ship . . .

———•◦•———

"We're havin' a venture, Mummy!"

"Yes, precious girl. An adventure."

Ragged, skeletal people spilled out of alleys, sleeping where they sat. Toddlers crawled among them, grabbed up by older children with blackened feet and haunted eyes. She kept her head straight, her gaze cloistered within the brim of her bonnet. Garbage and excrement littered the road. Smells, rubble and people crept up from cellars.

"Stay to the main ways," Missus Farrady said. "Stay in the open! There's starvin' Irish just off the boat and plenty of shysters as well—out to get yer' money."

Fires burned on the walkway. They stepped around a family eating from a pot, the mother spooning to each of the children, as attentive as birds in a nest.

"We've had no food for weeks." The flat statement came from a white-haired crone, small, bent over, eyes very black.

Elizabeth nodded to her and burned with embarrassment. The woman couldn't know how awful she smelled. They all reeked.

"Mummy!"

"Look for the ships, Sally!"

Jordan said he would command emigrant Irish. The potatoes were bad. She knew that, but she had thought there would be something else to eat.

All ways led down to the docks. A cacophony of dragging, hammering, and shouting lessened as they neared the water. Seagulls barked and the large ships groaned. Empty skiffs dwarfed stevedores on the wharves beyond. Her boys would be spellbound by these quays, each a study in block building. Sails winked against stone and brick. Hills of green trees and plaid fields rose up beyond them.

"Oh, Mummy. Papa should see all them boats!" Sally squinted into the sun as she looked up at her.

She gave Sally's hand a squeeze. Watching for Jordan, she reminded herself that he might not be here for hours. If he took the early morning train, he would be here in the afternoon. Of course, he didn't know she was there, waiting for him. She had grown used to scanning the horizon for him. It had become a habit, awaiting that lightening of heart, that blooming of her being that came from his simple presence.

A fence made of black pipes surrounded the overlook where they stood, a broad pulpit between granite steps that went down to boarding yards. Travelers gathered around bags and trunks, couples standing close, the women in straw bonnets, the men in knee breeches and swallow-tailed coats. Vendors nudged at their edges with jugs and pots.

A man played a penny whistle, its airs floating up to them. A midget man sat on an upended barrel. Children ran bursting up to stop short. When the song was finished, something was said that made everyone laugh. A young man joined the small man on the barrel, removed his cap and twirled it on his finger, watching his audience and waiting. *Not all misery anyway . . . .*

"He's telling a story, Mummy! Let's go down!" Sally's voice would have turned heads but for a breeze off the water.

"No, Sally-girl. They're in line for a ship." She turned to the sound of scuffling.

"S'fer the seasickness, Peggeen." A man was being steered by his wife. Her face, red with exertion, was dwarfed by the basket tied on her back. Her bonnet lay askew on her shoulder. His hat was pulled down so that the tops of his ears were flattened.

"Be careful with yer' reelin'. Boyo, get to the side of him for the stairs, will ye?"

The boy's shirttail wouldn't stay in his breeches. Broad-shouldered and long-waisted, the boy would one day be big like his mother. The man's tiny feet barely grazed the paving. Below, his son set him down, readjusted the canvas bag on his shoulder and swaggered away.

"Fine, great day for a sail, it is." A high hat was tipped and a sailing list waved before a checkered vest. "Are you interested in booking passage, Missus?"

"No. I am not." She kept walking, the silk of her dress baking on her back in the August sun. She could feel its pattern in the density of its colors and, just as she shifted her parasol, Sally yanked off her bonnet. Elizabeth took it from her and found an empty park bench. They sat, Sally splay-legged in her scalloped pantaloons. Harsh points of light bounced off the water, jabbing Elizabeth's eyes, and she pulled at the brim of her own hat. Docks pointed into the river like accusing fingers. The big boats sat weighted, lines all tight and rigid.

"Can we just go to Gram's, Mummy?"

"It will be fun to visit Blackpool, darling. We'll go tomorrow morning."

"I don't want Miss Harriet! I want you all!"

"You won't have me all to yourself when Mr. Locke gets here, Sallykins."

"I wouldn't have you to myself if Papa were here either, would I, Mummy?"

A man and woman lumbered along the quay below them, hauling a small trunk between them. They stopped to rest, he on a step, her wide skirt spilling over the sides of the trunk. They were not old but their children would be grown if they had any.

"Well, I just don't know if we've a good enough store," the woman said.

The man's dark eyes looked for something to rest on.

"Perhaps we should get some of that smoked fish. Of course, it's not possible to have too much fruit. I've heard it said we can sell what we don't use."

Far off, a boat's horn sounded. "Them figs would be good to get." The man never looked at the woman, although his eyes darted up to Elizabeth.

"I guess it sure would be nice to have a cup o' tea. Would you like that, Gus, a cup o' tea?" The man worked at his boot.

Sally rubbed at her nose. "Mummy, it stinks here."

Refugees camped everywhere. "A smell can't hurt us," she said, thinking of the workhouse, but her own head was aching and Sally was whiney and tired. The day was mostly spent. *Where is he?* Thirsty and slightly nauseated, she found her way back to Missus Farrady's.

Sally fell asleep with her feet still on the floor. She shifted her to the bed, took off her own skirt and shoes and lay down next to her. Thinking of Jordan finding them, she untied the ribbon at the top of her chemise to show off her cleavage and turned on her side to face the door. Blushing, she remembered Sally's presence and retied it. *None of that, Missus Grey.*

"Mrs. Locke has safely arrived with the child," the innkeeper would tell him. Jordan's black brows would rise with a start, and his flicker of confusion would be erased by a great smile of relief, as naturally correct as her own response of, "Soon, I pray," regarding the time of Jordan's arrival.

He would press the door open, close it gently, and kneel to kiss her. She opened her eyes to see if he'd be able to reach her. Yes.

Children's voices sifted in from the yard. Meridith, Emma, Owen and Matts . . . *I must write.* She wouldn't say where she was. *Grandma is feeling better and sends her love. Can't wait to see you.*

She slept and woke to Sally's small hands holding her face. "Mummy! It's tea time!"

Where is he?

In the dining room, an American couple chatted easily. "Some emigrants languish for weeks, I'm told."

"Oh my, yes. Paying for food and board, waiting for their ships to sail, for the cargo to arrive, for the hold to be full, for the captain to say goodbye to land, for the tide to turn, for the fog to lift."

Waiting. Waiting for Jordan. *Just for today* was becoming an uneasy threat. The day was almost over.

"When are we going to Blackpool, Mummy?"

"Sally. Use your small voice."

Eyebrows and lips moved in restrained appreciation, as her tablemates waited for Elizabeth to share some word of her plans. Spoons stirred inside cups. "Oh, just one biscuit, thank you." Cups clattered against saucers, and the topic was foregone.

"Are you on your way to the shore?" The American directed his question to her.

She returned his gaze. He didn't appear to be cheeky.

"Oh, I'm sorry," he said. "I thought Blackpool was the beach, the shore." His confusion and honesty showed plainly on his face.

She sipped at her tea. Jordan had said that Americans were different. Now she understood. "Americans are very direct," she said, turning to him.

"Oh, yes." He glanced at his wife, who stared boldly at Elizabeth.

"Hasn't the weather been a blessing now," offered Mrs. Farrady. "More tea?"

"Yeah, I heard it rains a lot over here."

She was stunned by the man's rudeness. How childish to not consider the feelings of the listeners when insulting their climate. But the waiting travelers wanted to know all they could about America.

Mrs. Farrady stood to pour boiling water into teapots.

Elizabeth kept her gaze down as she passed her cup and sipped her tea.

"My Gramma lives in Exeter. Near a castle," Sally said to the American.

"A real castle? No kidding?"

"No kidding. It's called Rougemont which means red mountain. I never met a 'Merican before. Are you a Indian?"

"No. I'm not an Indian. My grandmother used to live near a castle. In fact, I came all the way across the ocean just to see it." He ended the statement with a napkin wipe at his mouth. "But, you know what?"

"What?"

"America is so big that I've never even seen an Indian."

One of the guests asked, "Would you be from Boston, sir?"

"No, sir. I'm from New York."

Sally stood up and whispered in her mother's ear, too quietly.

"Try again, darling."

"Can we go to 'Merica, Mummy?"

Elizabeth beamed them her widest smile as she stood and said, "Goodnight," took Sally by the hand, and swept through the narrow hall to their room. Inside, she said, "No, Sally, we cannot go to America. We are here only to say goodbye."

She gave Sally a decent washing before bed, and then herself, but she was hot and already sweating in the chemise she had worn for two days. She had dreamed during her afternoon nap, and now the images nagged at her. With Jordan, looking for their reflection in a shop window, a black cat coiled around the crown of her hat and yowled at her. A photograph of herself at fifteen shattered like glass, and a black dog ran off with a baby in its muzzle.

She lifted her head from the wall, pressing her fingers into the muscles of her neck. The ache continued up the back of her head and curled throbbing at her temples. *Like the cat.* She made water in the chamber pot. There was no cover and the smell of her urine rose on its own heat in the stuffy, hot room.

The house had quieted to occasional thuds. Having sat in their room since dusk, she could make out a chair and the commode, its white bowl and pitcher, and the dark frame of an attached mirror. A hall lamp backlit the keyhole and made a vertical line of light at the edge of door. Paleness crept at the edges of the window, seeping in around the curtain. She had soaked her feet in the washbasin and she slid them, aching and bruised, under the sheet.

Meridith, Emma, Owen, and Matts would never know about this excursion. She'd be with them soon enough. A baby cried somewhere in the house, answered by murmurings, muffled thumping. The wailing grew stronger, took on fear. Colicky.

Daydreams no longer worked. She had fantasized and longed, and here she was waiting to say another goodbye. *If not for needing an address . . . .* She felt like she'd been there, waiting, for days. Tomorrow was Wednesday. What if he never came? He could be delayed—or stopped. The sheets were rough, gritty; Sally, a bundle of heat. She twisted and turned. She was here, so close! She had to wait. The black cat from her naptime dream yowled in her mind. She opened her eyes wide in the dark, so anxious that she panted.

"Our Father, who art in heaven, hallowed be Thy name," she whispered. "Thy kingdom come, Thy will be done, on earth as it is in heaven." She stopped her lips and continued silently. *Give us this day our daily bread, and forgive us our trespasses as we forgive those who trespass against us. Lead us not into temptation, but deliver us from evil. Amen.* The prayer calmed her.

Blackpool. She had done all this with the insidious innocence of visiting Harriet. Telling herself she was going to see a friend, she continued the affair, prolonged the goodbye. "My heart will break but once and your own will begin to mend." *God help me. I shouldn't be here.*

Tomorrow could not be the same. She would rouse Sally early and close up their bag, and get them to the train station. They would head for Exeter. No matter what the train connection, she must go to her mother.

Dress, breakfast, and leave the guesthouse. She would ask the cost and pay at table. She wouldn't explain a thing. Stand at the curb with the bag. Cabs watched for fares. There would be no problems. She pictured herself at the train station, looking up and seeing Jordan.

"Oh, Jordan," she breathed the words. Her eyes popped open to the murkiness of covered window, relaxation gone. She recited the Lord's Prayer, moving her lips when her focus began to stray.

Floating into sleep, she dreamed she was on a boat with engines vibrating through the soles of her feet. The stern was dragged around to a pier and Jordan was standing there. Behind him rose grassy slopes shorn as if by sheep, but there were no livestock or chickens, and there were no fishermen. He pulled his watch from his pocket, read it and shut it with a snap. Then, somber, he looked right at her. And it was Palmer.

11

Too late! Too late! The words screamed as her eyes opened. She reared up, started to cry.

"Darling, it's all right!" Jordan's hushed tones blanketed the room.

Oh, yes! Now it was all right.

He rocked her, his shirt soft on her cheek, kissing her wet eyelids and catching up the tears at her cheekbones. "Shh . . . shh . . . shh . . . "

She sniffled and wiped her nose. "Sally is with me. We were going to Exeter."

"Exeter? To your mum's?"

"Yes. I took a cab to the wrong station. I thought of going to Harriet in Blackpool. An express was leaving Euston pretty quickly so I had the cab take us there."

"And did you get to Blackpool?"

"No. Once I got here I wanted to wait for you—to see you off. I shouldn't have come."

"Don't say that." He put a finger over her lips. "That's not true. I prayed that you'd be here."

She thumbed his mustache, thick with white, then abruptly dropped her hand. She felt annoyed with him. "They don't always leave on time, you know."

"This one will. She's an American ship." He kissed her and pulled away. "I must get out of these boots." Bending to work them off, grunting, he pulled at a boot and bumped the washstand.

"Jordan, the candle!"

He caught the falling candle. "Ow!" His palm doused the light and Sally shrieked from the dark.

"You're all right, Sally. You're all right!" She pulled her close, hugging and rocking.

"Mama! Mama!"

"Mama's here, Mama's here."

Sally screamed until Jordan managed to relight the candle. When she could see the room, after the screaming subsided, she hiccoughed the words, "Fire, Mama. Fire."

"Shh . . . shh . . . shhh . . . . It was only a dream." She made certain Sally was past her nightmare. "Mr. Locke is here, darling. He burned his hand on the candle and that's what frightened you."

Jordan stood as far away as he could with his hand in the washbasin.

She spoke carefully into Sally's ear. "We took Mr. Locke's room, darling, so he needs to sleep on the floor." She saw that his coat and vest had been hung on the chair. Sally was sleeping again.

He whispered, "I'll get us some tea," and stepped out the door.

She got up and straightened herself and, folding the quilt into a pallet for Sally, placed it on Jordan's trunk. She opened the door to his knock and when he'd placed the tray on the bed, she said, "Can you move Sally onto the trunk for me?"

"Sound asleep," he whispered and laid Sally on the makeshift bed. Elizabeth folded some of the quilt over the child before wrapping her arms around her long-awaited man. She smelled his sweated shirt.

"I'll have a wash," he said.

He was, at the moment, her favorite perfume, and she held her arms tightly around him.

"Will you pour, madame?"

She laughed as they sat on the bed for tea. "What time is it?"

He opened his watch. "It's ten." He snapped it closed and returned it to his shirt pocket. "Missus Farrady was happy to see me in spite of her sleeping cap."

"I gave her a pound to make sure she'd let us in." She grimaced and sipped. "I thought you would *never* get here." But now she was lighthearted and laughed about the crumbs they were making.

Jordan was winding down. "I need to wash. I'm beat."

"You'll have to return the tray first. Someone will trip on it in the hall."

Looking at her standing in her chemise, he lifted his brows. "God knows I can't let *you* go," and he was again out the door.

She laughed, shaking out the sheet and re-tucking it, and when Jordan had washed and she had checked Sally, she wondered why she had been so anxious to leave. Being with Jordan—fitting together like the left and right palms of a single person—was a spiritual homecoming, centering and aligning her to some long-forgotten beginning. He slept, his snores—so foreign to her—thickened, and she lay collapsed in his arms, wanting only to rest there a while.

———◆———

In the morning she watched him assemble his food. "Jordan, this trunk is too heavy to move!"

"That's right! No one will walk off with it and the key will be around my neck." He rolled up his sleeves and began slicing a loaf of bread.

"You can't be serious."

He raised an eyebrow to her and continued sawing. "The brokers sell fares with no provisions. Most of these passengers don't know *what* they need. I don't mind sharing, but I won't be robbed."

"Vinegar, molasses, and brandy. Oranges, dried figs, and herring. Oatmeal, cheese, barley, eggs, bacon, and tea. Do you think you forgot anything?"

He bracketed the loaf with his hands and moved the bread aside. "Should I boil some milk?" His eyes cut to her.

The blood rose in her neck, prickled into her forehead. "We're taking the afternoon train."

"Can I help?" Sally directed the question to Jordan.

"It's 'May I,' Sally."

"If I *may*, I'll have a hug first." He held her, closing his eyes and smiling as she hugged him.

"Have you seen your boys, Jordan?"

"I have indeed. I'll be helping them emigrate." He let go of Sally and said, "Now. Your mama will toast the bread slices over the flame and put them on the table. When they're cool, you will put them in the tin. And I'm going to slice up another loaf."

Elizabeth kept her head down as they headed to the emigration office, avoiding eyes and blackened feet, dirty ankles, and ragged skirts, hurrying Sally past noxious smells.

Jordan leaned close. "There aren't nearly enough lodgings since the potato failure."

She chose not to shout over the clatter of hooves and wheels, wondering what he knew of the Irish situation. Her shoulders baked in the sun, and as they moved closer to the docks, breezes whipped her skirt and threatened her parasol.

"I'll just be a minute." Jordan entered a building papered with advertisements for ships' companies and sailings schedules.

"Look, Mummy. Letters. B-a-l-l."

"Ball. That spells 'ball,' Sally. The ships owned by that company have this black ball right on the sail, high up and in front."

"And on the flag, too, Mummy. Look! And here's a red cross."

"That's right." She read the list of ships: "The Leila, the Constitution, Versailles, Windsor Fay, Sea King, Creole—"

"B-l-u-e," spelled Sally. "N-o-s-e."

"Blue Nose," she said, and continued reading. *Black Ball, Red Cross, and Blue Nose.* She was bumped by a drunken man leaning on another, their stench lingering as they moved past her.

A placard shouted in large, bold type:

PASSAGE TO AND FROM AMERICA!

To ports of Baltimore, Boston & New York!

TRAIN'S Line Sailing Packets—Known for their STRENGTH!

Sail on schedule!! TRAIN'S Line Sailings as follows:

Washington Irving
Anglo Saxon
Ocean Monarch: Thursday Daylight, 24 August

Her stomach dropped. *His ship.*
"They've—"
She jumped.
"—started boarding." Jordan placed his hand on her shoulder. His eyes ran over her features, mirrored her sadness. "There's a park a few streets up. Here, Sally-girl, you walk in the middle, and we'll all hold hands."

Time to say goodbye. Again. They walked to the promenade where she had stood the day before, the same ship at the pier, with more travelers in the boarding yard, some leaning back to back, and when a ship's person came by with a checklist, those who stood up looked like half-naked skeletons. A flute sent out mournful sounds.

"That's my ship—the Ocean Monarch! Ah, she's a beauty! Do you see the flag? Look," he said as he pointed. "It's a white diamond against a red background."

From beneath the wall and out of sight, a child screamed, "Mama, Mama!"

A woman hissed, "I'll break yer' liddle neck if you rip this skirt!"

A man's voice scratched out, "Stop yer' gob yah' lidda bassid,' or ay'll stop it for yah.'" His tone chilled.

"There should be a large black 'T' in the fore topsail." Jordan looked over his shoulder as they started up the incline. "She'll have to be under sail for that to show." Sally was dragging and he picked her up. They walked along the ridge road, paralleling the docks from above the rows of guesthouses and cook-fires. A haggard-looking girl sold oranges, her deep-set eyes clouded, kind of stunned. When she held out a fruit, her unwashed skin was mapped lighter where liquid had run its course.

They found a bench and Jordan placed Sally, sleeping, against her. She untied ribbons and slid off the small bonnet, smoothing damp curls with the side of her hand. The back of Sally's neck, pink with sunburn, blanched white beneath her touch.

White clouds merged and thickened, mottled the sky. Beyond docks, gates, and depots, the dark river slithered under granite and brick, its wide bowl floating ships like toys, impervious to the devastating pull of ocean. From far away came a foghorn's muffled cry.

"My Liza." He took her hand. "You are a wonderful woman and a wonderful mother."

A train started up, groaning and keening.

"When I have gone, you will be wretched."

Green leaves waved and mocked.

"My darling, what are you going to say to your children when they feel your pathos? What is Sally supposed to tell her father when he asks where she has been? 'Why is Mama so unhappy, my little Sally-O?' How is she to answer?"

A cluster of blackbirds flew down and settled on the back of a bench and on the limbs of the tree above it. When the last bird had touched a perch, they lifted and flew off.

"Liza, you made the choice to come with me when you took the train to Liverpool. In your heart you know you did."

A wind roared through her ears.

"My poor darling. I don't think there's any going back."

A crow's caws—*hawk, hawk, hawk*—were like the cries of an infant. She looked down at Sally. *What have I done?!*

"We could not go on as we were, Liza!"

"Why so quick?"

"Why prolong it?"

Blackbirds fought in the leaves. The crow cawed.

"We will send for the children, my dearest. We will be offering them the choice of America."

"I went to the wrong station! It was an accident!"

"There are no accidents, Elizabeth."

She looked at him then. He shifted Sally to the bench and lifted Elizabeth onto his lap. "You couldn't *knowingly* leave them, my love. You tricked yourself."

"Oh! Oh, my God! No! No, that can't be! I must get them!" Palmer—Palmer would say she was leaving him with the entire burden. But it wasn't a burden! That's what she would do! Yes! "I will write to Palmer! I will tell him that I am taking the children! That he needn't be burdened!"

She climbed off his lap and sat tall to plan. "I must write my mother!" It must be a long, careful letter that her mother could share, in person, and Mama would be there to collect them and bring them to her. Matts and Owen were so little. Mama must stay with them. They needed holding and rocking.

"Oh!" she cried, rocking as if her little boys were in her arms. "Oh!"

Jordan squeezed her to him. "Darling Elizabeth, I must get back to emigration. Stay right here." On the promenade in three great strides, Jordan looked back with a broad smile.

Going with him! They were going with him! She wrapped an arm around Sally, pulling her close and feeling her sweaty back.

Sun glinted off the water, stung her full eyes. Her skin prickled all over. She had packed so little. But she had money—twenty-five pounds to buy what they needed on the other shore. Oh, but first she would need to buy passage for her children.

A telegram. She could send some words to her mother. *Sally and I are going to America. We will send for Meridith, Emma, Matthew and Owen.* Twelve words. She should keep it under twelve words. *Going to America. Will send for children, you. Stay with them.* And sign it Elizabeth and Sally? She would find out at the telegraph office. They had time. The ship didn't sail until tomorrow.

There. Jordan waved his hat from below and she watched as he ran to her. She felt sick to her stomach and suddenly hot. Trembling all over, she thought she might be sick, had picked up something from the refugees. *Sally!* Hot all over but the tiny, grimy hands were not feverish.

12

At the guesthouse, she packed her corset and traveling clothes. They were to wear nightgowns over chemises, Sally's with a smock and her own with a skirt. Crossing her shawl over her breasts and tucking it in at the waist, she began to sweat. Nerves, only nerves. Her heart ruling her head . . . Going to Liverpool was a mistake, not a decision . . . Had she decided?

The ship didn't leave until tomorrow, but they were to board this evening, saving the cost of another night's stay and sitting for a final supper with Missus Farrady. Jordan said they must savor the meal, but Elizabeth couldn't eat. She drank tea in quick gulps, the swallows sticking like stitches on needles.

"We'll send a telegram to Grandmama," she told Sally, and wondered then if she shouldn't also send one to Palmer. *Yes!*

"Sure now, if the Telegraph Company's in Liverpool, it's news ta' me!" Mister Farrady spooned gravy over his bread.

"It's in the works. Some say next month."

"London to Birmingham! One hundred 'n twelve miles away and your words are being read one minute after you wrote 'em!"

"Nothing less than a miracle."

Her insides dropped. No. This wouldn't go her way. Not the telegraph. Not any part of it. She would like to beg Palmer's forgiveness. The room was quiet. She looked up to see everyone watching her.

Jordan's hand closed over her own. "Darling, Mister Farrady has asked you a question."

Bushy brows curled over the big man's hazel eyes. "Are you from London, Missus?"

"Yes."

"Sure, and that's how yer' expectin' a telegraph. Now if you was to get a letter to the train, you could get word to your party almost as fast, don't you know."

"Malarkey, Mike! That's the bloomin' post!" Laughter looped around the table.

If she could get a letter to the train, she could *deliver* it herself. Her eye twitched and she stole a look at Sally who, old beyond her years, had said, "What about Papa?"

Jordan pushed back from the table. "We're set for a final freshening up, my girls!"

Out of the safety of the guesthouse, Jordan stopped a cab and deposited them and their bags and all of his things in it. Fugitive Irish stared from stoops, cellar ways and alleys. They cooked over fires, somehow laughing and singing. She wondered if her cheeks flashed red, if any could tell of her dirty flight and fallen state. She kept her back straight in the cab, clasping Jordan's hand on one side and Sally's on the other. Her ribs were squeezed so tight that she longed to loosen her corset and remembered that she wasn't wearing one. That was wrong, too. Everything felt wrong. This was going too fast. There was no telegram. The ship didn't leave till tomorrow. Maybe she would leave on the train instead!

The carriage rolled through the boarding yard and parked dockside where a large crowd queued, waiting for the boarding ramp to drop. Families of the poorest sort, cook pots in tow, were re-boarding. Jordan lifted down his trunk and hung his long canvas bag across his back, then reached up for each of them.

Thighs trembling, she scarcely breathed. Sally giggled. The huge black hull rose over their heads like a boot above ants. It creaked against the pier. In the watery gap between dock and ship, a body could be crushed and slip away forever.

Jordan hailed a vendor. Before she could tell what he was after, he handed her two white canvas bags, large enough to hold three or four pounds of potatoes. "Tuck these into your skirt, Liza." He folded one into his pocket, saying, "Very handy should we get stuck below in foul weather," and, assaying the shiny black sheathing, "Ah, she's a grand lady!"

She felt faint, out of sorts without her corset. Undressed and yet her middle felt squeezed tighter than any stays could ever achieve.

When they'd climbed the ramp and their names had been recorded, Jordan asked her to secure a top berth for them, placing the strap of his canvas bag over her head and one shoulder and saying, "It isn't heavy. Place our things at the back of the berth, dearest. And be sure to notice which deck and which berth. There should be a number."

He and Sally would find the galley and "learn the ropes" while most of the passengers went below. He set his trunk on the far side of the main mast, behind a large deckhouse. "We'll meet you here!" Face beaming, he leaned to hold Sally's hand and the two swept toward the ship's bow, Jordan's top half listing toward the little girl.

The deckhouse was for cabin passengers. A thick rope from its rear corner barred the after-deck from steerage passengers. *Steerage.* What was that?

Bare-legged sailors climbed in the rigging, their neatness mocking her own clumsiness that racked her into ropes. Pain laced across her back. She shifted her bag and filed past a low mahogany rail with piles of coiled rope and a mast thick as a tree.

She ducked into the small house at the steerage companionway, hunching her shoulders and head. Movement stopped as more people wedged into the dim space. Something caught on the canvas bag, a pot bruised her arm, and corded bedding fought her bag. At the steps she held her skirt and started down the funnel, heading into a steamy, unwholesome smell, the stairs curving to the right, each step narrowing to a point. Pigsty. It stunk like a pigsty, worse than the workhouse. Down, down into muddy layers of filthy smells— unwashed bodies, excrement, and sickness. The occasional tangs of vinegar and tar teased, and her nose craved more.

"Single ladies for'd!"

Her foot slammed into the deck and she plowed into a bony woman who cried out in pain.

"Single men aft! Families mid-ship!" The line jumbled up. "Keep movin'!" He pointed as he yelled. "Single ladies, for'd. Lads aft. No meetin' in the middle. Move along. Don't stop us up!"

A lantern cast yellow on their heads and shoulders and everything below in darkness. "Ow!" Her shin banged a trunk; her knee, the end of a bench.

"Four adults to a berth, missus! Two children makes one adult."

She placed their carpetbag and hamper in an empty top berth and stepped on the edge of the lower platform. Gripping the post and hoisting her skirt, she got her left knee on the upper berth and pulled herself into it, snagging the canvas bag and almost falling out.

"There's a ladder, lady! Under them clothes."

"Right." She crossed her legs and rested against the rough planking. Hands shaking, she lifted Jordan's bag off of her and leaned on it, and wiped her brow with a hanky from her pocket. They were supposed to ride *here*? In the bowels of the ship? *With companions the equal of workhouse inmates?* She crouched in the airless cave, shivering in the heat.

"Would ye be knowin' about the water closet, missus?" A thin girl asked a woman bent over like a clothed boulder.

"That I do." She panted. "Tis real close by. Them pails is dusgustin' and it's me that's wonderin' whose ta' empty 'em!"

As if wisdom lived in her innards, waves of knowing slammed Elizabeth, pounding at her middle. The girdle at her waist squeezed tight, tight, tight; impossible to ignore. *Get off this boat! Get off this boat!* Insistence cinched as if to cut her in half. *I will get off this ship. I will leave this ship.* Sensing it, saying it, knowing and meaning it, caused the invisible stays to loosen. *I need to collect Sally and get us back on land.* She prayed the Lord's Prayer, infusing rigid resolve with enough suppleness to act. She climbed down from the berth, picked up her things, and followed a shin-bumping path to the companionway. A lantern in this turn-around space threw her shadow black across the stairs. She stepped into its darkness and spiraled up, to the left, up, shifting for strangers at two other decks, up, and emerging into the dim interior of the deckhouse, and out to the deck and the sunless light of evening.

She looked for the boarding ramp and saw that it was tied inside the rail. "Why is the boarding gate closed?" She called to sailors on the after deck. "Where is the captain? I need to leave the ship!"

"No one gets on or off the ship till first light, ma'am."

"You don't understand. My daughter and I are not sailing!" She looked at the ramp and at the gate in the rail, locked in sailors' knots. Beyond the rail, smoke from the boarding yard beckoned her like paradise lost.

"Sorry, ma'am. You're not allowed to linger here." The young sailor appeared next to her without a sound, looking in her eyes as he spoke. He gestured to the sign: **KEEP CLEAR OF GATE**. "Best be movin' off afore you're sent below." He looked at her until she stepped backward, then gave her a quick nod.

She backed up until the low rail hit the back of her knees, and she dropped onto it. *We can climb over that gate!*

"Mummy, Mummy!" Sally rounded the corner of the companionway. Jordan sauntered behind, twisting the end of his mustache in preoccupied thought. She stiffened at the sight of him.

"Mummy, come see!" Sally pulled her hand.

Liza moved numbly along. Past the small white house that covered the companionway, past the huge deckhouse with the overturned dories on the roof and blackened smokestacks, past the forward mast to a deck filled with people.

"Look, Mummy! It's them ladies we saw at the train depot. My friends that talk different."

Yes. The train depot. That was where she had walked them into a noose—collared, like sheep.

Sally waved to the group gathered above them on the forecastle. "Hello! Hello!"

"Ya, ya!" they called.

"They're gonna' sing, Mummy!"

A man in spectacles pulled a pitch pipe from his pocket, gave them their keys and led them in song. They sang in German but she knew the tune and the English words:

> *Give us this day our daily bread,*
> *Our Lord taught us to pray.*
> *But make us thankful most of all,*
> *For Thine own self today . . . .*

Next to her plight, the prayer seemed trite. *Forget the bread! Just get me off this boat!* Irish girls bobbed up and down on the foredeck, tiny black feet pointing and prancing and skinny arms held straight by their sides. Starved out of their country, they had to ride like rats in steerage. But she had a choice. She had never made the decision to leave with Jordan. He decided for her. And told her (as a fact!) that she had decided to go with him. He was wrong! Thinking that he knew better, trusting him more than herself, she had let him pull her along. Her head and her heart were in total agreement. She and Sally were getting off this boat. Now. She needed to get off now.

"They take turns, Mama." Fiddlers and flutists played from the forecastle's steps, waiting until a hymn was finished before starting a tune.

She and Sally could tell of their visit to the seaport, how the musicians took turns, how they had taken the wrong train. There would be another train ride to Exeter and the visit with Mum before going to the shore, and lots more to talk about.

"Those are the water closets." Jordan pointed to four doors on either side of the bow. He asked the whereabouts of the berth and she gave him directions, not looking at him. He left them sitting against the wall of the large galley house behind the forward mast. Sally alone listened to ballads and watched the other passengers and tried to catch the gist of a story. Elizabeth looked beyond and around the passengers for a place on deck where she and Sally might spend the night. If they couldn't climb over the gate . . . .

"What's in this big house behind us, Sally?"

"A pigsty. And a galley with stoves and tables and hunrets' of people cooking! I like this spot best."

"We need to get off this boat. If we can't get off tonight, we will in the morning. How does that sound to you, Sallykins?"

"Good, Mummy. That sounds good."

She squeezed Sally and rocked a little, unable to say a thing. She had money. A bribe. *Let us off.*

At nine bells, the steerage passengers were rounded up to be sent below. She held back, watching for someone in authority to tell of her predicament, but sailors with crooks made rude comments and laughed when she asked to speak with an officer.

"Who lets us off earns a pound!"

"We're too far from the dock, lady! First light!"

With horror, she saw that they were no longer at the dock. "No! We need to get off!"

"First light, lady! No one gets on or off till first light."

She studied the boarding yard. Faces flickered in firelight, safe. On land.

Jordan rounded the companionway. "I've made oatmeal and tea, my girls." He wore clothes she'd never seen, a knitted shirt and a vest. He handed her a jar and crouched for Sally to climb on his back.

She could feel his eyes on her while her own locked on land.

"You'se can go down now!"

She held her head higher and used her bag and hamper to keep others out of her space. With grim satisfaction, she noted the descending passengers' hilarity grow more tense with each step, more brittle with each turn, and become dread. Hot, airless, stinking dread.

"Has the dunny-man skipped his post this week?"

"What dunny-man?"

Banter broke their tension, calmed their confusion at the unfamiliar decks where they probably hadn't bothered to note their position. Footfalls thumped and echoed through the companionway. Sounds of shoving, curses and growled threats followed them down to lower decks.

"You'll not be fightin' here, Bucko!"

"Mummy—I—don't—like—it—here!"

"Coming down is hardest." Jordan steered them through the turns. "Once down, we'll get used to it."

They stumbled onto the lowest level.

"Aye, we can settle in with safety this night. No harm can come in the Mersey River."

Sweating, she sneered at the lowly show-off in his knickers, gloating for those who had no idea what body of water it was. And dropping fear into the mix, fear of the crossing. She wanted to smack him in his smelly mouth.

Jordon crouched ahead of them. She planted her feet on either side of Sally's, avoiding wash-buckets and caches. Sick children threw up all around them. *Slippery, disgusting mess!*

They slowed, hesitated. Jordan said, "I'm sure this is it," and then louder, "Sorry to disturb you, mate, but I believe this is where we left our things."

"Ah, fer certain ye did, but we had to move ye below. Ye see, the couple sharin' yer' place—there's to be four grown folks ye understand—sure, that one is too big with child to be climbin' up above. Aye, so we switched. See, there's seven of us. So we put yer' things below there, we did. Good evenin' to ye."

This put them practically on the filthy floor. "That makes us four and a half." Elizabeth's tone was cold.

"So it does." The man's eye was hard.

"The trunk is handier to us at any rate, Liza." Jordan pulled a feather bed out of his bag and laid it to the left side of a blanket hung for privacy.

The couple lay under a quilt in the sweltering heat.

Jordan met her glance and adjusted his bag to act as a pillow for them. She and Sally crawled into the cave, hot as an oven. She pulled Sally's smock over her head and then her nightgown, letting her sleep in her chemise. Feeling along the rough partition for a nail or hook, she picked up a splinter in the side of her hand. "Blast!"

"This will help." Jordan pulled out a small hammer and banged some nails into the partition's post. "Your bonnets. Your shawls."

"Our gowns," she said, unsmiling. Jordan's eyes were visible in the dimness.

She unwrapped her skirt, knelt to take off her gown, contorting to lift it above her hips and over her head. "Ouch!" She scraped her elbow.

"Mama, my shoe!"

Jordan said, "Leave your shoes on. They're easy to lose and hard to get back on . . . just loosen the laces."

"We don't have laces! We have buttons, silly." Sally erupted in giggles, shaking with excitement.

Elizabeth, holding Sally against her and humming a lullaby, softened some. She smelled whiskey and pictured a small glass of amber liquid, a bulbous bottle and six liqueur glasses on a small silver tray. She poured glasses for each of the children and for Palmer and herself. She would do this when they were together. Soon they would all be at the shore. Sally had fallen into her deep sleep.

"Liza." Jordan ran a hand over her shoulder. "Darling Liza."

"We're leaving. Get me off this boat!"

He collapsed back from her.

"I'll pay you for the fare," she said.

"You needn't. It doesn't matter. Give it to someone." He blew air. "Are you sure?"

"Yes."

The ship groaned and thumped. The wood creaked, reverberated, breathed through a thick blanket, under a moan of low talk, the swish of whispers, vile sounds in the jaundiced light.

I want only to get off this ship. I won't let you stop me. Her heart was like ice to him.

"Forgive me, Liza."

Not until I get out of here. I'll forgive you when I have only myself to blame.

Hot. She let go of Sally and dropped onto her back. The sail bag's rough canvas smelled of kerosene. She sat up to reach for her shawl. "My shawl! Where's my shawl?"

"Liza! You'll wake—shush!"

"Don't shush me!"

With a loud sigh he reached up to the inner nail. "You put it here."

"Bring our bonnets and gowns in here, too. These people have nothing. I can't believe you exposed us to this."

Breathing loud, he crawled to the foot of the berth, collected their things and dropped them in her lap before lying back down.

She knelt to hang the bonnets and folded the two gowns far back on the bag. The other couple squirmed, turned over, spoke low. She placed her shawl over the canvas and lay down. Tomorrow they would put on their gowns and bonnets. She would carry her bag and when they were off the ship, they'd get back to the guesthouse to bathe and dress properly. She had no worry about accommodation. Missus Farrady couldn't turn away a shilling, let alone a pound.

Maybe the big man would take them to the train. "I decided to deliver the message myself," she would say. It was the truth. He was a kind man. He would help them.

Her eyes opened wide to Jordan's snore. She wanted to tear out his throat. She was ashamed to even think of Palmer. But he didn't know. He wouldn't know. And if he did, it wouldn't really matter. Neither one of them would turn their lives upside down to shake them all out on their heads. She would say good riddance to Jordan. She *did* blame him.

She went over in her mind gathering her gown and skirt—thought how best to get them on, then Sally's gown, and smock. She had the bonnets and shawl handy. Their shoes were on. She worked at the splinter. He could get it out—on deck, where they could see. Or Missus Farrady could see to it.

Sally whimpered.

Fearing a bad dream, Elizabeth placed her hand on the little arm and got up on her elbow. "I'm here, Sally. Mama's here." She wrapped her arms around her. "Mama's here." The entire deck would wake in terror if Sally had a nightmare.

The child squirmed, pulling her head from side to side.

Elizabeth shook her to wakefulness. She shook her until her eyes opened, and her whole body started. "Mama's here, Mama's here."

Sally caught her breath, rolled her eyes and closed them, and went back to sleep.

She lay back. Her older children never had such dreams. She wondered what would have happened if they had not been at the shore, if she had had some of their distraction; if she would have taken a train ride to Exeter. There wouldn't have been any thought of meeting this stupid ship. Sally trembled in her sleep. Elizabeth stroked her and began humming, "Rock-a-bye Baby." The rests grew wider, the hums smaller and quieter, until they stopped, and she slept for a while.

13

She woke with instant grim awareness. Jordan sat on the edge of berth, back to her, knees high, feet in the aisle. She said, "What time is it?"

He half-turned and pulled his watch from his pocket, holding it toward the aisle's dim light. "Six-fifteen."

Morning! She verified placement of gowns, skirt, smock, bonnets and shawl. "Is there water?"

"I boiled some." He handed her a tin cup and poured from a large jar.

She took it from him, ignoring the way his hand shook, and sipped it. "Oh! It's horrible!"

"It won't hurt you. It just tastes bad."

"I need to get out. Go up." *First light!*

"We can't go up until they open the hatches." He exhaled loudly and bent to tie his shoes. "I'll check." He moved away like a shadow.

She rinsed her mouth. With no place to spit, she swallowed. "God!"

Communal pots! She prayed he had a chamber pot.

Sally slept. Babies complained but the thumping commotion of rising was restrained. Hot and stiff, sore from the wooden platform, she crawled to the opening. She wanted to straighten up but could barely look in the aisle without being whacked by someone moving past. Urine sharpened the close air as buckets filled. She'd wait until she was on deck if she had to. There'd be a line, no matter how quick she was to get up there. When you're in the bottom of the boat, everyone is in front of you. She'd use a pot if she had one. She could hang her shawl. *What's keeping him?*

Jordan ducked into their bunk, reached into the sail bag and pulled out a tin commode with a hinged cover. "For when we can't go above. Like now. Ladies first."

Thank God. "I can hang my shawl across."

"Save your shawl. I've got a towel," and he dug in the bag again, hung the towel and moved away from the berth.

Gratitude lessened her anger. It wasn't his fault that they had to stay below. *But it's his fault that we're here! Stinking hot place.* Her chemise stuck to her back. She could smell her own sweat! She couldn't dress until the hatches were opened.

The space was so awkward that she let him brush out her hair, sitting with her feet in the aisle while he removed pins and massaged her scalp.

"I would do this every day of my life, but this one time will have to do." He kissed her neck, and she stiffened. He wove one long braid that hung down the center of her back. She pulled its weight over her shoulder to lessen the heat, and when he touched her skin, she threw off his hand.

"We'll have a farewell breakfast." He staked a spot at the table, where he peeled an orange, sliced cheese, and offered a jar of tea, adding brandy, "To remove the water's curse."

She held the orange peelings under her nose, but the fresh scent curdled in her stomach and she vomited in the cloth bag Jordan had bought.

Panting, clasping hamper and puke bag, she trailed Jordan and Sally onto the blindingly bright deck and shifted around bodies to get to the rail. She eyed the opened boarding gate cordoned at the rail and saw with horror that the ship had moved further from the dock. "Jordan! Oh, my God! Jordan!" Her knees buckled as he bumped into her and she almost fell to the deck.

"It's all right, Liza! It's all right." His hand squeezed her arm, holding her up. "The barge is still tied on. You can get off."

"Mama!" Sally's bonnet was far back on her head, her eyes creased against the sun. "Don't cry, Mama! Don't cry!"

She shook from head to toe. The boarding ramp descended to a flat barge where vendors sat with their wares. Clerks from the ship's company sat at a table with sheaves of paper and portable desks painted with the black diamond. She held Sally against her. A tug motored toward them, rocking, trying to come alongside the barge. A line was thrown, caught, and tied.

Sailors had forced everyone out of the hold. A surgeon moved among the sick passengers declaring them unfit to travel. Those who held them up were required to personally deposit them on the barge, splintering families and causing great anguish.

Steerage passengers were sent to the foredeck for roll call. Tension ran through them like the twine of a taut rope. Elizabeth gripped Sally's hand and barely heard terse whispers and guttural commands to not cough or scratch as passage papers were arranged and rearranged. The tug's engine growled from its far side, black clouds belching from its chimney.

A surgeon's assistant nabbed a man with a handkerchief around his neck and a brimmed hat hanging from a string on his back. The man stood straight with equal weight on his foot and a peg that was holstered in leather and strapped to the bottom of his knee. A girl mother-to-be, face grotesque with tears, sat leaning back against a bag at the rail. The crew poked and prodded every bundle and corner with long pronged sticks, and upended barrels, dumping out a ragged young man. He dragged himself over to the pregnant girl, who smiled through her tears.

The clerk called, "Locke, Locke, and Locke!"

She walked up to the clerk. "We two, Elizabeth and Sally, are leaving the ship. I should like our tickets to be used by the stowaway and his lady." Her voice was muted by the wind, blood pounded in her ears.

Jordan set down her carpetbag and stepped back.

The clerk looked over his glasses at her, assessed her dress and manners. His pale eyes took in Jordan, and he turned half a circle to see the pathetic couple who were being ejected from the Ocean Monarch. "Have you any means at your disposal, Madame?"

"Yes. I have means!"

"We'll wait on Captain Murdoch," he said, dismissing her and returning to the list. "McAlliff! Eight McAlliffs!"

The captain stood near the forward mast, listening as the peg-legged man contested the surgeon's opinion. She couldn't hear the words but saw Murdoch acquiesce and shake the man's hand. Murdoch walked him to the clerk, who took his name and checked him off and sent him back to the assemblage. She watched the clerk speak to the captain, pointing out Elizabeth and then identifying the stowaways. Both men glanced at Jordan, and the clerk spoke some more. The captain, somber and bearded, looked again at her, nodded his head yes, and walked to the afterdeck, hands clasped behind him. The clerk carried on with the list of names.

Passengers grew talkative as more and more were checked off, but she stood, thighs in spasm, squeezing Sally's hand, close to the clerk and away from Jordan. When the clerk finished, he folded his spectacles in his pocket, and said, "Okay, that's it." She pulled Sally toward the gangplank, following the clerk's tan-coated back and thick gray hair.

The clerk sent the stowaway and his lady across the ramp to the barge and turned so quickly that Elizabeth almost collided with him. "Captain don't think it's a fair trade, ma'am. We don't reward stowaways. But not to worry, he has a cabin passage for you." He smiled as if he had done something to make her happy and tipped his hat, then nodded to a sailor who held her by the arm.

"No! No! My name isn't Locke!" The tug whistle blared. "No! This is a mistake!"

Jordan shouted, "Please! Captain! A word please!"

A strong hand against his chest stopped him from entering the afterdeck. "Stay back or get below!"

She was sat down in the companionway. "Best to stay out' the way, ma'am!"

"Mama, don't cry! Mama! Mama!"

Elizabeth pulled her five-year-old onto her lap. Incensed and frightened, she heard cannons. Screaming and terror.

"It's my name, Mama! They're singin' 'bout me!"

God help me. They were stomping, singing as the sails went up.

> *Sally is a pretty girl—Sing Sally-ho!*
> *Sally she is fond of me—Sing sally-ho!*
> *We are for America, so cheerily we'll go.*
> *Then pull away strongly, boys, and sing Sally-ho!*

Passengers cheered and then hushed. A choking smoke crept through the windows. A fire could rescue her . . . . She watched the smoke disappear aft, smelled porridge burning in a pot.

She waited as if glued to the bench, her arm pressing Sally to her side. "I can't believe this. What were they thinking? We will get off. We will get off." Once the ship was underway, she would speak to the captain. He simply didn't understand. What did that clerk say to him?

Jordan ducked through the low door and sat at her side. "What happened? What did that man say to you?"

"He told me I could have a cabin. I don't want a cabin! I need to leave!" As her voice rose, her eyes filled.

"You need to stay calm, Liza!" He gave her arm an emphatic shake. "I'll take Sally forward with me. Think about what you're going to tell the captain. And watch for him."

"Mama? I think they was singin' 'bout me!"

"They were singing about you to help raise the sails, Sally." Jordan tweaked her chin. "Sailors like singing about pretty girls."

The truth. I'll tell him the truth. Elizabeth placed Sally's bonnet on her head and tied it. "Stay with Jordan, Sally, until I come for you." She picked up her bag and went out the door after them, barely four feet from the varnished rail that surrounded the mainmast.

Air slapped her. Huge, shrouding stretches of canvas strained into a high-pitched keening. Ropes steepled and creaked. She moved left to the starboard rail and stood, again, at the tied-down boarding gate. Her vista lay between the rail and the cordoned rear corner of a large deckhouse, a distance of about ten feet. She could see a section of afterdeck, sailors tugging rope, and now the deck was no longer flat, and she had to maneuver with care to get to the other rail and look through that alley, harder still with more canvas billowing and screaming. The smell of cooked meat coiled disagreeably in her belly.

Off the rail land was everywhere visible and she was encouraged. The waves ran into each other, chopping and colliding, denying any pattern or constancy. With each passing second, she was being pushed further from her children. She shook her head, wanting to deny the romantic lunacy that had gotten her to Liverpool. Her family was her current—the purpose and order of her life. But her husband and children didn't know she was missing. She was drowning and no one even knew she was in the water.

Feeling queasy, she swallowed saliva and scanned the deck again. She careened to starboard. The cockeyed deck pulled at her stomach and she turned back to the churning water. She leaned over the rail of the ship and threw up. She retched and cried, sobbing and heaving, and dirtied her shawl.

Spent, she dropped down, sitting on her bag and leaning on the rail. She closed her eyes and wished she could close her ears, stop the noise of people shouting and banging, and clanging pots, the discordant railing of flutes, fiddles, and drums, even singing, blowing at her, and the incessant thumping of feet, warring rhythms. She heard women speak of where their people lived, those who had gone ahead of them, expecting the huts and big houses to be like those they had left behind. "It's called 'The Acre,' don't you know. You can put a little house there, you can."

Her hand clamped over her mouth, she wanted to say, "At least you have your families." But they didn't, of course. Pig that she was, she was forgetting their famine. Thank God they didn't know she had so unwittingly boarded a ship without her husband and children.

Jesus Christ, what's wrong with me? She stood and vomited over the side.

God help me. Her throat was raw and she thought she might die before getting off this filthy boat. Her head ached. She dropped back onto her bag and pressed her hands to her stomach. A young woman sat against the deckhouse wall, a drawing pad propped against her raised knees. Tied in a bow at the side of her neck, a blue ribbon secured a straw hat, a fine bonnet for all its simplicity, designed to sit well back on her head. Blue sleeves had been rolled with precision back to the elbows, exposing small, sturdy forearms. The corners of her mouth pulled down in concentration, her thick dark lashes as still as if she were sleeping. She looked barely older than Meridith.

Thinking she could write something for the captain if the girl could spare pencil and paper, Elizabeth got up, pulling her bag, and sat a few feet away from the artist. The girl looked up, light eyes staring, her mind still caught up with what she had been doing.

"I'm sorry. I didn't mean to disturb you."

The girl's eyes, large and heavily fringed, were disconcertingly steady. She put down the drawing pad, sitting up straight to stretch, then crossing her legs tailor fashion. She glanced at the drawing, picked it up and softened the nose shadow with the pad of her second finger.

"I can't imagine being able to draw—" She stopped before even the thought made her sick and gave up any thought of writing.

"I was just sketching me mother." The girl picked up the drawing pad and turned it for Elizabeth.

Black luminous eyes stared into her. Dark hair had been parted in the middle, framing a strong resemblance to the artist in spite of the dark eyes.

"You are very good."

The girl said thank you and studied the charcoal drawing.

"You look like her."

"Do ye' think so? Tis how I remember her."

"Has it been long since you've seen her?"

"A year." The clear blue eyes settled on her. She took the tablet back.

I'll be with my children soon. "What is your name, dear?"

"Kathleen. Me name is Kathleen Rose O'Malley." She gestured at the drawing and said, "Rose after herself."

"You're traveling alone?"

"I've been travelin' alone since my family made the crossin'." She kept her eyes on her work. "She died of ship's fever, in quarantine. Off Quebec, they said."

"Oh! How awful!" Her stomach cramped, saliva filled her mouth and she ran to the rail; wiping her mouth before turning back and pressing a hand to her stomach.

The girl said, "Would ye' be knowin' where Quebec might be, then?"

"No."

"Oh." She made her pretty face blank and haughty at the same time. "I thought you might know, bein' English an' all." She leveled a hard look with the statement and held it.

Elizabeth reeled. *But she's a child! A grieving child.*

A slight smile played on the girl's face.

Her headache squeezed. She picked up her bag, saying, "Your mother would be proud of you. She would not wish you to be bitter."

At the rail, she heaved everything from her stomach, scorching her throat. If she died of seasickness, Sally, orphaned in America, would never see her family again. Jordan would become her family.

"Liza."

"I have to wee-wee, Mummy! Hurry!"

Jordan took the bag and walked her past the galley house to the fore deck.

"If anything should happen to me, Jordan, you must write to Palmer."

"Of course. Women use the starboard side. On the right," he said, still holding her arm.

There was a line. The door of the water closet creaked open as an occupant slipped out. It snapped shut with a bang, then creaked open again almost immediately, until the white painted door opened for them and she grabbed it and held it for Sally.

The hole was cut into a wide, flat board that ran through all four closets. The floor was puddled, the stench horrible. Sally started to cry.

"I'll hold you. Squat—on your feet! I'll hold up your skirt."

Sally left as soon as she could. Elizabeth gagged and retched and cried before getting her skirt up and over the back of her head.

Stomach cramping and throat burning, she pushed through the door and went straight to the rail, dragging her feet so she wouldn't step on anyone. Jordan wiped her mouth with his handkerchief and her tears with the back of his hand. The deck thudded into her feet.

Tea water was offered. He collected some and handed her the tin cup.

Shuddering at the rancid taste, she wet her mouth and gagged before making her way back to her vigil at the boarding gate, just off the main mast, where the artist sat engrossed in her drawing. She would talk with Meridith and Emma about bitterness, how it wrinkles a heart; wrinkles it like a prune and then petrifies it, turning it into a pit that is spent and rigid, incapable of giving succor.

She scanned the deck for the captain or his mate, for anyone who might be close to him. She watched cabin passengers cross the afterdeck. A steward, notable for his clean white pants and jacket, walked toward her. He came past the large deckhouse, straight toward her, and then he was unhooking one end of the rope that separated her from the afterdeck. She was sitting bolt upright, excitement boiling through her.

"Are you Mrs. Locke?"

"Yes."

"You're to come with me then. Captain has a cabin for you." He picked up her bag and held her elbow, ready to walk her aft.

"We need to collect my daughter." She let him walk her forward through the clots of passengers, passing the companionway, the galley dories extending off its roof, past the forward mast, the dancers and the water closets. Sally was on the forecastle, above the steps in the curve of an anchor.

"Sally! Come with me now." The little girl made her way to the ladder, and she took hold of her as she stepped down to the main deck. Jordan gave her a wink in the sudden quiet as all eyes watched, and they walked back the way they had come—Sally's sticky hand snug in her own—and into the passage by the great deckhouse and across the long expanse of clean deck.

"Ladders in the deckhouse and the companionway are also available." He spoke in straightforward American as they passed the rear mast and entered a door in the face of the poop deck. "In fact, they are better suited to your use as they are out of way of the crew. But this will give you a clear idea of where you are in the ship." He led them down a flight of stairs that had a brass handrail.

14

The tiny room smelled as fresh as the newly milled wood of its walls. Air came through a high window, its wooden cover slid open to a passage with portholes.

"It's like a playhouse, Mummy!" Sally sat on the narrow bed, made up with white sheets and a red and white blanket in a diamond weave.

A mahogany bureau served as a table, its hinged top folding out to double its surface. On it sat a white china tea service, a red flag with a white diamond painted on the side of the pot. The ginger tea was for seasickness, to be followed with apple slices. Then, she might try sea-biscuits.

She shifted the tray to a chair and pulled the pitcher and basin forward on the table. "Let's have a wash." This water smelled of roses. There were washcloths and soft white towels.

"There's a bathtub, Mama! Port. Steward said so."

Her stomach cramped. She didn't know how the bath worked, but it would have to wait. Since some cabins had water closets, the one at the end of the passage was almost exclusively for them. They also had a toileting chair with a clean pot.

She knelt on the floor, removed Sally's shoes, and pulled off the soiled nightgown. When had she put it on her? Yesterday. At Missus Farrady's. Just before tea. She began to shake, every nerve and cell in her body sputtering at the enormity of her blunder. She wanted to blubber, to cry out, to weep. She turned away from her child, pressing her back against the cot, planted her hands under her arms, and breathed away the tears.

Instead of undoing Sally's braids, with ragged movements she unhooked her own shoes and kicked them off. When she trusted the calmness of her hands, she turned again to Sally, kneeling to peel off her stockings.

"I like it here, Mummy." Sally traced the diamonds in the blanket.

"The captain will put us on another boat going back to Liverpool."

"What if he doesn't want to?"

"He has to." Otherwise it would be kidnapping. Her throat was too raw to speak. She stepped out of her skirt, pulled off her gown, and stuffed their dirty things in a laundry bag. Sliding the door open, she poked her head out, saw the alley empty, and hung the bag on a hooded hook; then returned to the rose-scented wash basin, so grateful that she wept a little, and washed Sally's face and neck.

"More red diamonds, Mummy!"

Embroidered on the towels. She made sure Sally was clean before washing herself.

"They have *no* water, Mummy—even to drink, and we have special water."

She weakened the ginger tea with boiling water and milk. "Try that before any more biscuits."

"It isn't fair."

It brought me to my senses. The rocking motion coiled through her and she threw up again—this time into the chamber pot—and looked up to see Sally covering her ears, eyes scrunched shut.

Sitting against her pillow, she sipped the harsh liquid. It stung her throat but stayed down, even calmed her stomach.

Sally fell asleep at the foot of the bed. Elizabeth untied her short braids, combed her fingers through the kinked plaits and didn't see anything unusual on her scalp. She checked her neck, arms, legs and torso before laying the cover over her.

They would be rested by tomorrow. They would have bathed and be fresh enough to ride directly to the train station after her talk with Captain Murdoch. She would dress in the blue silk blouse and black skirt, confident and correct in her corset, and offer to pay for their night's use of the cabin. She must have Sally out of earshot for their talk. After breakfast, she would walk her to the mainmast to wait next to the cord with Jordan just on the other side of it.

She wouldn't spend any more of her life daydreaming about him, but that was just the point. She *had* a life. She was a wife and mother before she met him. And he had compromised her. Had put her, and Sally, at risk. No. She didn't feel sorry for him. She had loved him. She didn't know if she did any more. It didn't matter. She set aside the cup and lay down, grateful for this tiny clean space, this exquisite comfort. Knowing that she would soon have them safely back on land, she slept.

In the morning, bathed and dressed, she and Sally followed the scent of toast and coffee through the hushed and carpeted corridor to the dining salon, where sunlight bounced off china and silver. A steward poured water into teapots and offered coffee, its smell heady in her nervous state.

Captain Murdoch sat at the head of the table, chatting with men sitting to each side of him. He nodded to her. "Good day, Missus Locke. I hope you're feeling better?"

She barely trusted her voice. "Yes. Thank you, Captain. And thank you for the ginger tea." She helped Sally onto the red velvet bench and sat. The table had a wooden lip around its perimeter. For a moment, she felt as if she were on a dais that spun to the right, but she grabbed the table edge and the movement stopped. A tray of butter and jams sat still before her. The steward set down her pot of tea and presented a crowded menu. She asked how the eggs were cooked.

"We have coddled, poached, fried, and hardboiled, Madame."

"Coddled, please, and toast."

"Bacon and sausage, Mama! And corn bread! Please?"

The company laughed. Poached eggs under a metal dome had been placed at their door the night before, and Sally downed custard, toast and jam.

Headache lingering, she drank ginger tea mixed with black, chewed some toast and managed to swallow it. Men sat for breakfast, ordering room service for their wives. Captain Murdoch spoke with a steward in a level fair-minded manner and departed. When Elizabeth was ready to leave the dining salon, the steward suggested she try to catch the captain at the purser's room and told her how to find it.

"I passed the purser's on my way here, thank you. But I need first to take my daughter to wait with a friend near the deckhouse."

"Then you'll want to use the forward ladder, Madame. It goes right up to the house. The companion ladder is the one you passed on your way here. It exits at the mizzenmast."

Prisms of glass built into the deck lit the passage and the red-carpeted stairs that led to the large deckhouse with shuttered windows, tables, and caned seating.

She stepped out into brisk air. The huge sails made an eerie humming, igniting uneasiness in her. Except for a few sailors scrubbing the deck, it was empty, hatches latched, steerage passengers waiting, sweating, below. She stopped the memory, protecting her newly bathed freshness.

Sun reflected blinding white off the water. She shielded her eyes to look for other boats, asking Sally to do the same. Some blacked-out spots turned out to be a sailing yacht that disappeared and resurfaced beyond the waves.

"There's a boat, Mama. Oh, it's burning!"

A sailor was instantly on his feet and running to them. "Where?"

"There!" Sally pointed. "There's smoke!"

"Aw, that's just a steamer, kid. We call 'em stink-pots." He went back to holystoning the deck.

Elizabeth scanned the horizon for a black haze, planning to follow it to its densest line, and waited while the sea arched, blocking her line of sight. *Stop or you'll be sick!* There must be sailors watching from the rigging, hidden by canvas, who could spot a passing ship. She wondered if they'd put out a lifeboat for them. The sound of rock scraping wood grated out the minutes. Steerage passengers would be lining up to get out.

A clear whistle released a fetid stream of men, women and children from the small house. Blocking glare, they escaped left and right and forward on the ship. Red-faced women with sweat rings under their arms carried babies who seemed too stunned to cry. Barefoot children clambered past whatever they could. She backed away from the smell of offal that was on them, on their clothes.

She must have smelled like that! The wooden bed fittings were brand new, designed to be torn out and burned on the other shore. The hold would be a day and a night dirtier. She steeled herself for Jordan, then considered turning around and going back before seeing him.

"Jordan!" Sally called.

Dazed, he turned, sprouting beard mottled with gray. Stooped over from the climb, he stepped away from the house to stand tall, arching his back and rolling his head before walking toward them. He wiped his face and neck with the red neckerchief and said, "Top o' the mornin', girls!"

"And the rest to you," said a small man stepping past him.

"Jordan, look!" Sally passed him her smeared and greasy breakfast napkin, nestled with bacon, sausage, and corn bread.

"What the hell?" A sailor grabbed Jordan's shoulder and spun him around. "No consortin' with the cabin trade, buddy!"

"But he's my papa!"

"Sally!"

"There's to be no contact between cabin and steerage, ma'am."

Jordan tucked the package into his pocket, gave Sally a wink, herself a nod, and strode away without looking back.

She took Sally's hand and hurried back across the deck, past the deckhouse, the skylight, the companionway, and the mizzenmast to the door she had entered yesterday, down into the hushed cabin area.

"Ow, Mummy. You're hurting my hand."

Never before had Sally told such a bold-faced lie!

In their tiny cabin, their bag, packed and closed, waited on the chair. "When I get back from speaking with the captain, young lady, I expect an apology for that brazen lie. In the meantime, you may wash your face and hands and wait here for me."

"Yes, Mama."

The captain would be at the purser's office. She smoothed her hair, rubbed her churning stomach.

"I won't have nothin' to do, Mama."

"Think about combing out Grandmama's long hair. We will be seeing her today, and all of this will be like a dream. Latch the door after me." Remembering Sally's deep sleeping, she said, "On second thought, do *not* latch the door. Just leave it closed. I'll be right back."

Sally sat cross-legged on the bed, looking glum. "Jordan won't never be able to cook his bacon, Mama. Not never." Her bottom lip began to quiver.

She looked so small—five years old. *This is all my doing!* She knelt and kissed a small damp palm. "It was very kind of you to give Jordan your food." Blue eyes pooled with tears. "Here is a menu card. Practice your letters until I get back. I won't be long." She kissed the rosebud mouth.

In the carpeted corridor, she retraced her steps to the dining room, having passed the purser's on the way to breakfast, walking aft past cabins and rounding the corner, passing water closets, a couched area with books known as the library, the bathing room, another water closet, and then walking forward past more cabins, and now she was upon it. The door was open. No one was there. A desk was built into the wall, its lid closed, chair tucked. Doors with locks covered small compartments. A square window like the one in her room had been slid to the right, opened, and she could feel its draft.

Anxiety roiled through her, sent her running past the companionway ladder to the dining salon, where the captain sat over a mug of coffee, two matrons at his elbow. Sunlight glinted off their faces. Boys the age of her sons played with marbles that rolled into the raised edge of the tabletop. Candles still warmed the breakfast pans, and the steward offered more tea.

Captain Murdoch spoke. "Missus Locke will have a ginger mix, steward. We'll take it with us to the purser's." Standing, he excused himself, accepted her mug and carried it before them down the passage. He closed the door after her, set down the mug and pulled out two armchairs.

Grateful for the ginger to calm her rolling stomach, she picked up the heavy mug and thought of her husband's blue and gilt shaving cup.

Captain Murdoch was a handsome man, his dark beard accentuating green eyes, quite disarming. He steepled his hands, fingertip pressed to fingertip, legs crossed; patient, expectant.

She sat perfectly erect at the front edge of her seat. "My name is Elizabeth Grey." She let her eyes drop, took a deep breath, and resumed speaking to his implacable gaze. "I live in London with my husband, Palmer Grey, and our five children, the youngest of whom is with me. We were going to Exeter to visit my mother. I—I never planned to board this ship. I came to Liverpool to bid farewell to Jordan Locke."

She watched Murdoch's eyes open wide. "I stupidly agreed to board. Within minutes, I knew I had made a mistake and tried to get off, but the ladder had been pulled in—"

"Have some tea, Missus Grey,"

She gulped air, forced herself to swallow some tea.

"There's no rush. Sit back."

No. She maintained her pose. "I told the clerk that my daughter and I were leaving the boat, that he could give our passage away. What did he say to you?"

Murdoch dropped his gaze and stroked his beard. "He said, 'This lady needs a cabin. She can pay for it. Can you accommodate her?'"

"Oh! Why did he do that? I told him I had to get off! Please! I need to get back to my family. My children need me. My husband— they need me!"

Murdoch's look was cold. "Missus Grey. What do you expect me to do?"

"Hail a passing ship! Put us on a boat heading back to Liverpool!"

Like a hawk about to take flight, Murdoch's chest puffed up and he sat taller. "Madame, you walked on this boat of your own free will. There must be some reason you did that. Was your decision to leave the ship prompted by the conditions of steerage? You'll be causing no risk to your child with a cabin passage. You'll be sharing a wonderful adventure. Take some time with this decision. Stroll on the afterdeck. Get to know some of the other passengers and their children. Spend some time in the library. And then write down your feelings. There are no accidents, Missus Grey. If you're on this ship, it's by God's design."

"No! This is kidnapping!"

"Rogers—the clerk—obviously misread the situation. He made a terrible mistake. He'll pay for it. But I haven't decided to turn my commission upside down for you, Missus Grey. You have put the business of this ship in jeopardy with your addle-brained actions." He pushed himself out of the chair and turned at the door. "I suggest you begin composing a letter to your husband, and maybe we can get *that* on a passing vessel." He left the door open.

Her body went into spasm. She shook from head to toe. He couldn't mean that! He couldn't. This was her life! Her children! Bloody bastard!

There were other boats within sight! They must be able to communicate. Bloody bastard! The bloody bastard!

Another man making another decision! Wasn't that how it started? First Jordan, then the bloody clerk, and now the captain.

She would make her own distress sign. Smoke signals like in that book. *Kidnapped.* The mug shook so much in her hand that she went to the dining room without it. The salon was empty, candles in gimbals close to going out. She slid open a small door, took out a fresh candle and stood to light it. She took three rumpled and greasy napkins from the table and used them to protect the flame as she went aft.

In the bathing room, she placed one napkin in the basin and poured water over it, soaking it, but if it was too wet the linen wouldn't burn. She wrung it out and held it with the dry napkins. The candle rested easily on its wide base, yet she burned herself and almost knocked it over. *All right. Calm. Compose. Breathe. I'm doing this for all the right reasons. God be with me.*

Sailors on other boats would see the smoke. Move fast. Just like that sailor this morning. She left the water in the basin and put the napkins in an empty tin pail, carefully picked up the candle and carried it and the bucket to the water closet that she knew had a through-hull fitting, lined with tin, and exposed to the sea. Put the pail in front of the opening with the burning napkins in it. She slid the door closed behind her, and rolled the dry napkins around the wet one, two to burn, one to make smoke, and placed them in the bottom of the bucket. Kneeling, crouching low, she lit the dry napkins. When she was sure they were burning, she set aside the candle, placed the pail in front of the opening, and carefully backed out of her crouch. She felt a reassuring draft as she opened the door.

Disoriented in the corridor, she went the wrong way, only realizing her mistake when she reached the companionway ladder. She heard feet running on the poop deck, a long high-pitched whistle. *It's working!*

Heading back, the passage was full of smoke. She alone knew what it came from and moved confidently past it to Sally and their stateroom. *I'm coming, Sally. Mummy's coming!* But she was stopped from going aft because of the smoke and sent forward to the companion ladder. *It's only smoke! It's only smoke!* She must have said it out loud because someone said, "Where there's smoke, there's fire!"

She climbed with the smoke to the upper deck and headed aft to the door behind the mizzenmast. When she was stopped, she said, "No! My daughter's there!" and they let her go. *Not far from here, very close, but the smoke is so thick!* She opened the door. "Sally! Wake up!" She lifted her. Smoke streamed into the cabin, pulled by the open window.

"Smoke, Mummy. Smoke!" Her cry turned into a shrill scream.

"Walk, Sally! We need to walk!" Outside their door, the smoke was so thick that they crawled, she above Sally, staying under the smoke, even on the steps. She felt heat, saw flashes of red. She couldn't breathe. The air was on fire, burning her lungs, but then she couldn't feel it. In her mind, she kept moving with Sally safe beneath her, and in her mind she kept breathing. It was all right if she couldn't see, as long as they kept moving and breathing.

She saw the ship burning from above. There was no sound. Sailors cut the forward lines and heavy white canvas fell and hung from the bowsprit. Passengers and sailors climbed down the lines, waiting for rescue boats that bobbed up and down, far out of reach. Flames chased everyone to the forward upper deck where people spilled off the bow.

The ship was in flames, fire outlined by ocean. Waves of heat distorted the flames, the ship. Sparks and smoke rose into the air, but she felt no heat. She smelled no smoke. She heard no sounds of fire, no shrieks of terror.

Nearby ships sent out dories. Sailors boarded the burning ship and lowered passengers into boats.

She watched the sea flood the after part of the ship and, as the boat gradually settled into the ocean, large volumes of flame, in silence, rushed into the air, until the ship disappeared under the water, causing a heavy swell. The sea settled, leaving only a few pieces of burnt timber and some spars floating on its surface.

15

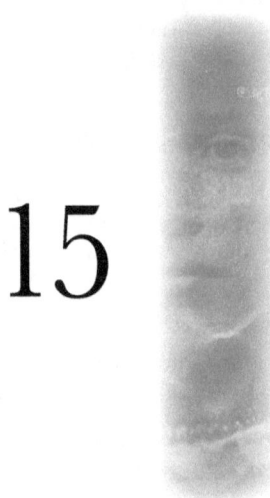

Head spinning, Jane pressed her hands together. The ferry's engine vibration jarred through the red bench into her backside, suddenly wrong. It numbed her ears, threw her stomach into cramping and she knew she was about to be sick. She reeled as she stood.

"Are you all right?"

She heard the voice, shook her head no, and clamped a hand over her mouth. Hands held her, maneuvered her to the stairs. In her mind she was Elizabeth being jostled into steerage. While Jane lay prone on a bench near the ferry's toilets, she knew only Elizabeth's shipboard ordeal. Seasick, water closet doors banging and creaking, she squeezed Sally's hand. Waiting, she held tight to the small hand.

When she opened her eyes, the hand she gripped was a stranger's, her head in the woman's lap, while another woman pressed a cloth to her forehead.

"You're all right, *de-ah*. You're all right. Just stay calm until you're fully awake."

The sea image burned in her mind. The ship gone, some spars floating around. *Sweet Jesus! Elizabeth set the boat on fire! All those people!*

"No, no! You must stay down."

Wanting to gasp, to cry out, she covered her mouth with her hands. *Oh my God! Oh my God!*

"I think you've had some type of shock, dear." The woman's front teeth protruded over faded pink lipstick. She replaced the cloth with a fresh, cool one.

"Yes." Her head ached. Fire on a wooden ship. *How stupid!* Hot and sweaty, she tried to sit and get out of the poncho. The women pulled it over her head and urged her to lie back. It was over. It had to be. Elizabeth died. The whole ship—Sally. Tears stung her eyes.

Someone pressed a tissue to her cheek to keep tears from running into her ears. *Funny,* she thought, in spite of her shock and sadness. "I'm all right now," she said, and they helped her to sit and offered a fresh bottle of water. She swallowed and thanked them.

"You gave us quite a turn." The gray-haired woman watched her.

Jane placed her palms together and breathed. "I thought I was going to be sick. Did I—?"

"No, dear. You just sort of fainted. But I see your color is back now. That's a good sign."

"Thank you . . . so much . . . for your help. I think I can get up now."

"Let's just wait a while. You're still a little wobbly. Don't you think she should rest a little more, Maude?"

The heavy-set woman nodded from the opposite bench, looking right in Jane's eyes. "There's no rush. Ferry's not dockin' yet. You're not needin' a doctor, are you?"

The question made Jane smile. "No. But some more water would help." She drank from the bottle and drank some more. "Thank you. For the water." She swallowed hard. "And for your help." Tears filled her eyes as she stood. "Now I really can go up."

"And that's exactly what we're doing, aren't we, Maude?" The women conversed with each other as they climbed to the open deck and took their original seats.

Jane collected her poncho and went up after them. In her own seat, sodden with gloom, veiling shock and grief, she found her sunglasses and covered her eyes.

The ferry was passing the naval repair barge that simulated dry dock, where a ship could motor in, be hoisted for riveting and painting, and dropped back into the water. She felt like one of them, hoisted into a different time and dropped back into the present; left to wonder what was repaired . . . if she was somehow fixed. Or forewarned.

The sea looked as it had where the ship went down. Dark, dark green.

A child made truck sounds. A boat bleated its horn. She heard the calls of men, the hum of engines, an electric sander.

She was numbed by the enormity of Elizabeth's mistakes and afraid of what it meant for her. Error rode the woman's attitude, from coach to station; train to docks to ship; like digging a hole in the sand, deeper and deeper, until the walls collapse and suffocate. Sliding along in a dream state, until someone else made a decision. Letting someone else decide. And, oh sweet Jesus, she started a fire! With a prayer! *God be with me. I do this for all the right reasons.* She meant only to make smoke. It was an accident. But what a stupid thing to do!

Poor Elizabeth, dying and thinking she was still moving, trying to get back to her family. But it was over. She recalled the bird's eye view, distant and quiet. She lingered with it until she felt sick to her stomach and stopped. Yes. It really was finished. She checked the pockets of the backpack and looked in vain for a tissue before stuffing in the poncho, again, and, sniffling, shrugged the thing over her shoulders.

She wondered if Jordan survived the fire and, in her mind's eye, saw him looking aft. The ship had turned, as if heading back to Liverpool. Something was happening. A distress signal was being hoisted. The anchors were released with a great scream of chains, throwing women and children into the water. Sailors and passengers rushed to the bow. Boats were dropping over the side. Flames licked at the poop deck, spread up the ropes and masts, raining fire, as everyone tried to run to the bow, tripping on cleats, ropes and heavy blocks that fell from the rigging.

"Don't run!" he yelled. "Don't run!"

Jane felt the gray-haired woman watching her while listening to her friend. The good women were talking about seamen's kits and how they needed to get some really large safety pins to hold them together.

"Those pins are hard to come by, Maude," she finally said, turning to the other.

"They had the most beautiful center on Staten Island, Rita."

"Who did? The sailors?"

Jane latched onto the conversation like a lifeline to the present.

"Yes. A wealthy industrialist donated the land and the buildings. He even paid for its operation. I don't know why they relocated to South Carolina."

"Were you ever there, Maude?"

"Oh my, yes. My mother was *from* Staten Island," she said, standing. "It's all changed, of course. Tchht. Mama would roll over in her grave if she could see it now."

Jane stepped up to the women, silent now, waiting to disembark, and said, "I have some of those large safety pins. They came with kilts."

"Well, that's just what we need, dear."

"Jane. My name is Jane." It felt so good to say it that she pressed their hands and continued. "Jane Eliot."

"This is Maude, and my name is Rita."

"How can I get the pins to you?"

"Well, Jane, you can bring them to the Methodist church on Friend Street. Do you know where that is?"

She went into the restroom at the Portland Terminal and saw her face, pale and warped, in the distorted mirror. She closed her eyes in order to picture the other face, testing, to see if she could, and saw the angry Elizabeth—felt an instant of intense rage. She blew out the feeling, to re-premise like an actor, and headed for the parking garage, remembering, again, that she left the Range Rover at the cottage. She started walking home.

If she were driving, she'd stop at the library and go straight to the reference desk, but it was too far in the wrong direction. She also felt unfit to face a stranger. "Somehow not quite myself." As soon as the words were out, she clamped her mouth shut. No one else need know what strange mantle had been dropped over her.

A woman's spastic hand caught her attention. It was her own reflection on a plate-glass window. The movement looked like someone shaking out a hand that had gone to sleep, but she hadn't felt a thing. *So much for getting fixed.* She pulled her notebook out of the pack and held it with her right hand. Squaring her shoulders, she walked up the inclines that were so like the steep rises from the docks in Liverpool.

She could approach it like a puzzle, figure out how Elizabeth's blunders fit in her life, or how knowing about it could improve her own way of living. Elizabeth left her children in search of more love. But she killed all those people trying *not* to leave them. Jane's own childlessness must be karmic payback. Jordan and David were one. Jordan was complicit—had gotten Elizabeth to Liverpool *and* on the ship. Double jeopardy: David and she together were to do penance. The promise of a child dropped sodden from her heart. While thinking she should pray, she escaped into rhyme:

> *Engage in rage oh vile sage!*
> *I rhyme to fill the time*
> *To stop my mind*
> *Cap it, wrap it!*

A school bus groaned up the hill. Church bells clanged and she thought of the lifeline of giant safety pins that Rita and Maude had thrown her.

> *Scream and dream of clean.*
> *Then clear, queer dear. Clear.*

She was tired of walking by the time she reached her house. Finding the front door locked, she went down the steps to the back door and opened it to a ringing phone. She ran to the kitchen. "Hello?"

"Jene? It's Renee. From the ferry the other day?"

"Oh?" She gripped the phone. The ferry . . . fainting . . . Renee. She could help her with hypnosis.

"How are you?"

"I'm . . . I just came in the door. I'm a little distracted."

"I won't keep you, but I'm going to be in Portland tomorrow. Can we meet for lunch?"

She agreed and wrote down the time and place. Dropping her backpack to the black and white floor, she took in the kitchen's yellow counter and soft green colors. She phoned the library and asked the reference librarian to look up a ship called the Ocean Monarch and left her number.

She moved through the comforting shallows of her house, up the stairs to the ticking of the hall clock, and into her soft pink bedroom. Perched on her bed, she thought of the silken green coverlet wet with Sally's drool. She called David's office.

The current receptionist answered David's line. "Oh, Mrs. Eliot! He's been trying to reach you. Are you home?"

"Put me through please." Jane had no reserve for small talk.

David picked up. "Jane? Everything okay?"

"Yup. Can we go out to dinner?"

———— • ◆ • ————

The pub was a popular nightspot in Portland. Darts, acoustic music, and banter wove a cocoon of protection around their booth. "David, do you remember that dream I was telling you about—I dreamed about you, but you looked different? Yesterday morning at the cottage."

"No. That seems like a long time ago, but—" He hesitated, raising his brows. "I've been reading up on dreams. They can be a link to the subconscious. The unconscious mind has access to information which the conscious mind does not."

Her eyes opened wide at this unexpected response.

"So tell me about the dream."

"Oh. A man comes out of a building. He's very tall. His hat is in his hand and he's wearing a black frock coat. I'm walking toward him. I see him through the veil of my hat and look into his dark eyes. Nothing much happens. They pass and greet, but it feels surreptitious. It's an ugly building with yellow brick."

She straightened, placed her palms together, elbows on the table, the movement calming her and helping her to focus. "That dream was a past life memory."

David looked for a server and placed their order.

She waited for his reaction while he sipped water, ice cubes clinking.

He grinned at her. "Edgar Cayce said that people can remember past life experiences in their dreams. I googled."

"What?"

"I googled 'Edgar Cayce/past lives'."

"Who's Edgar Cayce?"

"The sleeping prophet. My mom always referred to his 'Little Black Book' whenever anyone was sick. He died in 1944." He drank from the wine glass the waitress set before him.

"Well—good. Can you try being a little less smug about it?"

"Sorry. So I'm there, too?"

"Yeah." She wondered how much it would bother *him*. "Your name was Jordan Locke. You were master of the parish workhouse where I was schoolmistress. We fell in love."

He steepled his hands. "Sounds good to me."

"Well it wasn't! I was married. We were both married! You were leaving England. You were going to Lowell, the mill city. You'd been there before." She set down her glass and put her palms together, breathed. "I didn't want you to leave and you wanted me to go with you. I never even *considered* going. I had five children . . . " She broke off and searched in her bag for a tissue. David handed her his hankie. She blew her nose.

"Jane. How do you know this?" His look was direct and somber.

"I remembered it! I told you they were past life memories, didn't I? First at the cottage, and then on the ferry. The scenes just kept coming."

He began eating his salad.

"How can you eat?"

He chewed and swallowed. "I'm hungry, dammit. Why are you mad at *me*?"

She sipped her wine, the glass heavy in her hand. Fatigue? She tore off a crust of bread, chewed and swallowed it, and picked up her fork.

"How can you eat, Jane?"

"Don't be silly. I'm hungry."

"Another wine?" The waitress set down their plates.

She wound linguini on her fork and watched him place a piece of steak into his mouth. "It was pretty sordid." She waited while he chewed and swallowed. "We had sex in the workhouse tower."

He picked up his glass, laughing. "Great! Let's have a re-enactment!"

"David." She covered her face with her hands. "Don't be so—"

She watched him laugh and run a hand through his hair, the gesture similar to Jordan's. He wiped his eyes. "I'm eating steak here. Are you trying to kill me?" He reached for her hand, speaking quietly. "Learn anything new?"

Heat flashed through her face.

"Hah! You did!"

David's eyes weren't as dark as Jordan's, his brow was wider, but they looked somewhat alike. Their builds were different, her husband broader, not as tall. Jordan moved as if he were on center stage, very self-aware. David moved so as not to draw attention to himself. He was strong, as forceful as Jordan, but more controlled; more refined. His dimples were showing, and she couldn't help but smile back at him.

Now she shook her head and returned to her pasta. How much had Elizabeth looked like her? Blonde, strong cheekbones, large eyes that she only saw puffed and sad in a mirror. Bustier; heavier; corseted. "Different bodies, same souls."

David put down his fork and sat back. "Cayce said that karma is memory, not destiny. Let me get this right." He pulled an index card from inside his jacket and read it. "With free will, we can meet this memory as a positive or negative experience . . . each individual is ultimately responsible for shaping his life *in the present.*"

"It ended very badly. The ship caught fire. Elizabeth and Sally died."

David stared, motionless.

She was too tired for even coffee and grew more weary with each step to the car.

———————

She woke at one o'clock in the morning with David asleep beside her. Tedium from Elizabeth's life snagged through her mind: opening the garden gate; crossing the front hall; climbing the stairway; even her longing for a surprise encounter with Jordan. She watched for Sally but saw instead Elizabeth's mirrored face and felt grimy self-loathing.

She said the Lord's Prayer and the church bell chimed twice. She re-scripted the scenes. At the boarding house, with prayerful resolve, Elizabeth got up while Sally slept, put herself and their things together. When Sally woke—no. She would wake the little girl, help her get ready, and ask Mrs. Farrady to hail a cab. They would have a good tea before leaving for Blackpool. Fast and safe. Elizabeth would say the Lord's Prayer and put her rescue in Harriet's hands. No. She would pray and rescue Sally and herself by getting away before Jordan's arrival. Now that she knew when Jordan was coming, she could change the story.

Walking and talking at the shore, searching for shells, calmed by the ocean's swells, Elizabeth's loss would lessen, grow as distant as yesterday's wave, somewhere on the horizon.

> *Waves, awash with passion, covered my ankles,*
> *And buried deep—my feet—in a snug cave of sand.*

The ship would get to America.

But the ship didn't get to America. It barely got into the ocean and the memory of its burning forced Jane out of bed. She made coffee and watched the sky turn peach beyond the kitchen window. If she were to go out the door and down the street, she might see the sun rise quickly out of the ocean. Instead, she sat at the round kitchen table with her notebook and her laptop, outlining and transcribing the memories. She filled pages of details for each scene: the schoolroom, the smells, the children, that horrible broken window.

"Hey, what time did you get up?" David stood behind and held her against him.

"Early."

"Are you okay to go out to the island and get the truck? What are you doing today?"

"This. I'm writing it all down."

"Are you hungry? What would you like? Would you like bacon? Jane."

"What?"

He opened cupboards and banged pans. "What would you like?"

"Oh. Scrambled eggs would be good. I'll make them. Just let me clean this up." She continued to write.

When he brought the eggs over, she changed her seat and let him set the table.

Some hours later, as she answered the phone, her eyes fell on the note: *Lunch—1:00 at Demillo's.*

"Hello?"

"Hi. This is the Portland Library. You called about a ship? The Ocean Monarch?"

"Yes."

"What is it you wanted to know? Is there a specific aspect you're researching?"

"Just something general. What can you tell me?"

"It was built in 1847 at the Donald McKay shipyard, 301 tons, launched in July. Fifty-five meters long, eleven meters wide. August 24, 1848, it was destroyed by fire. Someone tripped over a candle. It's in seventeen meters of water in Liverpool Bay. It's a dive site, and there's pottery to be found."

Jane scribbled, pushing aside the sinking feeling at mention of the candle.

"There's a firsthand account written in 1848 by a Frederick Jerome: 'The Burning of the Ocean Monarch With The Noble Hearted Sailor Frederick Jerome.' The Boston Antheneum has it. The Peabody may also."

"Thank you, I'm writing this down . . . ." The librarian gave a web search name.

She hung up the phone. This was confirmation. But Elizabeth's starting the fire drowned out any desire to kick up her heels.

She created a list of all that she had seen of Elizabeth's life. Chills ran through her, settled in her knees. She wrote "mistake" in parentheses next to *Deciding to visit mother, Going to Harriet's at Blackpool,* and *Boarding ship.* The final entry was *Seeing the ship burn and sink. Braids turning into wet, soggy ropes . . . .*

With a gasp, she remembered a horrible nightmare. She phoned her sister.

"Jane. I've been calling your cell phone. Where are you?"

"I'm home. Sorry. I keep forgetting to charge my phone. I left the cottage after talking to you and headed home. I kept having memories—being in that other time—until it was over. On the ferry . . . I kind of passed out. I just finished writing out a list of the things I saw. And guess what."

"What?"

"I had this nightmare when we were on vacation, but I forgot all about it. I was on a boat, braiding hair, skinny braids and thick braids, but they turned into wet, soggy ropes that strangled me. It was horrible. And just as I wrote the last line of my list, the dream came back to me. It was all about this."

"So read it to me!"

"This is chronological, not the way it came to me. Okay." The list left a lot out but made the telling easier. "The ship caught fire. That's how Elizabeth and Sally died." She choked out the last words.

"Oh, my God! That's horrible!"

She paused to blow her nose.

"Jane, what about the blackbirds?"

"What?"

"Why were there blackbirds in your dream?"

The image of the birds flying in and lifting off was chilling. "Hideous. Jordan told Elizabeth that she had made the decision to go with him when she boarded the train for Liverpool. It wasn't true. He probably thought it was. They were sitting on a bench. A bunch of blackbirds flew in. Some landed on a bench and some in a tree and when the last one perched, they lifted and flew off."

Sadness eked through her. "That was it. That's when everything turned around."

Eileen was quiet. "Wow."

"Yeah. She trusted him more than herself."

Eileen groaned, and Jane said, "As soon as I got home, I called the library, and guess what? The Ocean Monarch burned and sank in Liverpool Harbor on August 25th, 1848."

"Jane, that's proof! This really happened! Aren't you excited?"

16

Halfway out the door to her lunch date, she spotted the empty driveway, went back in, and called for a cab.

David rang, offering her a ride. "You can get the truck after lunch, Jane. You'll be right there."

"I'm not going back to Peaks today."

"I can meet you at the ferry."

"No!"

"Jane." He let out a noisy breath. "I can go with you tomorrow, but I don't want to hang around all day."

"Do you think I want to?" She resisted slamming down the phone. "My cab is here."

She went out the front door to the cab parked at the curb and slid into the vinyl hollow of the back seat and the dank smell of cigarettes.

The cabbie rested his elbow on the doorframe, his forearm bared by the pushed-up sleeve of a gray sweatshirt. He wore sunglasses and conversed through the rearview mirror. "Where ya' headed?" He only nodded when she told him Demillo's.

Cabbies in that other time wore jackets and hats, day and

night. She thought of the clogged streets (going the wrong way), dragging her precious child into Liverpool's nefarious waterfront at night. Elizabeth never made a decision to go there. She just put all her energy into the daydream, and the daydream grew muscles and carried her. If only she had thought of surprising her children at the shore, of seeing their faces light up at the sight of her. But Elizabeth thought only of Jordan.

She wondered how much of this she could tell Renee and thought back to that ferry ride; how she had wanted hypnotic help for her hand, and then she had choked on smoke and fainted. Renee was studying hypnosis as a cure for phobias and said that Jane would be a good subject. Suggestible.

Soon she was led through a maze of tables and chairs, emerging in an area bright with ocean light. Her eyes met Renee's, each looking at the other with uncertainty.

"Jene? You look different somehow." Renee's voice was gravelly. "It is Jene, isn't it?"

If you only knew, she thought, and said, "Yes, I think so. *You* look nice."

Renee's white blouse was open at the neck, her hair in a French twist. "Pardon my attire. I spoke at Kiwanis Club this morning. You look lovely, Jene."

"Thank you." Jane had worn her longest earrings, heavy mascara and dark lipstick. "What was your talk about?"

"Hypnosis and my dissertation. I'm still off the ground from it."

"Nervous?"

"My adrenaline goes up. I feel like I've been flying—or something. Phew."

Jane felt a runnel in her belly. *It can't be!*

"What is it, Jene?"

"You look like her! Like Elizabeth!"

"And she is?"

"Elizabeth is from the 1840s—"

"Oh, *mon Dieu!*"

"How could there be such a coincidence?"

"There are no coincidences, *cherie*. All is by intricate design."

With no patience for waitress or menu, Jane ordered a Bloody Mary and the same salad as Renee.

"Tell me about Elizabeth." Renee's wide eyes were still.

"*Her* eyes were light, gray or hazel, but the same wide, high cheekbones and jaw. She was a strikingly beautiful woman, Renee, and so are you."

Smile-lines creased the corners of her eyes. "But, Jene, my husband said that you and I look alike. Remember? He even took a picture, but I don't have it," her voice trailed off in apology. "But thank you for the compliment."

Jane had liked this warmhearted woman with her gravelly voice and golden skin since they first met. "I've been having visions— memories from a past life. It started at the cottage, but I saw the whole horrible story while I was on the ferry." She pulled her notebook from her bag, removed the newly printed pages and handed them to Renee. "I wrote it down."

A Bloody Mary, large and sweating, appeared in front of her. She took up the stalk of celery and bit it. Droplets from the big cold glass seeped into the white table cloth, so like the ship's napkins . . . Jane hailed the waitress, ordered a pot of tea and sent back the drink.

"*Mon Dieu, cherie*! But of course, this must be difficult for you."

"It's been . . . pretty awful."

"I beg your pardon, Jene. When I get excited, I go into *Francais*." Slipping on tortoise-shell glasses, she went back to reading and, looking over the frame, said, "Fire?"

"They die in the fire." A lot of people died in the fire.

"*Cherie*, I am so sorry."

"The library confirmed the loss of the ship. August 25th, 1848." Almost a brand new ship.

"But that is wonderful for you! Many people spend their lives looking for proof and ignore the reason for having memory in the first place."

"You know other people this has happened to?"

"In hypnosis, with purposeful suggestion. But there are ways for seeing past lives without hypnosis. I don't know anyone who has experienced spontaneous regression as you have, but it happens. There must be a strong soul urge."

"Yes. I see very clearly how this relates to my life. Unfortunately." Jane twisted a section of tablecloth. Her napkin was paper and had fallen off her lap.

Renee studied her. "The higher self always pushes toward the positive. This remembering will be good for you."

"Renee, I've had two miscarriages. It's showing me why I will never have a child. And David, my husband, was Jordan, so that makes him complicit. Very appropriate, don't you think?"

"Complicit?"

"He is also responsible for what happened." She watched the trough made by a departing ferry deepen into the bay.

"At some level, Jene, this memory will help you achieve your life's purpose. How wonderful that you have found each other again."

She studied the woman's earnest face. "It's worse. Much worse. When the captain wouldn't help her, Elizabeth tried to get help by making smoke. She lit dry napkins around a wet one in a pail, and shoved the pail into a metal-lined hull opening behind a toilet. Elizabeth started the fire! She burned the boat and killed all those people!" She pulled the cloth to her eye, upsetting her water.

"*Cherie*! That was a different woman. That was not you. And she was doing all that she could to get back to her children."

Jane pulled away from the wet table while Renee wrote out directions to her house for the following afternoon.

"Your higher self will show us the way to go. I am very excited, Jene. You are truly gifted."

Nothing could be worse than what she had already seen. She accepted a ride home from Renee, walked in the front door and straight to her bed, where she lay in the sun and slept. She dreamed of the shipboard artist, the sullen-faced Irish girl. She kept seeing the girl shift the portrait, but each time it was swept away, just out of reach, again and again. She looked for the image as Elizabeth had seen it and found nothing, a vacuum, until, forced awake by tedium, the dark-eyed face flashed before Jane's closed eyes, setting off an alarm that made her heart beat faster.

The room was in shadow. She took off her silk shirt and put on her old Northeastern sweatshirt and, when David called, asked for the pizza she'd been wanting for two days. She took two aspirin for the thudding in her head and went down to the kitchen, made some tea and phoned her mother.

"Hi, Mom."

"Jane?"

"Yup, it's me."

"Well, what have you been up to?"

"I spent some time at Peaks Island, painting a friend's cottage."

"You went out to that island to work? Alone?"

"I went Tuesday morning and came home Thursday afternoon. It's a very quiet place, Mom."

"I'm surprised at David letting you go out there. Was he with you?"

"He came out Tuesday night—"

"Jane! Are you out of your mind? Oh! Is there something wrong with . . . just sitting still?"

"Oh, Mom. I wanted to have children!" She choked back a sob as tears burned her eyes. "Mom!" she cried openly. "I found out why I can't have children." Hot tears streamed down her face.

David had come in the door without her noticing. He came behind the stool where she sat, took the phone and said, "We'll call you back." He pulled her onto his lap and rocked her and, when she stopped to blow her nose, he said, "What are you crying about?"

"Isn't it obvious?" Her nose was stuffy, her eyes stinging. She got up from his lap. "You don't really think God's gonna give us more babies to abandon, do you?" She went into the bathroom, rinsed her face and drank some water.

When she came out, David waved a sheaf of papers. "Janey, this is what Edgar Cayce says. *You have to read it.*"

"No. I *don't* have to read it! Karma's a memory, David? Right. Just because you googled something doesn't make you any kind of expert!" Shaking and spilling, she tipped the pot to a cup.

David poured whiskey in a squat glass. Ice cubes rattled.

She mopped up her spill.

"I'll read it *to* you. After we eat."

He stood and brushed back strands of hair from her forehead, and she wrapped her arms around him, pressing her face into his cotton shirt.

———•◦•———

David put down his napkin. "How was lunch? What did you find out about the dog?"

"What dog?"

"I thought you were having lunch with the woman that has the Tibetan Terrier?"

"Oh, right. I forgot about the dog. Renee's a hypnotist. She—"

"What?!"

"She's a hypnotist. She said I had 'spontaneous regression.'"

"Wait a minute! This is the woman you met on the ferry the day you fainted?" He stood and then paced. "Now isn't that a dandy coincidence! Jesus, Jane. Are you sure she isn't a witch?"

"What?"

"My God, she could have put you under some kind of spell! Maybe she *already* hypnotized you! Jesus Christ!"

"Oh, my God. David! She's a nice woman . . . she's doing a thesis. She asked me if I had ever fainted before, and I said yes, once, but that was because of claustrophobia. Her thesis is on hypnosis as a cure for phobias. That's why she took my number—as research for her thesis." She had started cleaning up, wrapping the leftover slices and placing them in the freezer. "Okay?"

"She's a student?!"

"It's a thesis. She's not a kid!"

"Everything started with her. Coincidence?"

"She said, 'Zere ees no coincidence.' She's French. Oh, and guess what! She looks like Elizabeth! The same bone structure, wide set eyes . . . I can't believe it!"

"Maybe you shouldn't. Maybe it's your imagination."

She gave him a "you should talk" look. "Don't—do not start talking about my imagination."

"Is she first and foremost a student or a hypnotist?"

"I don't know. How 'bout she's a smart hypnotist?"

"Let's hope she's not too smart. Come on, I'll read to you upstairs and then you can read to me."

They went up to the living room, and she closed her eyes, put up her feet and listened as David read aloud from the Cayce pages. He spoke slowly enough for her to follow the heady subjects of religion, history, spirituality, dreams, relationships, conscious awareness, and soul purpose. She went deeper and deeper into his voice until he stopped reading to wake her and send her to bed.

———————•◦•———————

Jordan's black eyes stare at her as his jaw drops in horror. She is pulled swiftly away from him. Again and again, his face receding from her, fast, fast, until his mournful eyes clear into David's. He stands motionless looking at something, the collar of his blue oxford shirt loosened around a necktie.

She woke up. She turned on her pillow and reached out to David, sleeping on his side and facing away from her. She slipped into sleep and dreamed she nuzzled Sally's silken cheek. A curly tendril tickling her nose coiled into greasy smoke and yanked her awake.

Lying wide-eyed in the dark, she thought of Elizabeth's mistaken journey. It started with Jordan's goodbye note. *Missus Farrady's Guesthouse.* Ship, date, and place. That got her there, and then, in the park, he told her she had made the decision to leave with him when she came to Liverpool. He said there was no going back. Her stomach sank. Elizabeth trying to get off the boat, but was *too late.* She had listened to Jordan. David snored by her side. She wanted to sock him, push him right off the bed.

"David!" She got on her knees and shook him. "Wake up!"

He wheeled. "What's wrong?"

"It was Jordan's fault!" She whacked his shoulder.

"Christ, Jane!" He grabbed her wrist.

"Ow! That hurts!"

He let go of her and swung his legs off the other side of the bed.

Covering her eyes against the lamp's glare, she heard David's hard breathing.

He pulled over a chair and sat—his round shoulders hunched—let out a short breath and studied the ceiling.

"I'm not the only one responsible, David!"

"No." He closed his eyes and raised his hand. "No. I don't know if you had a past life memory. I know you *think* you did." His eyelids were low, almost menacing. "I don't care if you think I was Jordan. This is *your* dream. It's about you. If I had a past life, it isn't bothering me. But *you are*." He went into the bathroom, came back out, and shoved the chair back in its corner.

Leave it to David to make everything black and white.

"I take responsibility for everything I do in my life. In *my* life. Got that? And you know what, Jane? This is the only life that you can affect or change, improve or make worse and right now, you're making it worse!"

He left the room and she heard his feet slap across the hall. *I'm sorry, David.* Elizabeth was wishy-washy. "Do you think I'm wishy-washy?" she asked when he came back in.

"No. I think you're so resistant to change and compromise that you've become rigid." He tossed the stapled pages on the bed. "Now that you're wide awake, *read this*! Unless, God forbid, you should alter any of your drama with wisdom! It's Edgar Cayce, for Chrissakes! I didn't make it up!

"Page five and six relate to past lives." He walked away, calling over his shoulder, "I'm sleeping in the guest room. Don't talk to me until you've read it."

"Did you read my—"

He slammed the door. David didn't slam doors.

She read the sheaf of papers. They were theoretical, putting her to sleep, and she woke to the sound of the shower running. David's words shot into her mind. *Right now, you're making it worse!* If only she had told him she was sorry instead of talking about Elizabeth! Pretending sleep, she waited until he headed downstairs, postponing their encounter until she was fresh and respectable. She hurried, checking the driveway, hoping he wouldn't leave without seeing her.

The smell of coffee and toast coming up the stairs was reassuring. As she stepped into the kitchen, David caught a bagel ejected from the toaster. She walked quietly behind him and wrapped her arms around him. "I'm sorry, David. Forgive me."

He turned around, nodding, and brushed back strands of her hair. "Doesn't that bother you?"

She stepped back. "Yes! It does bother me!" She threw his pages on the table, poured some coffee and put half a frozen bagel in the toaster. "Did you read *my* pages?"

"Yes. I did."

"It's chronological—"

He pulled her to him and held her tight.

She felt like he was holding her together and loosed hot tears onto his shirt.

"Love is all that survives, Janeykins."

They both knew that was right.

17

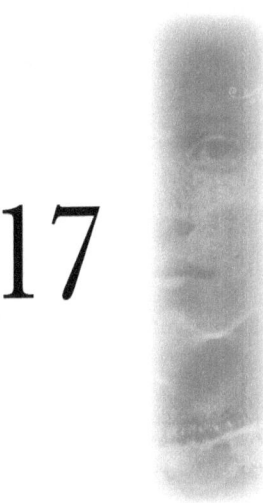

Renee's house had majestic columns and terrace windows on either side of the front door. It was opened by Renee's fifteen-year-old daughter.

"Hi. I'm Patsy. My mom is expecting you." Patsy showed her to the living room and ran off to answer a phone, leaving Jane to admire mahogany antiques on an oriental carpet.

Renee appeared between a set of pocket doors. "Jene, please come in."

While Jane took in the room cased with books, a loud thumping hammered and shook the inside wall. Renee slid the doors apart and said, "Zacharee! From now on, you use the back stairs!"

"Sorry, Mom!" The front door slammed on his baritone response.

Renee rolled her eyes and apologized. "Now we can both take some breaths! Please sit, Jene." She gestured to the side of her desk and a black leather chair with a handle for reclining, and seated herself. "I cannot tell you how much I've pondered your story. Are you well today?"

"Yes. I'm okay."

"Are you comfortable, Jene?"

"Yes."

"The more relaxed you are, the better it will be." She poured two glasses of water from a pitcher. "With your permission, I will record our session—for my research and also for you."

"Yes, that's fine."

"Good. I will push 'record' when we are ready. Have you ever been hypnotized, Jene?"

"No."

"Hypnosis is a state of extreme relaxation. It relaxes tension in the outer mind, so the inner mind may function with clarity. It is all self-hypnosis, since it cannot occur without the recipient's explicit letting go." She began filling out a form, checking off Jane's responses, her tone soothing. "Have you ever walked in your sleep?"

"Yes. I—um—sometimes draw in my sleep."

Renee's eyebrows went up and she made a notation. "Your higher self will monitor all that we do. If something does not serve your highest good at this time, it will not be forthcoming."

Renee sat in a chair next to the recliner, so that their right knees almost touched. She took Jane through three deep breaths, and began counting down from nineteen to one. "Every sound you hear will make you quieter and quieter." Her voice was soothing, each word a gentle stroke. "See yourself at a graceful outdoor staircase winding down ever so gently . . . as you descend you go deeper and deeper . . . in a wonderful relaxed trance . You may hear birds . . . smell the scent of kelp . . . more at peace . . . . One. Rest and breathe.

"Imagine a string tied to your right wrist. The string is attached to a buoyant balloon. It lifts your wrist gently up. Your right arm and hand are weightless. Very good. Your left hand holds a full bucket of sand. It is so heavy. Good. The balloon and bucket are gone. Your hands relax.

"Your subconscious will move a finger to show me a 'yes' response. Good. Right forefinger is your 'yes' . . . and 'no' is your left forefinger. I ask now . . . could Jene be more comfortable? Yes.

"Jene . . . be as a leaf floating on a brook . . . sky above . . . leaves waving . . . smell where the water meets the soil . . . smell your favorite flower. What flower do you smell, Jene?"

"White hyacinth," she answered, pleased that she could speak.

"You may breathe the scent of hyacinth and be calmed and soothed . . . . You are as perfect a creation of God's love as that flower. Your stem is strong, straight. Your leaves are shiny and smooth. Your scent as heavenly as the hyacinth. You are God's perfect creation."

Tears seeped from the corners of Jane's eyes.

"I ask Jene's subconscious: is this a good time to revisit the past? Yes. This will be as if you are watching a movie. You will maintain clarity and objectivity.

"Be again a leaf, floating . . . floating on air . . . wafting and light, to be set down wherever your higher self chooses. When you stop moving, when you are set on the ground, and all is still, you will look down and tell me what you see.

"Are you there? Rest at the spot."

"Spinning. I'm spinning."

"The spinning will stop." Renee snapped her fingers. "Tell me what's happening."

"I am above the burning ship."

"Tell me all that you see."

"Sailors cut the forward lines. Canvas hangs. People climb down. Drop into the water. Sink. Get bashed."

"Are there rescue boats?"

"Small boats take people off the burning ship."

"Keep telling me what happens."

"Open mouths. No sound. I can't hear anything."

"Go on."

"I call for Sally but I can't hear my voice."

"Stay calm. What goes on?"

"Sally—'Let's go to the light, Mummy.' We move fast through a tunnel. A bright light pulls us, surrounds us. Feels good. I stop. I have to go back. I slip back to the ship. I call out, 'Meridith, Emma, Matthew, Owen! I'm not leaving! I'm staying!"

"You are calm now. What happens?"

"Children screaming. I try to pull away." *Stuck. Tied to the spot where the ship went down.*

"Go forward in time—to another place. Where are you?"

"At the shore."

"How did you get there?"

"With thoughts of my children. I directed my energy to them."

"How are they?"

"Happy." *The crying is not theirs.*

"Go on."

"They don't know I'm here." *I practice making a stir, move some strands of their hair—*

"Go to the next important event. Where are you now?"

"With my mother." *I am sad. The crying never stops.*

"What happens?"

"I throw myself into my mother." *Mama! Help me!*

"How do you do that?"

"I rest in her. I cry in her ear."

"And?"

"We take the train to Palmer." *Face so white, his freckles all stand out.*

"What happens?"

"The passenger list." *I try to tell him I was coming back.*

"Go on."

"He sobs." *We were coming home!*

"You are calm, *cherie.*"

"The children scream and cry." *Grief distorts their faces and their hearts. Mirrors are covered.*

"Breathe and be calm. What are they told?"

"Harriet's rowboat capsized. That Sally and I were at the shore with her." *My children are drowned in sadness.*

"And Palmer?"

"Shamed. Everyone in London has read the passenger list."

"Go on."

"Harriet would marry him."

"And?"

"Meridith blames Harriet."

"Go on."

"They hire a house matron. I want to stay with my family. I try to keep Mama from leaving, but my spirit is attached to her and when she leaves I go with her." *Her shoulders are bent.*

"Why do you go with her?"

"My spirit rests in her spirit. I whisper in her ear when she writes to my children."

"What do you say?"

"That they are good. I tell them to always focus on good."

"How long do you do this?"

"Until she dies."

"How many years?"

"Three."

"How does she die?"

"In her sleep." *Papa waits to greet her. She leaves her body and laughs when she sees me. A big pink angel takes me up.*

"What happens?"

"We go through the tunnel." *The light is all the others welcoming us. I've done this before, many times. My heart leaps and expands.*

"What is happening, *cherie?*"

"In the light." *I am permeated in colors, each with its own healing, its own tones. Chimes sift through me. I reunite with the part of me that stays here—we are love. I remember soul family and group progress and our many earth visits, my recent life a single pearl in a long glowing strand, the luster on each orb defined by blemish.*

"Tell me, *cherie.* You can speak."

She chuckled. "We get so confused about love. And ego chips away at self—the soul's link." She laughed. *It was so funny!*

"Are you with your soul group?"

"Yes."

"What do you do?"

"This. We laugh and celebrate."

"Enjoy this feeling. And when you are ready, tell me more."

"Hmm . . . running away."

"Tell me please."

"Ha ha! Running away from running away!"

"Go on, *cherie.* Tell me something."

"There are 'pivotal points'—the words make me laugh. It's so funny! I saw myself butting heads with Palmer—addressing his peevishness. Palmer is in my soul group. He was *supposed to be* voicing his heart."

She laughed so hard that Renee said, "I ask permission to speak with the higher self. I ask Jene's subconscious. May I? Yes. Thank you."

The giddiness disappeared. Her voice cleared, became well-modulated. "Within the soul group, we are able to experience the course of our lives as if we had made different choices at life-altering situations. These are called pivotal points. The lessons are learned best with thoroughness and understanding. Elizabeth is ready to speak."

Renee said thank you, and Jane continued in a lighthearted tone. "By going along with Palmer, I was avoiding necessary confrontation. Learning to not defer to others is a very important lesson. I relived a different approach, facing down Palmer and calling on friends. As part of a group, I helped train young inmates to teach. This was much more fun, and my stints at the workhouse were never alone."

"Go on, *cherie*."

"The next life-altering opportunity regarding this aspect occurred after I had fallen in love with Jordan. Heartbroken with his leaving, I went home, climbed the spiral stair and lay on the bed with Sally. I pleaded exhaustion. Palmer was bad-tempered for feeling responsible, but I mended and was never again disturbed by his peevishness."

"You are describing choices you might have made. Is that right?"

"Yes, at each pivotal point, and how my life would have been affected by that choice."

"So by not having made that choice, you are going to the next life event that is a pivotal point. Is that right?"

"Yes."

"It seems very quick to me. How quick is it?"

"We get to live each choice."

"Please continue."

"We took the train to Exeter. Sally played with Mama and I had the space I needed."

"But?"

"Since I hadn't gone to Exeter, I found myself in Liverpool at midnight. I chose to take a cab to police headquarters, where Sally

slept on my lap. They gave us tea and got us on a train to Exeter."
She chuckled.

"Go on, *cherie*."

"Once at the boarding house, there was no alternative until morning. By focusing on Sally, I got us back to the train. Hmmph. On the second morning, I put my energy and purpose into Sally and me and left, instead of waiting on Jordan. This seemingly innocent time was most dangerous, allowing me to drop my guard and Jordan to suggest that I had decided to join him. So this is an opportunity for a different action or choice. My shock turned to anger at what he was asking of me, and I took Sally straight to the guesthouse for a cab to the train. I was badly shaken in Exeter."

"Continue, please."

"At Missus Farrady's I collapsed on the bed. I stalled for time, thinking, and after tea, took Sally and our things to the train, saying, "I don't care what you say! I'm going home! Whew!

"Having missed *that* chance, at boat-side—as Jordan climbed down from the carriage—I said, 'This doesn't feel right.' I told the driver to take us to the depot and kept my eyes on the driver's back while Jordan took down his trunk and the horse pulled us away. The shaking in my skin grew less until I was numb with relief. I knew I would be happy in Exeter."

"You seem so now, *cherie*. Can you say more?"

"The final reliving of a fateful choice was on the ship. Raging at the Captain, I collected Sally, paced the deck, and decided to write him a letter. Perhaps there was a way to get on another boat. If not, I would have to write to Palmer, tell him that I had boarded by mistake and couldn't get off. I wrote letters every day but the ship caught fire some other way. Sally and I made it into a rescue boat and back to Liverpool. Palmer was like a man punched in the stomach. Sally and I said, 'We didn't want to be on the boat, but we didn't want it to burn!' Still I thanked God every day for the rest of my life that I was able to get home. I didn't know if Jordan made it to America. I wouldn't think about him."

"And the burning of the ship?"

"A group tragedy is not left to the whim of one person. The

pieces are put together in a precise design, so that each individual is living karma."

Still smiling, she stopped talking.

Renee said, "I ask Jene's subconscious: is this a good time to stop? Yes. I will wake you to a count of five, refreshed and comfortable, all systems and organs functioning better than they have in a long, long time . . . ."

Jane opened her eyes. "Wow."

"Do you remember?"

"Yes! Palmer was in my soul group. There were others but . . . it's . . . I'm losing it. Too confusing . . . ."

"I cannot believe how deep you went! *Mon Dieu*! I have never before witnessed someone between earth walks. Cherie, this is fascinating to me. Soul cleansing on the other side of life!"

Jane wanted only to savor and protect her afterlife experience, rest in its sumptuous, soft jewels of dew-like petals and scents. She stayed silent and still, until she could bring herself to get up from the chair, drink some water, and hug Renee goodbye.

She drove to the beach, needing to just sit and remember. The sun, in comparison to that other light, felt as meager as a lighted bulb on a bright day. She gazed at the ocean and listened to the recording of her session. Renee's questions had prompted awareness of soul cleansing between earthly walks. Souls work in groups with others at similar levels, sometimes through many lifetimes. Their workings are indescribably happy and loving. She could—she would—hold on to images with words, but they were slippery, like recognizing a place in your sleep and not finding it seconds later when awake.

She left the car to walk at the water's edge, seeing in her mind's eye, Elizabeth planting her feet in the shallow skimming of surf; the alternate choices as vivid as the initial actions. She shook her head, remembered her spirit getting on a train to London but none of the ride, as if the dead are spared time and tedium, commanding a live person's actions and then fading out.

A jet ski whined and turned.

She wondered if she were delusional, that maybe this was all too good to be true. She wanted to revisit some of that pink brilliance, the incredible washings and waftings on the other side. Sounds. Colors.

The sun, like a beneficent hand on the crown of her head, led her up the beach, and she lay on her back in the warm pillow of sand.

> *Mare's tails banner pale blue sky,*
> *Ocean breath laps nearby.*
> *Water, earth, air and ethers*
> *shift and sigh . . .*

Basking in the beauty of this day, she used rhyming words to honor and paint it, but she wouldn't rush to write them down, filled with glory as she was.

Her right hand moved of its own accord, fingers digging down into cold, wet sand. This was third-dimensional reality. The other was memory of a visit to a greater reality, a world of unlimited dimension. Her smile widened across her face, a giggle rippled through her diaphragm. *Thank you, thank you, thank you, God!*

18

At home, she was quieter, slower. While emptying the dishwasher or filling the washing machine, she would stop, shake her head. A glass, a plate, even a knife flew out of her grip as her right hand took on new vigor. She swept up broken glass and laundry powder. She slept easily but woke in the laundry room wrestling with paper and pencils.

On Sunday, she considered going to church but didn't know where and wondered which churches spoke of life after death. After breakfast, sitting with her notebook and a dictionary, she reviewed the Lord's Prayer, writing it out and trying to clarify it.

'Our father who art in heaven (on the other side, in the light) . . .
Hallowed (bow before this) be thy name.
Thy kingdom (of love and light) come,
Thy will (love) be done,
On earth as it is in heaven (on the other side, in the light).
Give us this day our daily bread (love) and
Forgive us our trespasses as we forgive those who trespass against us.'

It was pretty temporal, she thought, dealing with the earth walk. *While in the light, we recognize and admit to incorrect choices on the earthly sojourn. Compassion and forgiveness reign.*

Lead us not into temptation. To forget the light?
But deliver us from evil (fear?).

She thought of the 23rd psalm recited daily by her fourth-grade teacher.

'Yeh, though I walk through the valley of the shadow of death, I will fear no evil. Thy rod and thy staff, they comfort me.'
If there were no need to fear death, what was there to fear?
Thy kingdom come, thy will be done on earth as it is in heaven. On earth as it is heaven was the hook (rhymes with crook, a shepherd's staff) that grabbed the unconscious mind, bringing us solace, reminding us at a subconscious level that we are only on the earth walk until we get back to heaven; that the light is as unavoidable as death. The prayer, direct from Jesus, who was on the earth but not of the earth, was the rod (truth) and the staff (hook) that comfort me.

She left her studying to sweep the kitchen floor, letting her heady thoughts settle. She swept crumbs, grit and errant slivers of broken glass into a pile and, crouching, into a dustpan. She stood, pausing to think, and the dustpan spread its contents clinking across the floor.

David looked up from the Wall Street Journal. "Are you alright?"

"Yes."

"When do you go back to her?"

"Tomorrow." She re-swept into the dustpan and emptied it. Leaving the broom leaning against the counter, she went off to the computer.

"How are you, *cherie?*"

"I am wonderful. Our last session feels like such a gift to me! I think I'll be forever sustained. Thank you, Renee."

"I feel honored and grateful to you, Jene. Are you ready?"

Renee put her in a comfortable trance and said, "Be again as a leaf in free-fall. Then, tell me where you are."

"I'm still in the light. It's time to go back."

"Back to earth?"

"Yes. I will be Emma's grandson. Elizabeth's great-grandson. William."

"Do you have goals?"

"To be steadfast and strong with family."

"Go to that life, *cherie*."

Emma's blue eyes pool as she lifts me and holds me to her heart. I am my Emma's grandson. I once held Emma as she is holding me. Elizabeth's second-born girl had kept her warm heartedness, in spite of losing her mother. I begin to cry.

"*Cherie?*"

"Emma is holding me." *Her love washes through me. I smile and Emma squeals.*

"Go to when you are ten years old."

"I work with Papa Palmer, my *great*-grandfather. I look like him and Grammy says we are 'cut from the same cloth.'"

"Do you have any problems?"

"Bad dreams. Mama gives me chamomile tea. Gramma sprinkles lavender inside my pillowcase. Papa Palmer takes me to the country to collect lavender and chamomile blossoms."

"Go now to when you are older. What kind of work do you do?"

"I make body creams, calming chamomile and soothing lavender. Grandma paints flowers and letters the jars."

"Do you support yourself this way?"

"I run the patent medicine shop. We sell the creams there."

"Do you marry?"

"Yes." *Mama has a stroke. Dies. It's not seemly to live in a house with female servants.* "I marry Letitia, a widow."

"Tell me about that."

"She teaches me how to knit." *With the soft clacking of needles, scarves emerged from their hands, and conversation was easy.*

"Do you have any children?"

"No."

"Go to the next big event."

"I enlist in the army."

"What year is this?"

"1914."

"What happens?"

"I go to France. Mud. Oh. I die. Gassed."

"I ask Jene's subconscious, did William meet his goals? Yes. Is there more to learn from William's life at this time? No.

"Be again as a leaf floating and when you touch the ground, look at your feet and tell me what you see."

"Black shoes."

"Tell me the first thing you see or sense."

"Woods. A lake. So quiet."

"Is there a path?"

"Yes."

"Follow it. It will lead to your life."

"A convent."

"When is this?"

"There are cars. 1950?"

"What is your name?"

"I am Sister Maria Agnes, but my birth name is Angela Marie Benedetto."

"What is happening?"

"I am a novice. Hmm. No mirrors. My knees are sore."

"Kneeling and praying?"

"Kneeling and scrubbing."

"Go forward to a happier time."

"Playing ball. We tuck up our skirts. I swing and hit the ball. Crack! A grounder. I run. I'm out."

"Do you miss anything?"

"I do! I miss the drawin'."

"Who is this?" asked Renee.

"Kathleen."

"What are you doing here?"

"Not much, that's for sure." She spoke with a brogue.

"Where are you from, Kathleen?"

"County Cork."

"When were you born?"

"22, January, 1832."

"How do you happen to be here?"

"I stayed with herself. I was determined to get to America."

"When did you stay with herself?"

"When the ship burned. I was in a boat and somethin' fell on me. I woke up above the water, and Elizabeth was calling her children, so I went to her. To stay there. To stay out of the beam of light that was takin' people away."

"And are you with the nun?"

"Yes, fer' certain. And I'm in America, too! I draw when she sleeps. I draw on the white walls of her cell. She keeps movin', so I keep drawin' on the new walls. I wait to see when all the rooms are covered, but every time I look, the walls are bare."

"Do you know Jene?"

"She is herself."

"Where did you go when Elizabeth died?"

"There is no death. I've been with herself since the ship burned."

"Where did you go when Elizabeth went to the other side?"

There was some hesitation, and Kathleen spoke more quietly. "I waited—with some of the others. We hid from the light."

"What others?"

"The children separated from their mothers and fathers. Herself cried, 'Me girls, me boys, me babbies!' and the children were instantly with her."

"How many children?"

"It changes. Some go to the light when herself goes."

"About how many?"

"I can't be sure. I never counted. And don't be thinkin' that I don't know how to count!"

"Five?"

"Closer to a hundred when the ship went down."

"Why did you not go to the light, Kathleen?"

"I vowed to make the crossing to America. I didn't want me mother to know that the ship went down."

"Maybe she's looking for you." There was a pause, no response. "Kathleen? Are you there? Tell me your name, please."

"I am Sister Maria Agnes, but my birth name is Angela Marie Benedetto."

"Where were you born, Angela?"

"Albany, New York."

"See yourself at seven years of age and tell me what you see."

"My mother brushes my hair. I have a lot of hair. 'My Angelina, my angel,' she says. She braids my hair. 'Love is patient,' she says. 'Five boys before the gift of my beautiful Angelina. Angelina of the *novena*.' She sings the Ave Maria."

"Can you see anyone else?"

"Brothers with big dark eyes and hair. Papa is smaller, a yellow tape around his neck—he is a tailor. But *my* clothes come from the store. I wear fancy clothes."

"Do you ever draw pictures, Angela?"

"No. I am good! Only Nonnie Benedetto doesn't like me."

"Stay calm, *cherie*. Why do you say that?"

"She looks at me dirty and says, 'Beauty is skin deep.' But I am good! I have the calling. I am going to be a nun. It is my secret. I play the accordion. I look back at boys, but I have the calling."

"See yourself when your calling is no longer a secret."

"The Sisters of Mercy are in New York. I will be near my family. Mama weeps."

"See yourself at the convent."

"I tingle all over. This is the happiest Christmas of my life."

"What do you do?"

"I pray. I play. I go to school to be a teacher. I love children. I have many nieces and nephews. I make them laugh. I make up songs. They roll over laughing."

"Go to the next big event."

"I am weak. Cannot breathe. Dying. When I leave my body, I see my mama flailing, and my papa so tiny—his suit hangs on him. My brothers—" She laughs out loud.

"What is funny?"

"My brothers want to have me canonized."

"Why is that?"

"I refused the 'Iron Lung.' Families need it. There is an epidemic. I have completed my life's purpose."

"What was that?"

"To be joyous and passionate and good."

"Go back to the time of death. Does anyone greet you?"

"Yes. My Nonnie Anna. She is with the pink angel."

"What happens?"

"We go up, up, up."

"And then what happens?"

"Beautiful light. Everyone cheers for me. Mmm . . . ."

"Do you recognize anyone from this life?"

"Nonnie Benedetto was the housekeeper at the workhouse. She helped strengthen Angela's character. Palmer played the father. Hmm . . . he expressed love with earthly forgiveness."

"I ask your subconscious, Jene: Is there more to learn from this life at this time? No."

When Renee wakened her, Jane reviewed what she had seen and felt. "What was that part with the brogue?"

"Tell me what you remember."

"I heard a brogue coming out of my mouth, but it's very unclear. I can see the convent life."

Renee turned on the tape recorder. "Let's find that part." At the question, "Do you miss anything?" a voice with an Irish accent said, "I do! I miss the drawin."

"It's the Irish girl on the ship!"

They listened until the nun's voice returned and Renee shut off the recorder.

Jane levered the chair into a straight-up position. "She was sketching her mother. I dreamed about that! How can *she* be in *me*?"

"It happens. Spirits sometimes 'go to the light' of another soul. She attached to you." A door slammed and the dog barked.

"Like Elizabeth attached to her mother?"

"Exactly." Renee went to her wall of books and selected one. "This book was actually the catalyst to my becoming a hypnotist."

She handed Jane a book about the "unquiet dead." "This is easy to fix. I'll be right back."

She thought of Elizabeth melding her energy with her mother's. But this felt creepy. *Ghoulish.*

Renee came back with a sketchbook and pencil. "Let's give Kathleen a chance to draw. Okay?"

"Yes." She adjusted the chair, holding the pencil in her right hand. The sketchpad rested against her knees.

Renee held a chain with a silver ball at the end. "Now be comfortable. Relax, relax, relax. Take three deep breaths, releasing all tension. At the count of three, I will clap my hands, and you will go into a deep trance. One, two, three!"

At the clap, she felt herself sink right down, her neck and head pushed forward by Renee's firm hand.

"Just rest, Jene. Kathleen! We have pencil and paper for you."

Without a sound Jane opened her eyes and lifted her head. She adjusted the pencil in her fingers and began to draw with sure, swift strokes. Dark eyes emerged on the paper, followed by rounded eyebrows, an oval face with dark hair smoothed and parted in the middle. The image grew. Her fingers smudged in shadows and dimples and filled in the soft lips that lifted to one side. She sketched in a neck and a diminutive collar with only the suggestion of shoulders, and rubbed highlights into the luminous eyes. She turned the page and started a second drawing, reproducing the same eyes and brows.

"Kathleen, it's time to go to the other side. It's time to see your mother again. She's been looking for you."

The drawing continued with sustained urgency.

"There is nothing to fear in the light, Kathleen. There will be great rejoicing. When you stop drawing on this paper, Kathleen, you will go to the light."

Her eyes closed, hands stopped in her lap.

"I call on Archangel Michael to accompany you and to take all others like yourself with you. When all have gone, I ask the pendulum to stop moving."

Jane felt dizzy, a whooshing, as if the pendulum were huge and whirling around her. Suddenly all was still.

"I surround Jene with angels, north, south, east, and west. Every vacated space is filled with God's pure white light. I do this in Jesus's name. Amen.

"Kathleen has gone. All are gone.

"Are you comfortable, Jene?"

"Yes."

"I want you to stay in trance. You will open your eyes to look at the drawing in your lap. Open your eyes and look. What can you tell me about this drawing?"

"My hand used to draw this face."

"When did your hand stop drawing it?"

"When I was nine."

When Jane was small, a dark-eyed face had superimposed itself on her coloring books, in purple, blue, red or green, whichever color she had been using. "Janey, that's very good!" said whoever was near. She would catch her breath and look at the crayon in her hand. No one believed her when she said she hadn't drawn the face.

Later, in art classes, she would start out with her assignment, circles, cubes or pastels, always pleasing her teachers with her natural ability. But as she relaxed into the assignment, the circles turned into eyes and the cubes into the planes of a face. Her teachers looked at her with awe and asked what she knew of Picasso.

The face's appearance came with a feeling of gloomy anger. She would try to scrunch up the paper before anyone saw it and apologize for not following the assignment if someone smoothed it out. But she was curious and at home she would sit alone in her room with pencil and paper, willing her hand to draw the face. Nothing happened unless she doodled or daydreamed until she felt sleepy. Then, as if by magic, her hand drew. All by itself. She watched her hand draw. The pictures were always the same, as large as the different sized papers would allow. She threw them all out after her mother woke her.

"Jane? Jane!"

"She's sleepin'!" came out like a warning growl.

"Jane! Wake up!" Her mother's eyes flashed black, a deep crease between her brows. "Never, ever do this again! Do you hear me?"

19

David was toweling the Range Rover when she stepped out of the car. "I'll do yours next," he said and moved a bucket of soapy water out of her path. "How'd it go?"

She leaned into him.

"That good, huh?"

"No. It was good." She opened the door, reached over to the passenger seat and brought out the sketchbook. "Remember I told you about an Irish girl doing a portrait? On the ship, David. The girl who zinged Elizabeth. Look." She held the portrait before him.

"I've seen this before."

"I know. Can you come in?"

"Yeah, just a second." He hung the towel in the garage and followed her in the front door and down to the kitchen.

Jane filled the kettle and turned on the burner. "I used to draw in my sleep."

David propped the thing on the counter. "I know you draw in your sleep."

"*This face*, David. Only this face!"

"It was on my spreadsheet."

"She's gone!"

"Who's gone?" He looked around and back at Jane. "What are you talking about?"

"Kathleen. The girl from the ship—Elizabeth's ship. She's gone from me!"

His eyes seemed to step back from her. He paled.

"I know—it's creepy, but it happens! Here's a book about it."

He took it, turned it over and read the back cover as the kettle screamed. "Does this have something to do with your spastic hand?"

"I didn't think you'd noticed."

"Does it?"

"Yes, David, it has everything to do with my spastic hand!"

"Has it stopped?"

"Yes!"

Doubt written all over his face, unable to smile, he watched as she poured milk into the small pitcher. She held her hands palm up. "See?"

She felt his trembling as he took her hands and kissed each palm, his eyes moist and somber, his emotion making them blacker than ever.

"Time will tell. You'll see."

He nodded with closed eyes. "My thoughts exactly."

"Here. I'll play the tapes. Do you want tea?"

"I'll have a beer." He flipped through the book before going to the refrigerator.

———•◦•———

Eileen said, "I don't understand. How could you possibly be happy about any of this?"

"Eileen! My hand isn't shaking anymore! It was the Irish girl on the ship who was trying to draw with my hand. She went into *me*— she went into Elizabeth instead of going to the light. And now she's gone. They're all gone!"

"Sweet Jesus! I'm happy about your hand, Jane, but this is freaking me out!"

"I am so relieved. I feel like a weight's been taken off me."

"I guess I don't—what did you say they call this?"

"Spirit involvement. There are books about it."

"Well, who was this Irish girl?"

She related Elizabeth's shipboard encounter. "I knew there was something weird about that drawing. I even dreamed about it."

"Wait a minute! Was this a dark-eyed woman with a part in her hair?"

"Yes."

"Janey, you used to draw that picture all the time! We thought you were an artist!"

None of this made sense, but the difference in how she felt was all the validation Jane needed. While spirit entities had been removed from her energy field, she felt as if *she* were the one set free, a bird let out of a cage barred by other people's spirits.

She laughed until her belly ached at David's expressions the third time he played the taped portion of Kathleen with her Irish brogue. They had sushi and sake in the living room, and wrestled and loved until their knees were sore with carpet burns. And when she went to bed, she slept the whole night and woke to a pleasant stillness.

David leaned on his elbow, watching her.

She said, "I hope our children have eyes like yours."

"Your eyes are beautiful, Jane. I love green eyes."

"Brown eyes are more expressive and they age better."

He ran his finger up and down her nose. "I've never known you to be so relaxed. How will we ever get up?"

"I'm getting up right now!" She swung back the covers. "I have to pee. Besides I want to see my mom today. "

"You're not thinking of taking that drawing—"

"I am absolutely taking it! And the tapes. Want to come?"

"I do. I'll check my calendar."

———•◦•———

Jane waited to bring the drawing out until after tea.

David stood from the table. "That just hit the spot, Mom. Now if you tell me where your keys are, I'll check out your car."

"They're in my purse. Goodness, you barely sat down."

"I've been sitting for three hours. Is it still hard-starting?"

"Mm-hmm." She nodded. "David, the brass key is for the front door. If you use that, you won't have to buzz us."

After he'd gone, they moved into the living room. Jane took the drawing tablet out of the bag and held it before her mother.

"Oh! That looks like the drawings you did when you were little, three and four years old even. Where did you get it?"

"I went to a hypnotist, Mom. I drew it while I was hypnotized."

"Hypnotized?" She gasped, her hands bracketing the air. "Jane! We are never, ever, supposed to let anyone else control our minds! That's exactly what happens in hypnosis!" She let out a loud sigh. "Get me an aspirin, will you, please? They're in the cabinet left of the sink." Her hands framed her head.

"Do you need water, Mom?"

"I have water."

"Just one aspirin?"

"Just one."

The orange couch sections pulsed in the afternoon light. "Do you like orange, Mom?"

"Not especially. It's all right. Everyone else seems to like it. I think of it as melon-colored." She swallowed the aspirin with some water.

"It's cheery. I like it."

"Yes. Eileen has nice taste and I can use some cheering up now and then." She put on her glasses and looked at the drawing, sitting forward in her chair. "There was something odd about it. You always drew the same picture, and as soon as you finished one, you'd start another. The same face, exactly, one right after another. If I spoke to you, you'd just stop. I kept some of those drawings for a while."

She took off the glasses and pressed her lips in thought. "Until—something unpleasant happened. I don't remember exactly what, but you seemed to lose interest in drawing. Suddenly you were very busy. Biking, swimming, playing the violin. You barely sat still. And you were—had been—the most placid of my babies. We couldn't get over the change."

"Well, Mom, you're about to find out. I'll start with the past life."

"There *are* no past lives, Jane! Only demonic trickery!'

"Mom! Are you aware that my hand *isn't* shaking? Or maybe you never noticed my spastic hand. Did you?"

"Yes, Jane, I noticed it. Has it stopped?"

"Yes! It has stopped. It's thanks to this woman, and I need you to listen to this tape. Okay?"

"All *right*, Jane. If you insist!"

Jane pushed the play button. Her voice filled the room. "I am a novice."

"Do you miss anything?"

"I do! I miss the drawin'.".

"Who is this?"

"Kathleen."

"What are you doing here?"

"Not much, that's for sure."

Her mother's mouth dropped open with a gasp. She took the pillow from behind her back and sat forward.

"There is no death . . . ."

"Yes, there *is* death." Her mom's eyes flashed.

When the portion with Kathleen ended, Jane stopped the tape.

"I remember now." Her mother closed her eyes in a grimace of annoyance. "The brogue brought it all back, more's the pity." She drank from her glass of water. "I went into your room because you hadn't answered when I called you. You were sitting there, drawing. I said, 'Jane,' and a low voice said, 'She's sleepin'!' Like saying 'Beat it!' or 'Scram!' Kind of tough, you know? That scared me. I yelled, 'Jane!' and you woke up. I suppose the look on my face scared you." She let out an exasperated breath. "It's all the work of Satan."

"Would you like to hear the second tape, Mom? That's on it."

She shook her head. "No. I'm— Who is this French woman?"

"She's a lovely woman, Mom. She's doing a dissertation on curing phobias with hypnosis."

"Well, bully for her!" Her mother's eyes darted. "Promise me, Jane, that you won't go back to her!"

"The entity is gone, Mom. My hand doesn't move unless I *want* it to! Can't you feel good about that?"

"Where one has left, seven others return, much worse than the first!" Her mother got up from her chair. "I think I'll lie down for a while. Why don't you see how David is doing?"

Jane found herself sighing as she cleaned up their tea things and put the cups away, and as she went down to David and the car.

"Hey. What's up?" He wiped his hands on a red garage cloth.

"Mom's lying down." Her lip quivered.

"Uh oh. Do you want to leave?"

"No. We'll take her out for dinner."

"Well stand back and check the directional and brake lights for me."

Jane watched a silver sedan pull into a "visitor" slot. Two men got out, one in a light-colored suit, the other in a sport coat and tie, and headed up the walk of her mother's building.

When they had checked front and rear lights, Jane and David went up the stairs, and used the key to enter the apartment.

The two men she had watched arrive stood to shake their hands, reaching across Bibles lying open on the coffee table. "Bob Oakes and Jeremy Hastings. Your mom asked us over."

———•◦•———

The next morning, rain covered the north windows as if thrown from a bucket, bringing to mind the deluge she had experienced at Chester's cottage almost a week ago. Last Thursday. This was Wednesday. Now she was safe at home, under her own roof. *And I am the only one under my skin.* But it was a far cry from the superb calm and celebration of yesterday. Unnerved, she phoned Eileen.

"You told Mom?"

"Oh my God, Eileen, it was horrible. She called the Jehovah's Witnesses, and two brothers came to pray over me. I told them— 'I already pray the Lord's Prayer. All the time! It's very important to me!'"

"What did they do?"

"They looked up scripture, chapter, verse, and line, all about

Jesus calling out unclean spirits. They read about Michael and his angels casting Satan from heaven. When I told them that Renee had asked for Archangel Michael's help, they looked at each other, shook their heads and started all over again."

"Was David there?"

"Yes. He kept squeezing my hand to be quiet. Every time I tried to say this was good—it was over—or even to ask anything, they started in again."

"Did you play the tapes for them?"

"No. I wanted to but David had them in his pocket. I told about Kathleen and the drawing, and they said, 'She doesn't sound evil, but the possessing ones are always unclean, always aligned with evil. Deliver us from evil is deliver us from the devil.'

"We all knelt and said the Lord's Prayer."

"Geez. Too bad they didn't have holy water or something, huh?"

"Yeah. The worst of it was the way they looked at me."

"What about Mom? Is she upset?"

"No. They told her I was safe, not to worry. She was practically giddy by the time they left."

"Then what happened?"

"We went out to dinner, and she said that she shouldn't have yelled at me and scared me like that, and David said, 'Kathleen was in Jane from the start. Now she's not.' He held my hand under the table and said, 'It's time to celebrate.' Mom had a Manhattan."

"But Jehovah's Witnesses don't believe in consciousness after death. What about the past lives?"

"Why do you think she called them? She was protecting me the only way she knew how. It didn't hurt me—other than being a complete buzz-kill."

Eileen was briefly quiet. "I think this Kathleen thing is really weird, Jane. How do you know it's true?"

"Didn't I tell you about Elizabeth's spirit attaching to her mother? Elizabeth backed out of the light to be with her kids and later merged into her mother." She was again aware that Eileen and her mother in that life were one and the same. No wonder her sister was always telling her what to do.

"Yeah, maybe. But I didn't really get it."

"Anyway, I'm the only one moving my hands. You don't have to believe it if you don't want to."

"It's spooky!"

"Yeah, it is. But it accounts for a lot of trouble that can be very easily fixed; even, sometimes, schizophrenia." She again gave her sister the title and author of the book Renee had loaned her.

"By the way, didn't you ever run into me in any of those lives? Are you going back for more hypnosis?"

"I have an appointment tomorrow. I want to see if Kathleen was with William."

"Who is William?"

Jane paused, then spoke carefully. "Emma was Elizabeth's daughter. William was Emma's grandson, and he was Elizabeth in her first incarnation after her death."

"Elizabeth's great-grandson!"

"After that, she was Angela, the nun."

"Oh, right. Okay, I forgot."

"Renee would be happy to work with you, too, you know. Just don't tell Mom. I'm getting off the phone now. Believe it or not, I'm looking forward to doing laundry."

She set aside her phone and placed dirty clothes and detergent in the washing machine. That would be the first step on the other side—washing earth grime off the spirit body. She wondered how begrimed Kathleen had been and then how many other entities had gone with the artist; if crying babies had always been there. No wonder she'd been tormented with nightmares and sleepwalking. How perverse to hide from the light, but Elizabeth had, too, just not for as long. Poor Kathleen, denying herself that brilliant richness.

The spirit bodies, fluffed by nurturing angels, could stay clean or return to the planet in a new body for another sojourn. Angela had stayed pretty clean . . . .

> *The wave washes in,*
> *Leaving its debris.*

She wrote out the poem, counting out the rhythm.

And is carried out,
Embraced by the sea,
Sweet, clean, and free.

Renee had cleaned *her* of debris, far worse than any third dimensional dirt.

She picked up her sketchbook. She wanted to paint a scene of shoreline lapping at feet, sometime when she'd mastered oil painting. The laundry room had been built with architectural lighting above a perimeter of counter tops and two stools on which to wheel around, and she would set up her oil and easel in here. She sat with a pencil. With a rush of gratitude to God and to Renee for the full use of her hand, she began a drawing of Sally, but she thought of the little girl she was so drawn to on the ferry. As she continued, it was as if she were drawing both girls in one place. She put soft loose curls around a smiling, dimpled face.

The gray-haired women who had taken care of her on the ferry were putting together sail kits with large safety pins, like those from bygone kilts. She had some, stashed in her old jewelry box with college exam grades on self-addressed postcards and old photo strips from Rye Beach. Neat, they were. Neat as a pin, and she would give them to those good women.

The kitchen phone was beeping when Jane came out of the laundry room, and when she pressed *play* Louise's voice said, "Hey, Jane, it's Wednesday. Are we having lunch? I'll be at the Chowder House at one, so I hope you get this in time to join me." A good dose of Louise and lunch was exactly what she needed. She grabbed a copy of her printout, pulled on her trench coat and drove down town.

Louise looked up from the menu as Jane slid into the booth.

"It's so good to see you, Lou!" Jane smiled and slipped out of her coat.

"Well! I'm glad to see you, too. What's going on?"

"A lot. But I am *not* going to start at the beginning."

They both ordered chowder with herb toast and tea.

"The big news is this." Jane held her hands out, palms up, and then placed them on the paper placemat in front of her.

"Your hand is better?"

Jane laughed. "Completely!"

"That's wonderful! What happened?"

"Hypnosis!" She told about seeing Renee on the ferry. "I've had two sessions with her, and I will see her again tomorrow."

Their tea arrived in small brown teapots, and was soon followed by chowder and baskets of toast wrapped in blue cotton napkins.

Jane said, "Umm. I forgot how good this was. Why aren't you eating, Lou?"

Louise was staring at her. "I just can't get over the change in you, Jane. Two sessions of hypnosis?" She began eating her chowder, keeping her eyes on Jane. "It is good." She put down her spoon and picked up some toast. "Did you shingle the cottage?"

"Yes. There's a whole story, and it's so involved that I had to write it down. But it's too big to tell you about now because you have to get back to work. I will give you a copy of it—after lunch." She poured tea into her cup. "I only got my hand back on Monday—"

"The day before yesterday. Well, what was it, Jane? What was causing it?"

She added milk to her cup and told her. "It was a spirit."

"A spirit."

"Yes. Of a dead person. They don't all go to the light when they die—sometimes they don't know they're dead, but not in this case."

Louise's jaw had dropped. The pink in her cheeks darkened to red.

"She—the spirit—was a very aggressive artist who was always trying to draw a picture of her mother. There were others, too."

"Okay." Louise held up her hand in a stop sign. "That's enough." Scowling, she shook her head side to side, sat back in the booth and dropped her hands in her lap. "Are you sure of this woman?"

"Yes. See?" She picked up a teaspoon, let it balance on her palm. "But, Louise, I want to take art lessons, oil painting, and I don't know anyone."

Louise, pink-cheeked and still, reached into a wide bag, a tanned red bag with round wooden handles, and pulled out her phone. "My neighbor, Elise, has been going to this place for years. Saturday mornings. She loves it, and she's really good."

"Aleece?"

"Elise, with an 's.' This is her number."

20

"Jene, you just picked up a pencil and drew this? No practice? *Extraordinaire!*" Renee looked closely at Jane's drawings and at the portrait drawn by Kathleen. "Your style is very different from the other—so much lighter, happier. So different."

"I've always wanted to be an artist, but it's thanks to you, Renee, that I can finally take painting classes! I signed up at a studio yesterday—in the third floor of a mill building."

"I am so happy for you, *cherie*. And who is this?"

"It's Sally, Elizabeth's five-year-old, but it's also a little girl I met on the ferry. We were drawn to each other—" She broke off, wondering if she were making more of it than it was. A wetness at her ankle pulled her attention down into Max's black eyes.

"Max!" She rubbed his silky head. "If it hadn't been for Max, Renee, I might not have reconnected with you."

"Trust, Cherie. Trust the good. There are no accidents, only signposts." Still studying the drawing, she said, "You are truly gifted," and set aside the sketchbook.

"So now you are good and relaxed."

Jane opened the sunroof and inserted the cassette and, once on the road, closed the windows to hear this last session from her life as William.

"What of children crying? Do you ever hear that?"

"In my sleep. I have bad dreams."

"Tell me about your dreams."

"Crying and looking, looking . . . I'll wake up, and I'll be out of bed, and I'll be sad, and angry."

"What are you looking for?"

"A pencil."

"Anything else?"

"Something to draw on."

"Do you ever wake up and find yourself drawing?"

"Yes."

"On what do you draw?"

"On books—on the inside covers. Or the desk blotter."

"What are the drawings?"

"A woman's face, dark eyes."

"What's troubling you?"

"Feelings of suffocation, and the crying."

"How old are you when you have these dreams?"

"A baby. I wake up screaming. Until I am too big to run to Mummy's bed."

"When do they stop?"

"When I am no longer frightened enough to wake up."

"And the drawing?"

"I draw in my sleep."

"When does that stop?"

"It doesn't."

"Is it the face?"

"Yes."

"How do you see it?"

"On newspapers. I throw them out."

"Does anyone else see your drawings?"

"The char would see them. And Letitia."

"What's funny?"

"Letitia thought it was an old love."

"Did you ever find out who it was?"

"No."

Jane turned off the tape and concentrated on finding the church.

Friend Street glowed like a seasonal postcard, the lawns dappled with sunlight and yellow leaves. She parked in front of a white clapboard church with two sets of green double doors, wondering if anyone would be there on a Thursday afternoon, and followed a concrete path to an ell with an open door. Trees shushed and leaves fell around her like blessings, an occasional one even touching her.

She stepped up and into a long hall to the sound of children's voices in the distance and, close by, a man's voice with a Maine accent, pitched with tension. "All I want's an announcement in your newsletter. Church newsletters are supposed to be a big help."

A deeper, calmer voice cut in. "Hi, I'm Rev Tom. Why don't you come in and sit down for a minute. You're right. That's exactly what our newsletters are about." A door closed.

She stepped into the office as the secretary, muttering about social services, turned to the computer.

"Excuse me."

The frail woman wheeled. "Yes? May I help you?"

"I hope so. I met two women last week who were looking for large safety pins to complete some sailor kits." The flat, round lenses of the secretary's glasses caught the light, hiding her eyes. "I told them that I could donate a few pins, and they said to bring them here."

"What were their names, dear?"

"One was named Rita."

"Let me see." She looked through a rolodex. "That would be Rita Haskell, and Maude? Was the other one Maude?"

"Yes. I can contribute three pins." She reached into her purse.

"Well, here is Rita's number." The secretary tore off a yellow sticky. "There's no sense leaving the pins with me. I won't be seeing those women until Sunday service."

The inner door opened, and the two men came out. "Lois, run this piece in the newsletter, please."

A red flush climbed into Lois's thin-haired scalp.

The other man spoke. "I thought maybe we could put it on the bulletin board . . . in the meantime."

"Sure." Rev Tom crossed to the copier. "I'll make a copy and we'll do that right now."

"Thanks, Rev. I'm much obliged."

Jeans, work boots, russet mustache. Jane knew him from somewhere.

"So you've already moved to the mainland?" Rev Tom spoke over the copier.

"Yessir. Moved almost a month ago."

That's where she saw him—the Saturday ferry. "How is your little girl?" she asked and, in answer to his questioning look, said. "We were on the same ferry."

He studied her. And blinked. "Buck Eaton," he said, extending his hand.

"Jane Eliot." *Strong grip, callused palm.*

"Cissy—Clarissa—is great. Cissy is short for Clarissa. She's the reason I'm here." He took the proffered copy from the minister and passed it to Jane. "This is my ad for childcare."

Five-year-old requires childcare around kindergarten hours. Some over-nights may be required due to single parent's work schedule.

The words almost took her breath away, and she said, "I'd love to do this!"

"Do you live in Portland?"

"Yes."

The secretary interrupted. "Do you still want me to run this ad, Tom?"

Buck said, "Yes."

Jane said, "No."

"Just as a backup," Rev Tom pronounced, accepting the large pins Jane dropped in his hands, and shifting them to shake Buck's hand.

"Thank you kindly, Rev. Guess we'll confer elsewhere," Buck said as he and Jane went out the door. They paused on the doorstep. "I'll be pickin' up Cissy at three."

"We can talk at my house, if that's okay. You'll want to see where I live anyway. You can follow me." She gave him the address, just in case.

"Thank you, kindly. Don't mean to put you out, but that'll simplify things."

In the car, she let out a whoop. "It's perfect! Perfect! I couldn't take my eyes off that little girl. I can't believe it!" Checking for Buck's red pickup in the mirror, she pulled in front of the house.

Buck stepped out of the truck and looked around. "My wife went to school over here. She liked to walk through the neighborhood—look for a small house." He was quiet, then said, "Simone died of a brain aneurysm during Cissy's birth." His look was direct until the statement was out and then he looked toward the park.

"I'm so sorry. What—how have you managed?"

"We lived with Simone's folks on Peaks Island. Simone was their only child." He studied the brick sidewalk that turned into the garage apron.

She walked the few steps to the front door, hoping it was unlocked. "Sorry. This door is locked. We'll have to walk down the back steps. The land drops off on this side of the street. Our house is built into the hill."

"So it's one story at street level and two stories in back? Makes sense. Is that the bridge to South Portland?"

"Yes." She opened the door, suddenly embarrassed that this one was *un*locked, but he was peering between trees at the harbor. The patio was already deep with leaves.

"This is about the best place I've ever seen. Do you have to mow *anything*?"

She laughed. "No. My husband is more interested in cars than yard work. In fact, we were looking for a carriage house . . . ."

"Your garage looks like one," Buck said as he came through the door and into the kitchen.

"Yeah. It's right on the street." She pulled out ham and cheese and started coffee, telling herself to stay calm. *And trust in a 'constant striving for good.'* Renee's words.

"Fact is, Clara's diabetic and she turned sick this summer. We needed to cut the cord some time, but Cissy's real close to her gramma and grandpa. They're good people." He studied the city map. Soon they would both drive to Cissy's school. "You're over here at Western Promenade and we live near the *Eastern* Promenade. That's where school is." He marked the map with a yellow highlighter and set it aside as she placed sandwiches on the table.

"Would you like water, milk, or coffee, Buck?"

"Milk's good, thanks."

They ate without talking.

"Do we have time for coffee?"

Buck checked his watch. "Ah-yuh. It's only 2:15."

She poured one cup. "How do you take it?"

"Black, thanks." He clicked his pen. Click. Click. Click. When she sat, he showed her the street map. "This is how we'll go. I think we can come back the same way."

"Yes, I think we can."

"Goshdarn-fangled kindergarten hours." He shook his head. "I wonder if she could go to a school closer to where you live."

His eyes were like brown cat's-eye marbles. Why had she thought they were blue?

"Are you sure about this?" Click. Click. Click.

"Yes! Nothing could suit me more. I left my job as a placement consultant—finding employees for companies, and I hadn't decided what I wanted to do. This will be perfect. And I . . . liked Cissy . . . as soon as I set eyes on her." Buck's silence caused her to continue. "My husband and I hope to have children. But I could still have Cissy— she'd be like a big sister. You'll need references—" She went to the counter and wrote down a name and number for her former boss, and also for Louise. "Louise is my co-worker. Are two enough?"

"It'll do for now." Buck told her about his hauling business and the need for midweek overnights. He slid a piece of paper toward her with an hourly wage written on it.

"That's too much."

"That's the going rate." He spoke with finality.

"All right."

"I'll need to meet your husband."

"Of course. We can do that this evening."

"How soon could you start?"

She could start tomorrow.

"Monday's what I had in mind," he said.

"That's perfect. We'll bring Cissy back here today, won't we?"

"If you don't mind. Thanks for the lunch."

She whooped again as she followed Buck's truck to Cissy's school and yelled, "Thank you, God! Thank you, thank you, thank you!"

——————•◦•——————

"Kindergarten kids have to be met at the door," Buck said as they walked to the triple set of glass doors. "And left there, too."

Cissy marched out the door and headed right to Buck.

"Hey, Cissy! How was school?" He squatted to hug her.

"Good!" A pink headband held back tousled curls.

"I have news, my girl. I have located a babysitter and she's right here!"

Cissy's eyes found hers. "I saw you before!"

Jane's heart skipped a beat. "I saw you too, Cissy. On the ferry with your stroller. I am so happy to be your babysitter!"

"Me, too! Even though I'm not a baby."

"You can call me Jane, if your dad doesn't mind."

"That's fine with me. Cissy, would you like to visit Jane's house?"

"Yes. Can I ride with Jane?"

"Yes, you may. I'll follow, okay?"

"Okay, Daddy." Cissy took her hand as they walked to the car. "Do you have an airbag, Jane?"

"A what?"

"An airbag. I can't sit in the front seat if you have an airbag."

"Oh. Yes, I do. Are you supposed to have a car seat?" She opened the rear door.

"No. I weigh over forty pounds, so I don't need one." Cissy pressed a finger to her chin. "But I need a booster seat."

"Here ya go, Cis!" Buck carried the seat from his truck. "You'll need to get one of these, Jane. I'll show you how it works."

Jane served cookies and milk, then showed Cissy and Buck

through the house and the room that Cissy would sleep in on overnights. When they left, Jane ran upstairs to wave, and Cissy's little hand wagged from the open window as the red truck pulled away.

Downstairs, she rummaged for the makings of American chop suey. Eileen's kids loved it. She pulled out noodles, canned tomatoes, soy sauce, and onions, which for some reason they never noticed. She found hamburger in the freezer and celery in the crisper. She was grating cheese when David called.

"How was your session?"

"It was great, wonderful. David! Guess who's coming for dinner!"

———•◦•———

David gazed over her shoulder as she studied the Cissy/Sally drawing. "Are you sure you can do this, Jane? Without breaking your heart?"

She turned and met his eyes. "I've never been more certain of anything in my life." It was as if the universe knew about this, and she had to be made ready. "If this child is being placed in my path, it's a gift. All I have to do is accept it."

"You don't think . . . I mean, it's not because you think she's that other little girl. Elizabeth's. Is it?"

"No. And it wouldn't matter anyway. It just feels right. She needs mothering and I'm available."

"Uh, uh. She needs babysitting, Jane, not mothering. You're not her mother and you never will be."

"Wrong, David. She doesn't have a mother, never did. She does need mothering, even if it isn't called that. She needs *loving* and I'm going to see that she gets it."

He pulled her close and she let her trembling dissipate into his body.

"It's a chance to love. That's all. It's for all of us."

———•◦•———

Buck looked up from his coffee cup. "Will you be watching any other children?"

"No. Cissy and I will be wanting to watercolor and make cookies, and we're going to get a puppy, so we'll have lots of walks."

"A puppy? I love puppies. Animal Planet is my favorite show. I know all about dogs, don't I, Daddy?"

"You sure do."

"My Grammy and Grampy have a dog. Duchess!" Cissy's infectious laughter had them all chuckling.

Buck's truck route required overnights for Cissy on Tuesday, Wednesday, and Thursday. He agreed that it made sense to have almost a second wardrobe at their house. "Cissy loves to shop, but I'm no good at it. Ever since Clara started feelin' poorly, I've been running to keep up. If you can do the buying, Jane, I'll pay for the clothes."

She emptied the guestroom bureau and put up rainbow ribbon tie-backs so the white curtains could be released to cover night-black windows. She hung the little girl portrait and warmed at the thought of brushing and plaiting Cissy's hair.

She bought white socks with lace edging, plain pink, and navy blue, a pink-striped nightgown and matching pajamas. She found a card of butterfly hairclips and a bag of hair ties that looked like doll bracelets. She wished Cissy were with her. She would leave the packages unopened and Cissy could open them if she liked them, and then they would shop together.

Louise's friend Elise had recommended her own art teacher, who had asked Jane to bring only a drawing pad and a number two pencil to her first session. The class was a drawing/painting class and allowed people to go from drawing to watercolor pencils or paint, or to acrylic or oil, when and if a student so chose. Some chose to stay with drawing.

At her first class on Saturday, Jane was asked to mask off a border on her sketch paper, then, using the side of her pencil, to lightly gray in the paper. When still-life items were added, shadows were darkened, and lighter areas were created by erasing. The exercise was helpful with depth and shading, but she asked Cara, her instructor, for a list of what she would need for oil painting. Still energized from the class, she went directly to the supply store.

21

She watched Cissy, in a bright pink backpack, climb down from the big red truck.

"Morning, Cissy!"

Buck carried two large baby dolls and a stroller. "Here's my cell. This is Gramma Clara's number, and this is Grampa's cell phone. School starts at twelve-fifteen, and I'll be back to pick up Cissy between five and five-thirty. Like I said, I'll be local this week so Cissy won't need to sleep over. "

"Daddy, I *want* to sleep over."

"I know that Cis, but I'm picking you up tonight. Now give Daddy a hug, and I'll wave from the truck. Bye Jane."

They waved as the truck pulled away.

"Who are these beautiful babies?" Jane held the door as Cissy pushed the stroller into the front hall.

"This one's Sarah Ann. Sammy goes in back 'cause he's bigger." She maneuvered the dolls into place.

"I'll carry the stroller down the stairs. You walk behind me. Okay?"

When they reached the kitchen, Cissy said, "I need to whisper."

Jane knelt as Cissy cupped her hand over her ear. "My Gramma had a operation. They cut off her leg."

"Oh!" She held Cissy to her, feeling the little chest heave with sobs, and sat on the floor to rock her. *Poor baby!* Her own eyes teared. She rocked and rocked, feeling her shirt grow wet and wishing she had a tissue to offer, until Cissy pulled away.

"I need a tissue, Jane."

"Of course you do. So do I." Sniffling, she got to her feet, "This is where I keep the tissue box. Can you reach it?"

Cissy stood on tiptoe and pulled out a tissue. "I know how to blow," she said and proved it.

Jane chuckled and blotted Cissy's cheeks.

"We need to call my Grampy's cell phone."

"Would you like me to dial?"

"Yes." Jane helped her onto a stool, input the number and gave her the phone. "Grampa?" Cissy smiled, her hands tiny on the receiver. "Hi, Grampy." She squirmed on the stool and giggled. "Here's Jane."

"Hello?"

"Name's Roland and I'm pleased to make your acquaintance." Cissy hadn't seen her grandparents since the surgery four weeks before. The amputation had laid Clara low, and her husband had barely left her side. "The neighbor women have pitched in a lot, but I need to get back to work. I sure do miss that little girl. Fact is her Gramma's too ornery to see even Cissy. Clara's a prideful woman."

Jane suggested he call an agency and pulled out the Portland directory. "You talk to Cissy while I look up some numbers."

After hanging up, they made a get well card for Clara and put it in the mail. Soon they were rushing to get to school on time. Jane kissed Cissy on the cheek and watched the big glass doors close behind her. She sat for a while—at a loss for what to do, but getting dressed had been difficult. She needed to buy some casual clothes. She drove to the store and, looking at everything with an eye toward Cissy, bought herself jeans, cotton jerseys, and a pair of clogs before heading back to the school.

Cissy studied the ground, walking slowly to her.

"I'm so happy to see you." Jane held out her hand and they walked to the car. "It's such a pretty day. I wish we could walk home, don't you?"

"I'm kind o' tired." She acted like a different child.

"What do you like for a snack, Cissy?"

"Maybe peanut butter."

There was no conversation in the car. *Maybe a little homesick.* At home, Jane put peanut butter, jelly, and crackers on the table with a butter knife and sliced up an apple. "Would you like some milk, Cissy?"

"Yes, please." Cissy's mouth turned down.

"Would you like to say hi to your dad? Call him on the phone?"

"Yes." Cissy put down the knife.

Jane dialed and handed her the phone.

"Hi, Daddy. Uh, huh. Yes. Peanut butter." As Cissy spoke into the phone, she moved against Jane's knees. "Okay. I love you, too."

She lifted Cissy to her lap. "You know, I like peanut butter crackers, too. I'll show you how I make them, okay? Sometimes I use jelly and sometimes honey. And then we can read a story."

Cissy fell asleep at the end of "Clifford to the Rescue." Jane put aside the book and snuggled them down, keeping her arm around the warm little body. Looking at her drawing that had started as Sally and turned into Cissy, she knew in her heart that Sally had been returned to her, not *as if* by design but *by design. Trust a constant striving for good.* Hot tears seeped from her eyes. She pulled the bedspread over their legs and, knowing that nothing in her life could bring her more than this precious now, she accepted her gift and slept.

That week they got to know all the dogs that were walked in the park. Cissy brushed her own hair, and Jane clipped it back with butterfly clips that broke apart in her thick hair. They switched to hair elastics, and Jane finger-brushed the curls enough to make a topknot.

———•◦•———

At painting class, Jane mixed odorless turpentine and yellow ochre into a light wash and covered the canvas with it. She learned how to hold the brush at the very tip. Similar to her drawing, she used the same still-life model and marked the dimensions of pitcher, grapes and plate with yellow ochre. She asked Cara's advice for colors and mixed the paints with oil to a good consistency and filled in the curved items. She was heady with the rich smell of paint and still buoyant when she got home.

On Sunday, Buck asked Jane and David to meet him for brunch. "From our side of things, this is working very well. My girl is acting like her own bright self." He placed his knife and fork on his plate, and waited while the waitress filled his cup. "Now Sharon, she was Simone's matron of honor, is happy to babysit Cissy, but Junior, her youngest, has turned resentful." He sipped his coffee. "Fact is, I took an apartment on the east side of town just to be near Sharon."

The waitress filled Jane's cup and collected their plates.

"I'd like to enroll Cis in the school on Brackett Street, if you folks think this is going to work out for you."

Squeezing David's hand under the table, Jane said, "My cup runneth over."

"She zeroed in on you on that ferry ride." Buck's look was frank and steady. He turned to David. "This good with you, David?"

David stirred cream into his coffee.

Jane stepped on his foot. "David?"

"Oh, absolutely."

"Then I'll find a place on your side of town, and Cissy can live in the same neighborhood as her schoolmates. This feel right to you?"

Jane said, "We're delighted, Buck. I can't even think of being with Cissy as work."

David stepped on *her* foot. "You think you'll ever move back to Peaks?"

Buck studied his coffee cup. "When I lost Simone, I could barely function. Of course, Roland and Clara were also grieving. Cissy could turn our sobs into chuckles—a life ring for each one of us. Our lifeboat. We called her Simone so many times that Clarissa turned into 'Cissy.'" His gaze came up. "I don't want her to see Clara suffer, and moving off the island . . . has given some—" He gestured palms up and left the sentence unfinished. "We'll visit when Clara's up to it. Cissy needs them and they need her, but it's time to get off their doorstep. It's time to widen our emotional circle, so to speak. Ay-yuh. So . . . probably not."

Jane asked, "Did you and Simone live at Peaks?"

"We lived there for six months before moving to Portland. Simone worked at the city library." Buck's eyes were dark with heaviness, and she wished she hadn't asked.

Walking home from brunch, Jane said, "Why did you hesitate, David?"

"I'm trying to add a little balance. You and Buck are like the opposite ends of a seesaw. You're both so . . . desperate!"

"What are you talking about?"

"Jesus, Buck is ready to move! He's planning his life around us!"

She kicked an acorn out of her path. "He's planning around his child! What's the matter with you?"

"What's the matter with *me*? I'm the bloody fulcrum! I feel like the only stabilizing force . . . I just wanted to make sure he's planning on sticking around for a while."

"He's been alone for a long time—"

"Yeah. And now he's *really* alone."

"Poor Cissy. A baby in all that mourning."

"Poor Buck. What if he meets another woman?"

"I hope he does."

He stopped her then, his eyes black and serious. "Are you lying to yourself, Jane? Cissy would have a mother."

She shrugged. "So? She'll *always* have me—for as long as she needs. For whatever!"

"And when she doesn't need you?"

"I'll still love her." She wrapped David's arm in her own and pressed forward. "Wow. Imagine! Monday morning and Cissy is my *work*. Yippee!"

After cleaning up their supper mess, Jane washed and dried the apples and placed them in a large bowl at the center of the table. The phone rang, reminding her that she hadn't called her mom. "Hello?"

"Hi, Jane. It's Buck. There's been a change of plans. Can you talk?"

"Yes. Of course."

"Gramma Clara has gotten back in the swing of things, and she insists that if Cissy must go to school on the mainland, she's going to Waynflete. Simone did elementary at Peaks, but Clara did *all* her grades at Waynflete. She grew up with someone important there and she plans to call her in the a.m. So if you're plannin' on walkin' to the school with Cissy, I believe it's on Spring Street."

"Wow! That's practically across the street from us. We'll walk over unless you tell me otherwise. That's great, Buck!" She hung up, found David at the computer and told him the news.

He raised his brows. "She *is* their only grandchild. Good. I didn't want to say anything, but that other school is pretty rough, and Cissy's coming from Peaks—like a lamb to wolves. Good for Clara!"

———•◦•———

She held Cissy's hand as they used the crosswalk with the stop sign to cross Danforth, walked up Vaughan Street past Orchard and one block further to Spring. The school took up the whole block and some of the next and, rather than intrude, they walked down Fletcher, stopping at a gate that opened into the school property. If they stayed on Fletcher, it would take them down the hill to Danforth. Admiring a large stucco house with long green shutters, she turned right onto Orchard.

"Look, Jane! For rent!"

"Very good, Cissy! I didn't know you could read."

"I know *that* sign. Let's tell Daddy."

"We sure will. Are you nervous about your new school?"

"Uh-huh."

"You'll be fine. You make friends easily. Remember how quickly *we* met—on the ferry?"

"That was different. We already knew each other."

Jane laughed. "Look Cissy. Two little girls—"

"With red hair!"

The older one spotted Cissy and rode her tricycle to the sidewalk. "Hi. I go to kindergarten." Her voice was as gravelly as Renee's.

"Me too," said her little sister.

"She doesn't really."

"I do," said Cissy.

———— ·•·•·•·————

Buck picked them up at noon and drove across town to the old school, where the teacher said, "Clarissa, you'll see all your friends again in middle school. Can we all say in one big voice, 'See you later, Clarissa'?" She took some things off the wall and placed them in a purple folder that she handed to Buck. She hugged Cissy, and everyone waved and called, "See you later!"

The glass doors closed behind them. "Whew! I'm glad that's over! Can I have my folder, Daddy?"

"Yup. Do you want them to call you 'Clarissa' at the new school, Cis?"

"Yes. That's my name. I already have a friend at school, don't I, Jane? And Daddy! We saw a rent sign!"

Buck found a parking space. "You'll probably just walk, Jane. Isn't that nice, Cis?"

Cissy was quiet.

Buck introduced Clarissa and 'Mrs. Eliot' to the administration, and they were all shown to the kindergarten class in the Founders Building.

———— ·•·•·•·————

Jane walked out the gate and straight ahead to Orchard Street, passing the house with the red-headed girls, before turning left on Vaughan. This was a thousand times better than driving across town. Fletcher Street was closer to her house, but crossing at Vaughan was safer, and the hill was less steep.

She timed the walk (ten minutes), started a kettle for tea, and answered the phone.

Eileen said, "I thought you could come down to see us while you're not working."

"Cissy has school. You have to come meet her!"

"Maybe after Christmas. We close that week."

"You can help me make plans with the house."

"Plans for what?"

"I need to do something with the lower level. Maybe put in a guestroom. You can listen to the tapes and see my drawings."

"Can't you bring them at Thanksgiving?"

"Isn't Mom coming?"

"Oh, right. So next month. Maybe you could hypnotize me, and then I could hypnotize you. Wouldn't that be fun?"

———•◆•———

Cissy pulled the girl with red hair to Jane. "My friend's name is Ellie!"

"There's my mom," said Ellie, dragging Cissy to a woman pushing a double stroller. Tracy had straight coppery red hair and a shy smile. The women introduced themselves and walked together.

"I'm actually Cissy's babysitter. How old are these two beauties?"

"Sarah is almost three and Amy is six months."

Jane said, "Hi, Sarah. We met this morning."

Sarah focused on the big girls. "Out, Mama! Out!"

"No, Sarah. You have to stay in the stroller or we won't be able to go for a walk." Tracy handed her a sippy cup and picked up the pace. "Ellie! Come back by your sister." As they neared her portico, she said, "We'll walk on with you, if you don't mind. Once everybody's strapped in, I kind of hate to stop."

Jane said, "Do you have to do that on the way to school, too?"

"Pretty much, unless my husband doesn't have a flight. It's a challenge."

"Would it help if Cissy and I collected Ellie on our way to school and back? We're going right by."

"Could you? Oh, that's a wonderful offer. Getting Ellie to school on time has been really hard. Are you sure?"

"I'd love to."

"I can't thank you enough. Maybe after dropping them off, you can come by for tea, or lunch. I could use some adult conversation."

"Thank you. I'd love *that* too."

Cissy and Ellie collected red, orange and yellow leaves and handed them to Sarah who dropped them on the ground.

"How did you come to babysit Cissy?"

Jane told her about the ferry ride and delivering the pins to the church, and then blurted, "I had two miscarriages."

"I'm sorry. But you have plenty of time. Before you know it, you'll be practicing birth control! Believe me. I *know*!"

Jane laughed. "I hope you're right! My house is just down the hill. Should we walk on to the Promenade?"

"Sure. Which house is yours, Jane?"

"The small stucco with green shutters."

"With the carriage house? The one that's a cape in front and two-story in the back? I love that house!"

"We've been almost-neighbors all this time, Tracy. I'm so glad we met!"

———•◦•———

She let Cissy cut celery and fill the stalks with cottage cheese or peanut butter, slice carrots, and sprinkle a little of each spice into a dish for the cook-pot. Cissy liked to kneel on the warm dryer and fold wash-cloths, towels, pillow cases and hankies. Watching Animal Planet, they witnessed the birth of all kinds of animals, and at night they read a story in the new rocking chair, and Jane rocked and sang a medley of songs.

On Fridays, Cissy took her school pictures off the refrigerator and put them in her suitcase. "Daddy and I have to go to the store before we go home." She stirred an egg into brownie mix. "We never know what to get."

"Do you think you and your dad would like to eat dinner with us on Friday nights?" Jane scraped some of the dry mix into the center of the bowl.

"I don't know. Maybe. I just wish we knew what to get at the store."

Jane poured in the oil. "How about making a list? Have you ever tried that?"

"No. But Gramma does."

"When we finish the brownies, we can make a list."

"Okay. You can finish."

Jane scooped the mix into a pan and put it in the oven, set the timer, gave Cissy the spoon to lick, and filled the bowl with soapy water. "You wash the bowl while I clean up."

Cissy, chocolate on her cheeks and arms, gave up on the spoon and used the brush to wash the bowl, spoon, and spatula, while Jane cleared and wiped the counters.

"Okay. Let's sit at the table."

Cissy said, "I want to write it!"

"Okay. What do you think you'll need to get?"

"Milk. We buy a small bottle so it won't go bad." She held the pencil above the notebook. Jane spelled and Cissy printed. "Bread, and chips, and Honey Nut Cheerios. And a cooked chicken, and we can make a salad at the store. We might eat with Grammy and Grampy, so we don't want to get too much. We always buy soup."

The oven timer went off. "S-O-U-P."

Before Buck arrived, Cissy had filled her tote bag with books and dolls, and her suitcase held skeins of blue yarn for Grammy to knit into a sweater. She watched from the window and ran to the door when Buck's truck pulled in. "Daddy! Daddy!"

Buck lifted her and swung her around and hugged her tight before setting her down. "Are you all ready, Missy-Cissy?"

"Yes."

"And Ms. Jane? Did she have a good week?"

"I had a wonderful week, thank you. How about you?"

"Fair to middlin'. Can't complain."

"We made brownies, Daddy. Would you like one?"

"Yes, I would, but I don't want to eat alone."

"Coffee or milk, Buck?"

"Milk's good, thanks. Do you want some milk, Cis?"

"Yes, please." She climbed on his lap.

"Ummm . . . . These are good brownies."

"Guess what, Daddy. I made a list for the grocery store."

"You did?" He read the list out loud. "Good job, Cis. That'll help a lot. And that reminds me. Save my seat, Cissy. I have something in the truck."

"Have you got everything, sweetie?" Jane ran a finger round

the smooth curve of Cissy's cheek. Cissy moved over to her lap and wrapped her arms around her, and they hugged and kissed each other's cheeks.

"Aroostuck County potatoes." Buck presented the bag to her. "Last to come out of the ground."

"New potatoes? Wonderful! Would you like to join us for dinner next Friday night, Buck? I promise to cook some of these potatoes."

"We could do the shopping after, Daddy. When we're not so hungry."

Buck smiled. "We'd be grateful."

David came in the door. "Hey, Buck! Got time for a beer?"

"No, thanks anyway. Me and Cissy—*Cissy and I*—have shopping to do. Cissy wrote a list. But I'll look forward to havin' one next week."

On Saturday, Jane painted in the background of her painting. There was a lot wrong with it, even though she had asked for help every step of the way. Cara said, "It's all practice and it's all fun. You're going to have to leave it here to dry anyway, and next week you can change whatever it is you don't like. But I think it's very good for a first, so congratulations! Here. Do you mind if I do something to it?"

"Not at all. Be my guest!"

Cara picked up a cloth and carefully smudged off some of the background paint, which lightened and brightened the painting. "There. Next week you'll think of ways to tweak it a little, maybe drop some white on the grapes. But you might, my dear, actually have a painting worth hanging, and that is no small feat for a first."

22

Jane e-mailed Chester. She wrote, "I finished the shingling, old buddy, and guess what! I had spontaneous regression at Pigeonhole. We were good friends in the 1800s, so no wonder I felt like I'd known you forever." She started to tell him that they were married in another life, but that suddenly seemed too personal, even embarrassing, and she deleted those words.

Chester was fascinated. Impatient with texting, he called her on the phone. "Oh, my God, Jane. That explains it. You know, you were the only thing I liked about that job. I'm not kidding. I can't wait to hear everything about this. We'll get together over Thanksgiving, and I have the best news! My company has a new facility in Portsmouth, New Hampshire, and I'm transferring there in January! I'll be right across the bridge, and we can get together all the time. Isn't that great? And hypnosis! Jane, we can find all the answers to all the questions!"

Jane was smiling, her heart light, when she got off the phone. Chester had that effect on her, but he was also impatient with his questions, which she couldn't answer all at once. She set the timer for picking up Cissy and began typing out a third-person narrative. As it grew, she included hypnotic regressions, inserting more information every time she wrote. She would share it with David and forward it to Renee, Eileen, Chester and Louise.

———•◦•———

Cissy told Jane and David about Mrs. Wilson, who had a glass eye, and who ran the Ducette household so that Grammy got to make all the decisions. Grampy had put a little kitchen in Mrs. Wilson's rooms so that lived right there in the house. "Grammy gets to be boss and Mrs. Wilson gets to do any hard stuff, so Grammy is smiling again. And guess what! Grammy is getting a artificial leg.

"Mrs. Wilson fell off the couch when she was three. She fell on a toy truck. That's how she lost her real eye. She has a new one but she can't see through it.

"Daddy says Peaks Island is better for riding bikes because there aren't so many cars."

David said, "Your Daddy's right about that, Cissy. Jane and I love to ride bikes on Peaks Island. In the summer we rent a cottage and we ride our bikes every day. Would you like that?"

"Yes! And we could see Grammy. We ask Mrs. Wilson first. Mrs. Wilson knows when it's good to visit."

After Cissy pointed out Tangle-Free-Conditioner-For-Tots at the grocery store, Jane was able to comb right through Cissy's shampooed hair. "We could put your hair in a braid and in the morning it will be easy to comb. Would you like that?"

"Yes, please." Cissy's eyes were serious in the mirror.

"Ooh, sweetie, your hair is so thick that I think we'd better do two braids. So that it can dry." Jane smiled from ear to ear, and Cissy smiled back.

After reading *Frog & Toad are Friends*, Jane sang a medley of "Nightingale, Cockles," and "Danny Boy." She rocked slowly, humming a little.

"She's asleep." David stood in the doorway.

"I thought so. Can you help me get her to bed?"

"Of course." He picked her up.

"See if you can walk her."

"Why?" He carried her to the bed and set her down, pulling covers up to her chin.

"Because I wouldn't be able to carry her. I wanted to see if she could be walked."

"Next time." He kissed the sleeping child, turned off the light and steered Jane to the couch and a glass of red wine. "It's organic. Tell me how you like it."

She sat with her elbow on the arm of the couch, leaned her head into her hand and let out a heavy sigh.

"Jane. What's wrong?"

She crossed her feet beneath her and sat straight. "I blew it." Sometimes she wished David weren't so patient, sitting opposite her, waiting, eyebrows raised. "I called Gramma Clara."

"What for?"

"Just to be nice. Cissy talks so much about her, I thought it would be kind to . . . 'ring her up.' I wanted to say thank you. For Wellflete."

"It's Waynflete. And?"

"I don't know what happened! I said, 'This is Jane Eliot, Cissy's babysitter—' and she said, 'I *know* who you are!' Ooh. 'Why are you *calling* me?'

"I said, 'Cissy is so devoted to you, I just thought I'd give you a call—'

"You just *thought*. I'll bet you just thought! Thought you'd just step right into my daughter's shoes! Well you can just *un*-think it. Cissy has a mother! It wasn't you, it isn't you, and it never will be you!' And she hung up.

"I couldn't believe it. I wrote it down. I've gone over and over it."

"Ouch! I think we better talk to Buck."

She pulled a cushion onto her folded legs. "Grandpa Roland *said* she was 'ornery.' 'Clara's a prideful woman.' Poor Mrs. Wilson!"

"Jesus. I'm calling Buck."

Her stomach roiled. She had no interest in wine.

David handed her the phone. "It's Buck."

"Hi Buck."

"Sorry I didn't warn you, Jane. Clara's good people. I never said she was nice. Fact is she can be meaner than a rattlesnake. Now, Cissy's been talkin' up a storm about you. It's kinda' gotten Clara's nose bent out o' shape. I'm real sorry. Come to think of it, Roland was speakin' kindly of you, too, and *he* really ought to know better. Best if we don't say anything to Cis about this. I'll put it to bed right away, so don't be frettin'.""

When they'd hung up, David presented her with an aperitif glass of fine Irish whiskey. "Sip it slowly. It's Buck's Clara remedy. He says you should only need it the one time."

———•·•———

At Tracy's house, Jane changed Amy's diaper, kissed her plump neck, carried her to the kitchen, and strapped her into the highchair. When she sat, Cissy slid onto her lap. "I love you, my girl." Jane squeezed her and Cissy melted into her. "You know, Clarissa Anne, I will always love you. And if I ever have a baby, we will love that baby together, and we will still love each other."

Cissy hugged her and ran off to find Ellie.

Tracy sat down with a dish of baby cereal and began spooning it to Amy's open mouth.

"Mommy!" Ellie pulled her mother's arm. "Can we have a dog? Can we have a dog, Mommy?"

"Some day we'll have a golden retriever. We'll take him to the beach. When Amy is big enough to throw a Frisbee."

"When she's as big as me?"

"Bigger."

"Cissy's getting a dog!"

Cissy leaned into Jane. Amy thumped her tray, while Sarah, climbing on a chair, reached for a cookie. Tracy and Ellie looked at Jane—two sets of brown eyes exactly the same.

"When the time is right." And quietly, into Cissy's ear, Jane said, "Now that I have a little girl to love, I'm not so anxious to have a dog." Their eyes met. "Okay?"

"Okay!"

"Let's play babies, Cissy!"

"Me too!"

"Wow." Jane took the teapot to the stove and turned up the burner under the kettle.

"I know. They don't miss a trick." Tracy focused on the path of the spoon, going from oatmeal to applesauce. "Do you know anyone else who's diabetic, Jane?"

"No. I don't think so. Do you?"

"One of my grandparents might have been, but I don't know which one. I'd like to check out their dispositions. I've been reading Louise Hay . . . . She connects illness with behavior. Kind of saying that the body will manifest an illness to get a person's attention."

"Really?" Jane poured boiling water into the pot and brought it to the table.

"For instance—if someone is using his hands to do something he hates, he might develop carpal tunnel. Instead of having surgery, he could just start doing something he likes and get better."

"You sound like my sister!" Jane picked up a ring of red plastic measuring spoons from the floor and sat. "Tracy, what do you think about reincarnation?"

"Makes sense to me. Every major religion has embraced it—including Christianity. Didn't Aristotle say, 'It's no more remarkable to be born twice than it is to be born once'? Or something like that?"

Jane poured tea into her cup, added milk, and sipped it. "Want to hear about some of my past lives?"

Tracy's eyes left the business of the spoon and rested on Jane's.

———◆·◆·◆———

Eileen was the first to call about the emailed narrative. "What were they wearing?"

"Who?" She pulled glasses from the dishwasher.

"Elizabeth and Sally—on the train."

"Oh! Their traveling clothes. Wait a minute." She closed her eyes and pictured them in daylight, near the docks. "Sally was wearing a blue flowered cotton dress, with sleeves that ended just above the elbow, and a straw bonnet with blue ribbons that were sewn across the crown and tied under the chin. The dress had white piping at the shoulder seams and waist. She had a blue knit sweater with sleeves that were wide at the wrist and cuffed—I guess so they could be dropped and grown into. Buttons were at the neck. The lower part was cut away—longer in the back.

"We wore low boots with white canvas tops and silk stockings that tied at the knee. I wore pockets over my petticoat that I could reach into through the sides of the skirt. My dress came to a V below the waist. It was blue and pale green plaid with a line of pink, a lot shorter than what you see in pictures, and Sally's was even shorter. My bonnet had a black grosgrain ribbon folded and stitched across the crown, and silk ribbons tied under the chin. Oh!" An image of a coiled black cat flashed before her. "That awful dream just came back to me! The dream with the black cat wrapped around the crown of a hat. Maybe a reminder not to get caught up in this—"

"So don't. Just let me know about their clothes."

"I—*Elizabeth* wore a linen chemise with a corset and a petticoat above it. She slept in the chemise at the boarding house. They washed in cold water. I—*she* had a salt crystal for her underarms, but still smelled. So did Jordan. He washed, but he still smelled."

"Yuck. What about toilets?"

"Chamber pots. We didn't use the outhouse. Maids brought pitchers of water."

"Uh, yuh," said Eileen. "I guess that'd make a difference. What about underwear?"

"What? Are you writing a book?"

"Maybe. Underwear?"

"Linen pants came down to the upper calf. Sally's tied at the waist. Elizabeth's buttoned, embroidered on the bottom, pretty. But get this! The crotch was open to the knee. You pulled them open to void."

"Ooh! What about on the ship?"

"Water closets were built into the bow of the main deck. Toilets hung over the water. With all that rocking, people missed, and—oh, don't remind me!"

"How many were there?"

"How many what?"

"Water closets."

"I don't know. Maybe five? or six on each side. " She coughed. Why was her throat irritated. "You know, Eileen, this makes me feel—"

"Weird?"

"No! Lousy!"

"Just tell me one more thing. What did Sally look like?"

"She looked—a little like Cissy . . . ." Jane was both sad and cross. She wanted a drink of water. "None of this matters, Eileen."

"It's fascinating! How can you say it doesn't matter?"

"It's past, it's heartbreaking, and there's nothing anyone can do about it." That cat had snarled or something. "Eileen, did I tell you about my painting class? I have finished my first painting, and I have started another. I love it! Three hours go by like lightning, and sometimes I get to stay a little longer."

———•◦•———

Jane dreamed that Elizabeth's daughter Meridith had become Cissy's mother. She sketched Simone with clear blue eyes and black hair bowing out behind the ears, and considered a blue striped jersey.

"David, is there any way to get more living space downstairs?"

"Not if you want windows. Why?"

"I would like to put a guest room down there."

"Who are you thinking of?"

"My mom, your parents. Eileen."

David dropped the magazine to his lap. "All we'd need is a hide-a-bed. Or we could put a bed in the study."

"It's pretty small. Would it be too far away for a nursery?"

"It's only across the hall."

"I'd keep a newborn in our room, but the study is such a nice sunny space."

David knelt and took the sketchpad out of her hands. "Have you got something to tell me?"

Tears filled her eyes. "I haven't been to the doctor yet."

"Do you want me to buy one of those kits?"

"I did."

———•◦•———

David cut Cissy's chicken into bite-sized pieces. "Where is Daddy taking you for Thanksgiving, Cis?"

"To Gramma Anne's house. In the county. With the cousins."

"How many do you have?"

"About a hundred!"

"Do you have fun with them?"

"Yes. But Daddy promised Simone that we would never move there."

The next morning, the Tuesday before Thanksgiving, Buck was in town but brought Cissy in the morning so that she and Jane could make molasses cookies for the school banquet. "I'll see you both a little later," he called.

Cissy said, "I need to whisper."

Jane knelt to listen, her whole left side tickling as Cissy's warm breath kissed her ear.

"Can I call you 'Mommy'?"

"Oh, yes, Cissy! I would love that!" She looked through her tears into Cissy's wet eyes, and they hugged and rocked.

"I love you, Mommy," said Cissy.

"Oh, and I love you. You are what I am most thankful for!"

Before they stopped for Ellie, looking straight ahead, Cissy said, "I picked you out on the ferry."

Jane squeezed her hand. "I felt like I already knew you. Like I already loved you. Did you feel that way about me?"

"Yes. I did!" Cissy's blue eyes were as round as buttons.

She pushed the buzzer on Tracy's front door and smiled at the commotion inside before it was opened.

"It's carrots and ranch dressing," Ellie said in her husky voice.

"We'll join you soon!" Tracy was spoon-feeding Amy.

"You have plenty of time," said Jane. "Don't rush."

They walked the short distance to the cross-street and soon through the gate and up the path to the kindergarten building.

Cissy whispered, "Bye, Mommy," when Jane knelt to kiss her, and she whispered back, "Bye, my darling girl," and called out, "See you soon, girls."

Jane watched the five-year-olds turn suddenly shy, looking a little lost as they joined a crumpled line.

Guests were asked to wait forty-five minutes before entering the school. She sidestepped arrivals. She must tell Buck. She must ask Buck! Tears leapt into her eyes. Cissy had never met Simone. She wondered if she had called her grandmother 'Mama', if she had called *anyone* Mama. Buck might marry again and give Cissy a new mother.

I will take good care of her, Simone. She knew that Simone had been Meridith. She could trust that Simone's death had served a karmic plan, so complex as to make the intertwining branches of far off trees appear simple, yet as purposeful as the energy that would again course through them. If she were to lose this baby, hateful as the loss would be, it would serve some purpose . . .

Heading down the walk, she pulled a red beret out of her pocket and over her ears. Limbs and fingers of trees mapped an intricate pattern against sky. Soon the delicate twigs would be limned with snow, safe and still, until spring-sweet sap coursed through their veins once more, forcing life to erupt and blossom. She resisted the urge to cup her belly. Morning queasiness was back, and her breasts were swollen and tender.

Maybe it would have been unsafe to have an infant with her previous hand bobbing . . . She had so innocently dedicated her life to tension, deciding to never relax until she was safely in bed. While repressing all memory of sleep-drawing, her right hand found every lapse, forcing her to ratchet up conscious preoccupation of her hands.

Maybe bodily stress pulled at fibers of her internal baby basket, turned them taut and brittle, and little beings could only adhere to soft and flexible. Now she could soothe a baby while mothering a five-year-old. Nothing could separate her from Cissy. Their bond would bridge an ocean, lifetimes even, but she needed to talk with Buck.

Wondering if David and Buck had arrived, she reversed her steps and headed back to the school.

Inside, she peeled off layers and stacked them on top of coats laid on a table. The children wore paper pilgrim hats and Indian feathers. Cissy's red paper headband slid down over her eyebrows, and Jane maneuvered close and slipped it back to rest on her ears. Indians showed Pilgrims how to plant corn with fish, and they recited group poems and sang short songs. Other parents had cameras and videos, and Tracy filled the gap by taking stills of Cissy. Jane introduced her to David and Buck, and they all nibbled on carrots and celery, popcorn and cookies.

Everyone trundled out of the school together, Buck appearing as ready to confer as she was. Jane suggested a hot drink at a nearby restaurant and, on the pretense of planning a surprise birthday party for David, she asked Cissy to keep him busy in the outdoor playground while she and Buck went inside for coffee.

"She not only wants to *call* you Mommy, she wants you to *be* her *mother*." Buck fingered his mustache, avoided her eyes and clicked a pen. "She has lots of aunties but she's never asked to call anyone 'Mommy' before. Believe me, I'm happy she feels—or *has*—that strong a connection to you."

You don't look *happy.* "I love her, Buck. I'll always love her."

A waitress created a draft as she moved past their booth.

He looked hard at her. "She's my life. I'm all she has." His eyes glistened. "If you had any idea—I'd give my right arm for Cissy to have a mother!"

Trust me, Buck. Just trust me! She swallowed hard and prayed. *God be with me.* And plunged. "I think I was her mother in another life." She held her breath.

He glanced at her. "That would explain it." He made a sad laugh. "Makes some sense of that ferry ride. Do you know what she said to me?" He pinned her with his eyes. "*I found my mommy, Daddy.* All happy. Just like that." He shook his head. "And you're sittin' there—with your husband, and I'm thinkin', 'Somethin's wrong with this picture!' And, much as I like you, *Jane*, there's still somethin' wrong with this picture!"

Her head began to ache. "Waitress, I'd like some hot water, please."

Buck clicked his pen, again and again. "I'm sorry." Grief was everywhere on him.

"No, *I'm* sorry."

He dropped the pen and began working the fingers of his left hand, squeezing each segment, massaging and pulling; pressing the pads, knuckles, and palm. He switched hands and started on the other, relaxing as she watched, taking breaths. His muscles seemed to fill out. He sat taller. "Reflexology." He squeezed the base of his thumb, ringing it with the opposite thumb and forefinger. "Simone studied it." He loosened his neck and rotated his shoulders.

"She studied reflexology?"

"She studied everything."

"I wish—"

"Don't we all." He cut her off, watching David and Cissy compare their long shadows in the play area, and went back to his hand, his strong thumb manipulating knuckles and pads. "It's saved me but I still have to remember to do it."

A waitress filled their cups.

"I'm sorry, Buck."

"It's not *your* fault. My girl wants a mother." His eyes teared up; he palmed them and cleared his throat. "And she's found one." He closed his eyes and stopped his lips, dropping his hands to the table.

Help us, Simone. If it's possible, Simone, if you can help, if you think it's right. She said, "God's will be done."

"Amen." Buck let out a breath. "It's a good thing. It's good for my girl." Cissy's moving arm caught his eye and he waved back. "Poor little pet's never even *had* a mommy. I *know* she needs a mother. She needs one *now*. If we can give her that . . . She deserves it."

His wet eyes, blurred by her own tears, asked a silent question.

She nodded, wiping away tears. "Yes, Buck. You can trust me—to my dying breath. I'm sorry I said that. Forgive me."

He shook his head. "It doesn't matter. Simone is not coming back." He dropped his head in his hands momentarily, white imprints fading from his weathered skin when he lifted it. "She'd like you." He nodded, drank from his cup and folded his hands on the table. "You may be my daughter's replacement mother, Jane. But I am always her father. I am her only daddy. Is that clear?"

She nodded. "Yes. Of course. That's clear."

"If I ever get married again—" He rolled his eyes. "My second wife would be Cissy's stepmother." Shrugging a little, he said, "Who knows why things happen the way they do."

"I will love her forever, Buck."

"Who wouldn't?" He pulled a red bandana from his pocket and blew his nose. "Are you sure about this, Mrs. Eliot? People will think you were married to the likes of me." He folded the hankie in his lap and returned it to his back pocket.

"It would be my greatest pleasure." She dissolved in tears.

Buck reached out his hand.

She dropped her soggy tissue to return the shake.

"I am truly thankful, Jane, that Cissy's found you. We'll just be like some divorced couple. Who knows? Maybe we were married in another life." He clicked his pen: click, click, click.

"May be." She fingered her silver cross. "What about Clara?"

He raised a brow to her. "Cissy is very open about your being her mama. Clara's had a rough year, on top of a parent's greatest loss. She'll come round."

While she fished in her bag for a tissue, Buck said, "Cissy's wanted to call you Mommy all along. I gave her permission this morning."

She blotted her nose with a napkin and sniffled.

"Here comes our girl now!"

David and Cissy radiated the fresh smell of cold outdoor air. Cissy slid onto Buck's lap.

"Whoa, that face is cold!"

Cissy giggled and locked eyes with her.

"Temperature's dropping like a rocket." David placed his hand like a cold mitten over hers.

"David and Cissy, we have an important announcement. Are you ready? It's official. Ay-uh! Jane is to be Cissy's Mommy."

Cissy's face dimpled into a smile, and her hands flew to her mouth. Then she hugged him. "Forever, Daddy?"

"Forever, my beautiful Clarissa Anne Eaton. But just like your name says, I am forever your daddy. I am your only daddy."

David stared from Buck to Jane and back again. He reached in his pocket for a hankie and handed it to her.

Buck steadied his gaze on David. "Are you with us on this, Uncle David?"

David nodded. "One hundred percent." He reached over and shook Buck's hand.

"So you live with your daddy," Buck continued, "And you visit with your mommy and your uncle David. How's that sound?"

"Good." Cissy hugged his neck. "I love you, Daddy."

"I love you too, baby."

David coughed. Jane wiped her eyes with David's neatly ironed handkerchief.

"I fold your hankies, Uncle David, and I fold my daddy's too."

Jane laughed into the handkerchief.

"Don't cry, Mommy," said Cissy. She looked at Buck, and climbed down, and David got up from his seat so that Cissy could sit near her. They hugged, and Jane whispered a question into Cissy's ear.

"No," Cissy whispered back. "Can I?"

She nodded.

Cissy leaned on both elbows. "Guess what, Daddy! Mommy is going to have a baby!"

It sounded so funny that everyone laughed, but Buck's eyes filled. He took her hand in his and said, "Congratulations, Jane," and he shook David's hand. "I wish you all the best."

Cissy beamed. "Uncle David, is this a good time for hot chocolate?"

The End

ABOUT THE AUTHOR

Bette Lischke lives with her husband in Newburyport, Massachusetts, where she is active in theater and the Newburyport Choral Society.

In addition to fiction, Bette enjoys writing songs. She has produced a compact disc of her story, "Santa Claus & the Elf Scout Leaders," which includes seven original songs. There are eight melodies in "Santa's Magic," a three-act play for children's theater.

Bette paints with watercolor and studies yoga, dowsing, tai chi, and all things spiritual. She has worked as an executive recruiter, social worker, writer, hypnotist, and nanny. She is both teacher and student of seven grandchildren, and further blessed by their proximity.

In the Waters of Time

Bette Lischke

www.bettelischke.com

Publisher: SDP Publishing

Also available in ebook format

TO PURCHASE:

Amazon.com

BarnesAndNoble.com

SDPPublishing.com

 **SDP Publishing**

www.SDPPublishing.com

Contact us at: info@SDPPublishing.com